Jeannie and Suggs

In

Texas Hearts

This book is a work of fiction. Any names, characters, places and references only refer to this work of fiction. Any accidental reference to any content that is not owned by me is unintentional and was referenced therefore to support this manuscript.

Thank you to all who have prayed and supported me. Blessings.

TEXAS HEARTS

Introduction

Suggs couldn't help a quiet grunt as he sat up when he saw Eric Ranald entering his hospital room. His head was fuckin' pounding. In fact, his head hurt worse than his left arm. And he didn't know where his fuckin' Stetson was either. What he needed was something to smoke and a woman, in that order, with another smoke afterwards for good measure. He put his head down for a moment while he pulled the sheet off of himself and when he put his head back up what he saw or should he say *who* he saw made his mouth drop open. He could not take his eyes off of her. Ranald was oblivious to Suggs' stupor as he started to speak.

"Hey man! How're they treatin' ya in here?"

Suggs attempted to choke out a strangled fine. Ranald still hadn't keyed in on Suggs' expression and kept talking as he started to look around the room. "I'm glad you're alright brother."

Suggs tried to calm his pounding heart as he continued to stare at the enchantress who walked into the room with Ranald. What the fuck was wrong with him? He didn't like his reaction to the woman, not at all. Maybe he had been knocked on the head harder than he thought. Ranald startled him out of his thoughts as he had finally noticed how quiet Suggs had been thus far.

Ranald stared at Suggs with a disturbed look on his face. "Bruh, you're sitting there with your mouth hanging open. Are you doped up? You have a concussion? That Russian fuck knocked the shit outta you, ya know."

Jeannie chose that moment to blurt out, "Oh, no Detective! You mean that big Russian you told us about? The one that likes *men*?"

Ranald's head whipped around at the sound of Jeannie's voice. "Aw man, I'm sorry Jeannie. I haven't even introduced you to my good friend." He lowered his voice and continued, "And let's not mention the big Russian who likes boys, ok."

Jeannie's eyes were large and round when she nodded her head that she understood what Eric was saying.

Suggs clearly heard what Ranald said to the beautiful little sprite that stood slightly behind him. He turned red with rage as a few things suddenly clicked into place for him.

"I can hear you, ya know."

Ranald leaned back up and looked at Suggs with a wary expression on his face. He cleared his throat and responded, "Yeah well, that, uh, has nothing to do with you so, yeah, anyway...I need to introduce you to the lovely and incomparable Jeannie."

Suggs glared at Ranald quickly right before he switched his attention to the sprite. He knew what Ranald was doing. And he promised himself he would talk to Ranald about that later. Pushing down his frustration and impatience, he smiled lightly. He had to get it together. It wasn't often that a woman caught him off guard or in any situation that he didn't want to be caught in. He also didn't like the inference that he might have had a run in with the *big Russian who likes men*. Especially not around the sprite.

Leaning down a little and forward, he extended his hand to Jeannie. She walked closer to him slowly and because she was a small little thing she still had to look slightly up at him as she extended her own hand. When her little hand sat in his he had to fight the urge to kiss her hand like some gallant fool. Yeah, so not him. He would have to steer clear of this one. She peered up at him and opened her mouth to speak, but he beat her to the punch. Nice lips, he noticed.

"So, I believe Ranald said your name is Jeannie?"

"Yes, Officer, it sure is."

Before Suggs could stop himself, he responded candidly, "I've never heard a woman with such a whimsical appearance and musical voice sound like a Texan cattle ranch hand as well. I like your little twang, Sprite."

For some reason Jeannie couldn't explain she didn't like his comments and she was sure that he felt *entitled* to mention his observations about her. *Men,* she thought to herself scathingly. She did had to admit, he was the most good lookin' man that she had seen in a long time, but so what. She was done with men. They always felt like they were God's gift, no matter who they were. She bet it had been a while since *Officer* Suggs had experienced any kind of let down. Chuckling on the inside, she came up with a plan of attack. Suddenly smiling sweetly into Suggs eyes, Jeannie smirked on the inside as Suggs attention immediately went to her lips. The imp inside of her caused her to ever so slightly catch her breath so her breasts strained against her shirt and she lightly licked her lips with her moist pink tongue. When Suggs' breathing started to become choppy and he started to get that look on his face that a man gives a woman when he is aroused by her, she snarled and snatched her hand away from his.

Suggs almost forgot that his head was hurting as he watched her breasts strain against her shirt and when she licked her lips, he really almost forgot. Just when he had almost forgotten as well that Ranald was in the room, she snarled at him and snatched the warmth of her hand away.

Her emerald green eyes flashed as she told him, "Next time I ask for your opinions about the way I look and talk *Officer Suggs*, I'll let ya know. And my name ain't Sprite." With that, she turned around sharply, her red curly hair flying everywhere and stomped over to Eric. She turned around and stood next to him. She made herself put a blasé look on her face and casually look around the room as if she were completely through with him.

Ranald looked over at Suggs with an amused, but perplexed look on his face. "So...I can see that you two are getting on pretty well. *Not.* Anyway, I need to go and check on Vette. I was going to ask you if Jeannie could chill with you for a while bruh and now, well, I don't know."

Jeannie answered before Suggs did. "It ain't a big deal Detective Ranald. Vette'll need space and *you*, I imagine. I think I can handle a wounded officer of the law without too much fuss." She looked at Suggs and smirked, "After all, he ain't whole right now as it is. I think I can take 'im if he forgets himself."

Ranald looked over at Suggs again with a dubious look on his face. "Suggs, you gonna be safe with this beautiful terminator?"

Jeannie couldn't help a half laugh that escaped her lips. "Very funny, Detective." She pushed him playfully, which barely moved him and ordered, "Now go on and take care of my friend. Don't let that nasty Max Bates hurt 'er."

"I'd rip him apart first."

Suggs eyebrows rose to the top of his head. "Hey brother, you sound a little crazy over Miss Sylvette over there. Didn't you tell me that Bates would probably be paralyzed? And I know Russini beat his face to mush."

"Yeah, he did Suggs. Anyway, I need to run. Jeannie, just come to Max Bates' room if you need us. Otherwise, we'll come back here to get you."

"Got it Detective."

As soon as Ranald left the room Suggs allowed his focus to turn back to the fiery 'sprite' that was eyeing him warily as if she didn't trust him. This woman interested him and that in itself was interesting. "So, you look like you are a lil' bit nervous despite that big show of bravado and all that yapping you were doin' about me not bein' whole and all."

Jeannie glared at him, "Ya know, you have verbal diarrhea and for an officer of the law, that's a damn shame."

Ignoring her waspish reply, he continued, "And you're concerned about me being an *officer of the law* more than I am." He stopped to leer at her. "You like the law, Sprite? Cause I am the law."

Primly, she turned her nose up at him. "I beg to differ with your stupid self. I know what the law is. That's what I'm gonna go to school for."

He guessed she was about 25 or 26. He liked it that she was going to go to school. She had goals for her life, which was always attractive. He wasn't going to tell her that though. He knew he had just met her, but he already liked trying to get a rise out of her. She seemed fun. It had been a while since he had this much fun sparring with a woman.

"Well, good for you, Sprite. Ya know, you're gonna have to tweak that twang and grammar before you can go around quoting the law to people." His lips twitched while he waited to see what her response would be. He didn't have to wait long.

"Why you no good, high falutin, punk ass cop! Ya better consider yourself lucky that I don't have my daddy's pellet gun cause I sure would pellet the hell outta your ass!"

Suggs threw back his head and roared with laughter. His head was banging, true, but he ignored it. Oh yes...yeah, he was definitely going to have to get to know her.

Jeannie was lightly touched on her shoulder from behind and still in a rage, she whirled around and was gonna give hell to whomever she saw when she noticed that the person was an elderly nurse who was smiling at her curiously. Jeannie quickly changed her expression and did her best to speak politely to the innocent nurse.

"Oh! I'm sorry, Mam, for whippin' 'round on you like that."

The nurse smiled kindly. "That's alright, sweetie. I just heard a loud barking sound or maybe some yellin' and was just tryin' to make sure that Mr.Suggs is doin' alright."

Before Suggs could speak to the nurse, Jeannie threw in, "Oh, that obnoxious noise was *Officer Suggs* howling about his wounds like a baby."

"Uh, hey-," Suggs started to call out, but Jeannie cut him off. Putting the most concerned expression on her face that she could muster, she said fervently, "Oh please help him, mam. I'm so glad that ya heard him callin' out in pain cause he didn't want me to say nothin'. I think he needs another one of them shots."

At this point Suggs was glaring and blustering on his bed, but the nurse looked at Jeannie and winked at her in an understanding manner. "You're right. He's objecting, but I can tell by his color that he must be in pain. I'll go draw up some good stuff and bring it right back." Turning her attention to Suggs, she continued, "And young man, you should be glad to have a woman who cares about you and doesn't want you to be in pain." With another kind smile, she turned around and rushed out of the room.

Jeannie smiled sweetly at Suggs while he glared bloody murder at her.

"Now you listen here Sprite-," Suggs began.

"Oh no, no, no," she interrupted. "I don't think I do have to listen to you. Seems to me like you better listen to me. I'm callin' the shots. So if you don't wanna get the happy juice you might wanna ask me how that can be stopped."

"Why you little, mm." He paused to collect himself. Through clenched teeth he continued, "So what is the next move, *Jeannie*, so you don't have the fooled nurse give me the happy juice?"

Jeannie thought fast cause she really didn't know what she wanted him to do. "Mm mm, I'd like for you to stop givin' me your opinions and callin' me a sprite."

"You mean to tell me you created this stupid situation and that's all you want?"

"Well, I can make it more involved."

"No. No. No need for that. I'll promise to do what you say... *if* you come close to me."

She gave him a look that said, yeah right.

"Seriously Spr- uh, I mean Jeannie. It would be more comfortable for me if you came closer."

Narrowing her eyes at him with obvious distrust and what she hoped he would think would be distaste, she slowly and cautiously moved towards the bed. "Now you behave yourself *officer* or I'll take your gun and shoot you."

He smiled a very unworried smile. "Mm hmm. I hear ya. Come on Jeannie."

She grumbled deep in her throat and when she was about a foot away from him, she stopped with her hands on her hips. Waspishly she asked, "So, now ya can hear me well? Is your poor little neck still being stretched? I never would've thought a police officer would be so fragile, Officer Suggs."

Suggs eyebrows shot up and at that point he knew that the sprite needed to be taught a lesson. And he was just the asshole to do it. Besides, the lesson was going to be ever so enjoyable. She was really close to him, even though he could tell that she felt like she was a safe distance away from him. Grinning on the inside, he moved his arms into a more comfortable position.

With her hands on her hips, she narrowed her eyes at him and complained, "Oh great! I'm here now, against my better judgement, an' you ain't even talkin'."

He looked into her green eyes and distantly realized that he had never really had a thing for green eyes before, but he really liked hers. "That's cause I'm really not tryin' to *talk* to you *Sprite*."

Before she could ask him what the hell he meant, he reached out really quickly and grabbed both of her arms. He pulled her close to him and trapped her legs inside his by wrapping his legs around hers. She was still blustering when he swiftly put his hand on the back of her head and met his lips to hers. He was not a fanciful man by any means, but he swore that time stopped or all the noise of the hospital seemed to fade away. All he knew was that he felt his heart racing and damned if he didn't love the sweet smell of her breath and the feel of her soft lips. When she sighed and leaned further into him, he shifted her to his lap. She wound her silky flesh around his neck and tentatively offered him her tongue. Damned if she didn't feel like she was an innocent as he kissed her. She was so soft and she smelled like lemons. He lightly stroked his tongue against hers so as not to cause her to bolt in alarm. She was making little noises that were driving him crazy. God, he could kiss this little hellion of a woman forever. And he knew at that point that he was in serious trouble with the future lawyer-to-be, Jeannie.

<u>Chapter 1</u>

Jeannie had big crocodile tears rolling down her cheeks as she watched her best friend walk down the aisle with a man that was truly made just for her. What made it even better was that Sylvette's man was proudly grinning from ear to ear with his Stetson on next to the Minister. Jeannie and anyone else could clearly see how much he loved her friend. Jeannie would be telling a falsehood if she said her secretly romantic heart wasn't just a tad bit envious. Jeannie's ruminations were interrupted when she heard a particular squeal of anger come from a little one in the congregation. Rolling her eyes, she just prayed Sara wouldn't make too much fuss. Jeannie located her mom in one of the front pews and her mom looked well and harassed, that was for sure.

Two hours later, Jeannie was just coming up from planting a big wet one on Sara's chubby cheek, when Vette came rounding the pew closest to her at full speed. And she was still in her wedding dress so it was an awesome sight. Jeannie quickly handed Sara to her Mom and turned to the breathless and flushed Sylvette. Lord, what did she have goin' on?

"Lord Vette! What're ya doin' honey and in your beautiful dress?"

Vette grabbed Jeannie's little hands and squeezed them tightly. Breathlessly, she gushed, "I just had to see you before we left. I haven't talked to you."

Jeannie laughed. "Seriously? Girl, I think it can wait. Ya got a whole new husband to look after now. You betta get goin' Vette."

"I know. I know. I am, but I know you've been avoiding me girl."

Jeannie's heart started pounding. Oh no, she thought. She knew! Ranald! Damn Eric for telling her! Jeannie still tried to play stupid.

"Vette, I don't know what you're talkin' bout. You sound like a crazy woman."

"Hmph, I bet. So, what's goin' on with you and that fine ass Officer Suggs?"

"You're cussin in church," Jeannie replied caustically.

"You're tryin' to evade me. That's alright, Jeannie. I'll get Auntie Moran to get it out of you."

Jeannie started to respond, but Vette said hurriedly, "You're right though. I do need to go. Ranald is probably pacing, even though he's *always* late." Rolling her eyes, she turned away to bolt out of the church, but stopped abruptly and turned back around.

Jeannie rolled her eyes. If she was impatient for Vette to get to her man than she knew Ranald was probably chompin' at the bit.

"Vette! Ya gotta go!"

"I know. I just wanted to tell you to have a good time with *Officer Suggs*." She threw a cheeky smile in Jeannie's direction and then giggling like a schoolgirl, ran out of the church.

Frowning, Jeannie turned to her mom to grab Sara, saw her mom's questioning look and said, "Ma, don't even ask."

T.J. Suggs stood beneath a massive fern tree. It was the only place where he could find some relief from the blazing Texas sun. It also provided a good meeting venue that he was hoping to take advantage of with a certain red-headed hell-cat. He was getting frustrated because he still had not had a chance to talk to her. Still keeping an eye out for the red-haired imp, he briefly allowed his mind to wander. He had not seen her in about a month. Eric and Vette had decided to do a quick marriage and then have an extended honeymoon that would last for three weeks. He was clear that was the only reason he was going to see Jeannie today. He didn't have her number or anything. He didn't want her to think that he was desperate or looking for a girlfriend because he *so* was not. Relationships were not his thing, but he did have to admit that he was intrigued by the incomparable redhead that Vette had befriended. He had put the bug in Ranald's ear that he was interested in the little minx and apparently her response had been less than favorable. Why was he not surprised. That was okay though. There would be no way she would be able to bypass him today. He was seeing to it.

Jeannie walked out after her mom and Sara. She felt a pang of pain on her ankle right before she reached the double doors and stopped short as she bent down to adjust her heels. Slightly ahead of her she heard her mother make a feminine sound of appreciation, which could only mean a good lookin' man was somewhere around. Jeannie chuckled at her mom and teased as she was standing back up straight, "It must be a man, Mama. Somebody shoulda told whoever he is to look out for Sally Shayer."

Her mom giggled like a little school girl. "Oh, hush Jeannie. I swear! I'm just admirin' his, uh, figure."

"Mm hmm. I know what you was admirin' Mama."

"Hush Jeannie! He'll hear you!"

"Oo, that means he's close Mama." Giggling with her Mama, Jeannie stepped to the doors, looked up and out to see this fine cut figure of a man that had her Mom so titillated. Jeannie did not have to look long before she did see a fine ass man standing beneath the shade of a Fern tree. He had on a slate grey suit over a white vest and, of course, a bone white Stetson on his head. And even though the Stetson shaded the top part of his face, she knew how that suit had to be complimenting his stormy grey eyes. Officer T.J. Suggs was indeed a good lookin' man and against her will she was so drawn to him. She had done absolutely nothing but moon over the man since he had kissed her senseless in the hospital room. He sure hadn't acted like he had been injured. And, just then, she could see his pearly white's gleamin' in the sun as he smiled in their direction. Jeannie was stuck as soon as his eyes met hers. Lord! What was it about that infuriating man? Slowly, he started walking towards her and her heart, damn it, started beating so fast that her breathing got faster too. She was damn near panting by the time he ambled on up to where her and her family were standing. When she heard his deep, mellow voice she wanted to melt right then and there. She hated her reaction to him, absolutely hated it.

"Well, my my. If it isn't miss lawyer-to-be, Jeannie."

Smiling tightly, she responded, "Officer Suggs."

"Tsk.Tsk. I did tell you to call me T.J. You *do* remember that day that I told you, don't you?"

While she glared at him furiously, he casually rubbed his fingers over his lips. In a very suggestive manner he continued, "Mm, yes, *I* do remember that day, even if you don't."

When a nervous giggle escaped her Mother's lips, she belatedly remembered her manners, but, of course, the glib-tongued Officer Suggs beat her to the punch.

"Why Jeannie, you didn't introduce me to the lovely ladies that are with you. Shame on you." He leaned down and forward to accommodate her Mom's height. He grabbed her hand and smoothly brought her hand to his mouth and gently kissed her on the back of her hand.

"I can see where little Jeannie gets her beauty from."

All her done-in mother could muster was a breathless, "Oh my."

Jeannie tightly said, "This is my mother, Sally Shayer. "

Smiling warmly at Sally, T.J. removed his Stetson and said, "Sally, it is my pleasure."

He looked down at Sara, who was wrapped snugly in her grandmother's arms. Jeannie had thought she was sleep, but she was wide awake and staring into Officer Sugg's beautiful eyes. Even the baby seemed to be transfixed. He flashed her his million-dollar smile and Sara squealed with glee.

"And this beautiful little tike must be Sara."

"Hey! How did you know my daughter's name?"

"Oh, I've been finding out as much about you as I can."

She couldn't help it. She really did want to melt right there. She had tried so hard to ignore his existence and definitely what had happened in the hospital room a month ago. But she consistently remembered the feeling of being in his strong arms *and* the taste of his lips.

"Oh! Jeannie you didn't tell me you had already met this handsome gentleman."

Smiling roguishly, T.J. said, "Oh we've done more than met mam. You could say we're on our way to becoming really good friends."

Beaming, Sally responded, "Oh! That's great! Jeannie has always had trouble makin' friends ya know."

"Momma!"

Suggs chuckled. Sally continued, "Ya know, sometimes I think it's cause she has a temper, yes. But, of course, all that red hair that she got she gets from her daddy's side, ya know. But I really think it's because she's always been such a pretty little thing. Other girls didn't quite like that and they didn't care for her learnin' ways either."

"Learning ways?"

"Yeah. She's a damn genius. Her IQ is so high she skipped grades in school an' everything. Her father was alive then an' we were so proud of our little girl."

T.J. processed that and responded, "Well, that doesn't surprise me at all, Mam. And you and your husband obviously did a great job raisin' little Miss Jeannie here." He looked at Jeannie and continued, "And I didn't know you had skipped grades while you were in school."

Jeannie glared at him. "Why the hell would that even be any of your business to know, Officer Suggs?"

"Jeannie!" Sally looked back at her daughter. "You stop that rude behavior young lady."

Suggs chuckled and could not contain throwing a gloating grin at the silently fuming Jeannie.

"Jeannie messed up in her junior year on account of tanglin' up with Jed and his kin."

"Okay, okay Momma," Jeannie threw in irritably. "I'm sure Officer Suggs has better things to do than stand here jawin' with us."

"Oh Lord! I've been prattlin on and I'm sure you're a busy man."

Smiling charmingly, T.J. responded, "Oh Mam. Being in the company of such beautiful women has done my ole heart good."

Blushing furiously under his regard, Jeannie's disgustingly taken mom replied, "Well, young man, ya sure do know how to please a lady. And old, hah!" Sally was almost smacking her lips when she continued, "Believe me when I say *young* man, I can't see nothin' old about you."

T.J. threw back his head and laughed uproariously. "I see I'll have to be careful with your flattery as well, Miss Sally. Maybe you can pass some of that flowery language on to your daughter. Her mouth sure is filthy sometimes."

Sally laughed and responded, "Yeah, she does have a foul one sometimes. Comes from her daddy's side too, ya know."

"I'm sure it does, Miss Sally. Well, I must be amblin' on. I'm on duty today." Flashing a smile, he tipped up his hat and looked at Jeannie. The look was so hot that Jeannie almost forgot where she was and jumped into his strong arms. Almost. He smoothly said his goodbyes to her Mama and Sara.

He gave her another smoldering look and said, "Jeannie, it is *always* a *pleasure* to see you. I hope to see you again soon, Sprite."

Nine hours later T.J. pulled into his condo's garage and instead of getting out of the car, he leaned back and closed his eyes. He was frustrated with himself because all day on duty he could not get the red haired, green-eyed witch, Jeannie, out of his mind. He had to get it together. Like earlier, at the church, he had wasted so much time standing under that tree waiting for a *glimpse* of Jeannie. T.J. prided himself on being a happily situated bachelor. Before Jeannie, he wouldn't have been caught dead waiting on some female, especially to only *talk*. And only talk for about 10 minutes at that. Yeah, he was definitely going against the grain with Jeannie. Wearily, he ran his hand down his face. Maybe he should just cut it off before it even got started. She obviously was attracted to him physically, but for whatever reason he didn't think she liked him too much. That was probably his fault, he grudgingly admitted to himself, but it was so much fun to tease her. Jeannie was a challenge, yes, but she was so much more than that. She seemed honest and actually had convictions and depth. That was such a refreshing change from his usual. And just as he thought that, he also realized that meant she wasn't the type of woman to be trifled with. Again, definitely not his type. She was the staying kind and would want the same from her man. Sighing to himself, he promised himself right then and there that for once he would be considerate of the situation and who she was and back off. Miss Jeannie was too *good* for him and he would only *hurt* her.

Chapter 2

Moran put her ear to the bathroom door by Jeannie's room and grinned to herself. She felt no shame at listenin' to her young friend, not at all. She was too busy thinkin' up some possibilities for the pretty little redhead and the super gorgeous Officer T.J. Suggs. Jeannie wouldn't admit nothin', but it was obvious to everyone around that she had caught the love bug. She was humming and dancin' all around the mansion. She already was a busy little thing, especially now that she had started her classes. And she was already a sweetie, most times, but it was like now nothin' could affect her. Little Sara had messed all over her car seat one day and it was nasty and funky by the time Jeannie came home from class. It had gotten everywhere and normally Jeannie would have really been putting her surprisingly foul mouth to use, but Jeannie had not one frown on her face as she tended to her motherly duties. In fact, she had been singing. Moran would have vomited everywhere. Thank the good Lord she could just be an Auntie. She knew Jeannie's super upbeat attitude was due to a man. It had to be. Couldn't nothin' make a woman smile and sing like that but a man. And after conversin' with Vette, she had to agree, it did sound like Jeannie might be likin' that handsome police officer. Now, the officer wasn't rich, of course. But from what she had heard he did alright. And while that would not have been enough for Moran, she knew her independent little friend would be right comfortable with that. Hmm. T.J. Suggs. Smiling, Moran walked away from the bathroom and headed to her own room. She needed to get ready to go and see her little sister, Macey, at the county jail.

Jeannie looked at herself in the mirror critically. She had her fluffy shower robe on so she looked like a drowned little waif further drowning in a huge robe. Frowning, she took the robe off and wondered what a man would see when he looked at her. Of course, she was blushing just at thinking about a man looking at her in nothin' but her bare skin. She had only ever been with that rotten Jed, Sara's daddy. Her ex-husband had been as wild as she had been as a youngin'. The problem had been that she had grown up and he hadn't. Towards the end of her relationship with Jed he had been so abusive, physically and verbally. Since she had left him she had really realized just what kind of damage he had done. Jeannie wasn't sure how appealin' she really was anymore and she felt out of whack with her femininity. That's one of the reasons why T.J. Suggs' attacks on her senses had caught her so off guard. Jed had told her on many occasions that the only hot thing about her was her "tits". *After all, they're right plump for such a puny ass woman.* Sighing, suddenly a bit unhappy, she turned to the side and looked at her imaginary derrière. It was so unfair that white girls didn't often have the *lusciousness* (Sylvette's favorite word for butt) in that department that Vette was so proud of. Jeannie smiled as she thought of her friend. They were both being silly and were also a little tipsy to tell the truth and were talking one day about the perfect body. Vette felt like as long as you had clear skin (every now and then Vette would have small bouts with acne and Vette hated that), a voluptuous ass and swangin' hips you were good. She refused to discuss breasts because she didn't have much in that department. She said it was so unfair that Jeannie was so petite and had such an awesome rack. They had laughed like henwits and Jeannie had replied that if she had Vette's ass she would never have to pay for anything or have any problems. Cause even Vette couldn't act like she didn't know that whenever they would be out and about, men would always be stumbling all over themselves cause of Vette's *lusciousness*. Jeannie knew that drove Ranald crazy too. Yeah, she definitely wouldn't mind the perks that came from having ass. Moran had chosen that moment to come into Vette's room. She remembered it clear as day. Moran had sashayed in with her hands on her hips and said,

"I don't know what's wrong with both yawl silly little girls. Men want a body on a woman like a woman over 30. All our jiggle shows we know how to take care of a man, if ya know what I mean. *I* have the best figure in this house ladies and don't you forget it. How do you think I nabbed all of my hubbies!"

The three of them had fallen all over each other they were laughing at themselves so hard. Jeannie felt a little better after reliving that memory. Vette and Moran were beautiful women, but they weren't *plastic* women. They had real imperfections like any other real woman and it didn't detract from their beauty, if anything, it added to it. Like, they loved her freckles. Jeannie couldn't understand it because to her they were a real imperfection, but they loved them and to them it added to *her* beauty. Jeannie had always been on the shelf about her flaming red hair, the freckles and her green eyes. Sighing, she knew beauty was in the eye of the beholder and that there were all different kinds of beauty. She would only admit this to herself, but she really hoped her kind of beauty appealed to the gorgeous T.J. Suggs.

Suggs ran on the wooded path that ran behind his house all the way out about 20 miles south. He usually ran on the path 3 times a week, about 2-4 miles each time. Today he was flying through his run as his mind was truly on other things. Normally, he let his mind go blank if he was able or he focused on all the natural sites that he saw during his runs. By about his 3rd mile he could usually feel a little strain on his muscles. Today, he looked down at his watch and he was already at 5 miles. And, of course, he was *fucking* distracted by the incomparable Jeannie. The power of pussy. And what was sad was he hadn't even gotten the pussy. And if he stayed true to what he had told himself he was going to do, it didn't even matter anyway cause he wouldn't be talking to her. He still believed that would be the best thing, but, damn it all, he couldn't get her sassy ass out of his head.

"Hey, Suggs!"

At the mention of his name, Suggs turned around. It was Officer Torres from Missing Persons. He was walking up the front steps to the precinct and Torres was hailing him towards her. Grinning, he trotted over and gave her a bear hug. He really liked Torres. She was fine *and* cool people and had no strings she needed to attach to a man. He purposely checked her out and realized he hadn't *had* her in a while.

"Hey Torres! Looking *good,* love."

She had a big beautiful smile and she was obviously happy to see him. She gave him a saucy wink and replied, "Well, ya know, you're *always* lookin' good Suggs. Mm mm."

He laughed good-naturedly. "Mm hmm. I bet you say that to all the guys."

Laughing, she replied, "Yeah, I do."

"So how goes it Torres?"

"Well, I was tryin' to see how Ranald was doing. Ya know I've been out for a while. I was doing undercover surveillance for a FED case. I heard Ranald headed up a ground team on a sting for the Hammer. I know the Hammer is detained now, but I heard some things didn't go so well."

Suggs so did not want to talk about that case. And he did not mind admitting to himself that he was still having issues with the big *Russian fag tag* that liked men. He wanted to throw up just thinking about it. He also wouldn't mind beating the dog shit out of the guy for even trying him like that. Thank God for Ranald coming in the nick of time, even though a part of him hated that Ranald even knew about what went down. He admitted to himself just then as he thought about the situation that he didn't want to just beat that Russian fuck's ass, he wanted to torture him...and then...dismember him; erase the fuck from the earth. Maybe then he would be able to let the shit rest.

"Hmm. Well, yeah, you're right. It did get interesting. We lost an officer during a shoot out. One of the accomplices, Max Bates, was shot in the spine. His girlfriend was injured as well."

"Wait," she interrupted. "I feel like I heard something happened with you as well. Is that right?"

Knowing it was going to come, he sighed. "Yeah man, some shit went down that wasn't cool at all Torres."

"Wow. What the fuck happened Suggs? You alright?"

He looked around at all the people walking around the precinct. He looked at the cars going back and forth, people walking on the sidewalk going about their way. And he blanked out for a moment. Life was beautiful and it was also hell. He realized at that odd moment that he truly was mortal and his life in this world is fleeting and he was but one small speck of the human existence.

Torres peered at him curiously and with some concern. "Hey Suggs, you alright. You're phasing out."

Suggs shook himself and it was weird, but it was like his vision *cleared.* He hadn't known that it was fuzzy. He wondered briefly if he should seek some help, maybe some counseling. "I'm good, Torres. Just..just, I just feel strange and a little off."

"Damn Suggs, you're worrying me. What happened to you?"

Suggs smiled vaguely. "I just got banged up a little bit. That's all. I guess it affected me more than I thought." Trying and seriously wanting to shake off his melancholy mood, Suggs suddenly laughed and said, "This is not the way to start the day. Don't worry about Suggs, baby. I'm always alright Torres. Let's go on in and start another hell of a day."

Torres looked into his face searchingly for a moment. His face was closed off now so she couldn't read anything, but still she worried. Suggs was known for his lady killer charm and devil may care attitude. He was also a badass. Not a lot seemed to phase or shake 'im. Today, though, he seemed different. Torres knew that the Lieutenant was trying to get him to be a Detective. Suggs had always groused at a mainly desk job. She wondered if maybe he shouldn't take it. This last sting may have been enough for him.

Later on that afternoon Suggs was leaning on a locker in the basement of the precinct by the gun cage. He had his headphones on and was trying to clear his mind of his day before he left for the day. He had made it a rule that he never carried stuff home with him from his job. That was how he always felt cops got burned out. It *had* been a rough day though. He had to shoot someone earlier and he didn't think the guy was going to make it *and* he had to turn two kids into child services, amongst other things. He was beat. Maybe his mom was right and he needed to look at another career path. He didn't know when it had happened, he was still a cop, but he was getting disgusted with what he saw every day. He couldn't get the man he shot out of his head. He remembered he had been standing in their living room and they had clearly hated him and everything he stood for from the beginning. No matter that he was just doing his job and trying to protect his own life, in their minds they were justified for their shit and *he* had come to them bringing madness and destruction. Well..maybe he had.

One of the perp's children, a little boy, had yelled at him and he could still hear the little boy's high and cracking voice as if the boy were right next to him, "Get outta my Daddy's house! I hate police! You hurt my Daddy! You hurt my Daddy!"

He had tried so hard to not have to shoot the man, especially in the man's home with his wife and kids there. One of his ex-partners had gotten a tip off about a big time drug dealer and Suggs had went with him for back up. Of course the situation had gotten out of hand once they got there. The little son had opened the front door for him and had been scared by the two cops barreling into the room with guns drawn and yelling freeze, get down. The perp and his wife had rushed into the front room, also terrified. A teenage girl, their daughter, he had assumed, came running from the kitchen with a butcher knife. The other cop, Brandon Knowles, had an itchy trigger finger some times and had not hesitated. He shot the girl in the hand and all hell broke loose. The perp howled with rage and charged directly at Knowles. Knowing that Knowles was going to have to take care of himself for a moment, Suggs heart had pounded with dread. He had ran over to the girl and quickly ripped a piece of her shirt off and wrapped it around her hand. He wished he didn't remember the look on her face when she had stared up at him. She had tears rolling down her face as she just kept saying over and over, "Please don't hurt our Father. Please don't take him."

The mother had started towards the girl right as her husband rushed Knowles. At that point, Suggs quickly stood and waved the wife over hurriedly.

"Hurry Mam! I need you to sit with your daughter and make sure you keep applying pressure!"

"Connie!" She reached her daughter and quickly moved her behind the couch.

Suggs had then stood quickly and pulled his gun on the perp. The perp was still going berserk. Suggs yelled freeze at the exact moment that Knowles shot off and hit the perp in the shoulder. The perp was so enraged the jolt of the bullet tearing through his shoulder did not stop him.

"You fucking mother fuckers! You shot my daughter!" He had tackled Knowles head on and the two had fallen over an easy chair and landed on the floor, grunting and punching each other. When Knowles gun skid to a stop near Suggs foot, Suggs kicked Knowles' gun towards the front door so the perp couldn't reach it. Quickly, he looked back at the family, saw the mom and the son were sheltering the sister behind the couch, and knew he more than likely wouldn't have to worry about an attack coming from behind. He could hear the little boy calling to his Dad though.

"Freeze, sir!" Knowles and the man continued to fight. "Freeze! Freeze, sir, or I will shoot you!"

Knowles was starting to tire and the man could tell. The man punched Knowles in his face and blood sprayed all over the perp as Knowles' nose broke from the hit. He crashed back to the ground and the man scrambled quickly towards the knife his daughter had dropped, grabbed it and held it out in front of him as a warning to Suggs. Backing up, never taking his eyes off of Suggs, he had delivered a swift kick to Knowles mid-section and after one barely audible grown Knowles had passed out.

The man glared at him with hate. There had been unshed tears in his eyes. "Why have you done this to my family? You get the fuck outta here cop if you know what's good for you."

"I can't do that, Sir."

"Hmph. Yes, you can."

"Sir, *I'm* holding the gun. Put your weapon down and put your hands in the air."

"Fuck you and fuck your gun! You shot my daughter and you've threatened my family! You gonna have to kill me cop."

"I don't *want* to kill you, Sir and I didn't shoot your daughter. Now put your weapon down! This is your last warning."

"I don't give a fuck about your warning. I give a fuck about my family! Everything I do, I do for my family. Kill me if you have to. You wouldn't understand pig, but I'll die for mine."

"I'm *not* going to hurt your family, *Sir*! Put the weapon down!"

The perp's wife spoke up. "Tommy, baby, put it down. Don't get shot again baby. Put it down." Her voice trailed off as she tried to control the emotion in her voice. She then addressed Suggs. "Please, officer. Please. He's all we have. I'm sick. I'm really sick. We need him here."

"Shut up, Yolanda," Tommy interrupted. "This mother fucker don't care about our problems."

Trying *not* to care because he was still in a critical condition, not to mention Knowles needed help, Suggs steeled his heart and did not respond to the wife.

"Are you putting it down, sir?"

The perp clearly took his words as a slap in the face *and* affirmation of what he had told his wife. Snarling viciously, the man had said, "You fucking pig bitch. Didn't you hear what she said? You take me away and they're not okay. That's my family, so you gonna have to kill me today."

"No!" his wife yelled as she jumped up. "No, Tommy! No!"

He barreled towards Suggs and Suggs had no other choice. One discharge went off and the man's body jerked to a stop. The man's eyes grew large with disbelief and shock and then he looked down at the blood that was spreading along his side. He looked up and though in obvious pain, he straightened himself and held his side where the bullet had struck him and opened his mouth to say Suggs knew not what. Blood filled his mouth and he spit that out instead. Groaning, he then dropped to a knee, but still did not drop the knife. Cautiously, Suggs walked towards him to assist the man with the flesh wound, but had to stop abruptly as the man emitted a guttural yell and stood rather quickly. Straining to speak, he said, "Fuck you...toy cop."

He rushed towards Suggs again and this time Suggs put a bullet in him that would stop him. The force of the bullet struck the man so hard that he flew back and landed on Knowles where he was finally still, laying on Knowles and the floor, with blood pooling all around him. Of a sudden screams broke out from all of Tommy's family members. Suggs had shot him in his shoulder and due to the close range, the shoulder was shattered.

It had definitely been a bad day.

Torres eyed Suggs leaving the gun cage and trotted after him. She caught him quickly.

"Hey, you ok? I heard about it." When he turned around and just stared at her vacantly, her heart melted. Poor Suggs.

"I read the report, T.J. You did everything right. It's Knowles whose behavior is in question. Try to let it roll off."

She jumped a little as he abruptly grabbed her arm and spoke tonelessly, "I looked into the family's history. The wife has cancer. Stage 3. The husband has 2 felonies from when he was in his early 20's and can't keep employment, probably because he's profiled. They really have some legitimate issues, Torres. Did I *help* them? Did we as a police department help those people or make their situation worse? I mean, what the fuck are we doing out there, Torres?"

"Suggs, what's wrong with you? We're the good guys, remember? We're the best thing going for the people."

Truly disturbed by his thoughts, Suggs mumbled, "So you say."

Torres looked him over speculatively. The fact that he was a hurtin' Texas man made him all the more appealing and she felt she knew just what he needed to take a load off.

"Why don't you come see me tonight Suggs. It's been a long time. We can have dinner and then take your mind off of things for a while."

Suggs processed her invitation and had to shake himself. He really was Mr. Doom and Gloom right now. Maybe he did need a tumble in the sheets with the ever vigorous Marcella Torres. It had been a month or so since he had drowned in a woman's warmth, definitely longer than he was used to. He blamed that lame ass reality on Miss Jeannie Derit. Since he had met Jeannie he hadn't thought about any other woman, even his regular,Torres. Thinking to himself again how ridiculous it was for him to be chasing a woman that he would be all wrong for in the first place, he figured he may as well indulge in some feminine companionship. Maybe she *could* take all the other shit that was on his mind off his mind, including the delectable Jeannie.

<u>Chapter 3</u>

Jeannie cursed as she stumbled over her shoestring. "Shit!"

Of course her loud ass mouth woke up the baby and the wail that rent the once quiet mansion filled her with even more frustration. She had just put Sara down for her nap.

"Dammit!"

Moran stepped into the hallway from the sitting room attached to her room and looked at Jeannie with an amused look on her face.

"You keep on doin' all that cussin and thumpin' Jeannie, she ain't gone never go back to sleep."

Muttering to herself before she answered Moran, Jeannie fell to one knee and started tying her shoe. She looked up at Moran.

"It's not like I even meant for none of this to be happenin'. I tripped over my damn shoestring."

"Girl, what did I tell you about them damn shoestrings. Honestly Jeannie, you're gonna break your damn neck one day."

Wryly, Jeannie responded as she stood up, "Obviously, you're right Moran. Hate to admit it and I feel silly for even having this conversation Miss Moran, but I really ain't never been good about my shoestrings. I just never think about the damn annoying things." Jeannie stretched quickly and said, "Come to Sara's with me Moran."

"Oh, I was comin'," Moran assured her. "My Sara needs me."

Jeannie discreetly rolled her eyes and smiled to herself. Sara was finally quiet and playing with her toys instead of Moran just a bit later. Jeannie looked at the time and groaned in frustration.

"Moran, I really gotta go. It's the first day for this class and now I might be late."

"Oh, of course Jeannie dear. Well, who's watching Sara?"

"The new housekeeper."

"I think you better let me have sweet little Sara. We don't know that woman well *and* she ain't me, darlin."

Jeannie laughed, "Moran, I love you so much. Of course that's best. You're right. Thank you."

Moran regally waved her hand. "Never you mind, Jeannie. You just get to class. Sara and I will go shopping."

Jeannie was still smiling about Moran when she pulled up to the building she was supposed to have class in. God, she still wasn't used to being in anyone's classroom yet. Luckily, some of her previous college credits had transferred so she wasn't starting from scratch at least. Jeannie entered the building and looked around, familiarizing herself with her surroundings so she wouldn't get lost. She hated the feeling of being lost, even to a small degree.

"Hey! What're you looking at?"

Jeannie jumped and peered into the murkiness in a hallway that was right across from the hallway she stood in. The lights flickered off and on giving it a real creepy kind of feel.

"I can't see you," Jeannie called.

"Yeah, cause I'm leaving the darkroom and the hallway is kinda dark and creepy too. There's no light escaping into the hall at all. This part of the hallway is a dead end."

The voice finally materialized into a sandy-haired, brown-eyed guy with a friendly and open smile. He was a little on the short side like Jeannie.

He walked up to her and smiled into her eyes.

"It's nice to meet you. I'm Cam. Don't worry, if you're not doing film or photography you never have to go down that hallway. And most people are here for the social and civic sciences... and law, of course. And I'm betting you're here for the latter."

"I sure am. I'm gonna be a lawyer."

He chuckled ruefully, "You're a better person than me. I couldn't handle studying the law. I would always fall asleep in class."

Jeannie laughed. "That boring huh?"

"Oh, definitely." He looked at her with an appreciative smile on his face. "But nothing about you screams boring. Quite the opposite actually."

Jeannie gulped in nervousness. She could swear he was flirting with her! Enjoying it and his easy manner, she responded with genuine alacrity, "Well, that certainly is nice. I'm glad to know I seem interestin' to ya. I'm pleased to meet ya. I'm Jeannie."

He did a cute little gentlemanly bow and in a funny interpretation of a British accent, he said, "And the honor, my dear, is all mine." He gallantly presented his arm. "May I be of assistance, Mum?"

Knowing she couldn't even attempt a British accent, she laughed and replied, "You really don't know how much that would save my life right now Cam."

He bobbed his head in a stuffy butler sort of way, which made her burst into laughter.

"Well then, my sweet, off we go."

She belatedly grabbed his arm and they walked to her classroom, laughing with each other like they had been friends for years.

Two and a half hours later a different Jeannie was walking out of Professor Ronald P. Meyers classroom. Frowning, Jeannie grimaced as she heard the professor calling for her to wait. She already could tell his class was going to be hell. Professor Meyers had already commented on her being 2 mins late, her terrible diction and obvious outspoken manner. Really, all Jeannie wanted to do was run 'im over with her pick up. As soon as Jeannie had the thought she felt bad, but, hey, she was a redhead. She was glad her thoughts weren't worse.

She walked back through the doorway and began the long descent between the stadium seats to his podium where he stood glaring at her. Jeez, she thought. She had just met him. Was it that bad? And it was just the *first* day of class! Old weasel, she thought meanly.

She reached his podium and tried not to stare at his bushy grey eyebrows. She had to admit, it was pretty hard not to. Someone could have written a whole book on them for what your eyebrows should never look like.

"Miss Jeannie. You finally decided to *grace* me with your presence."

Jeannie was taken aback by the meanness in his tone. "Uh, Sir, y-,"

She was cut off.

"It's Professor Meyers, young lady, and don't you forget it. I don't like sass."

"Mm hmm. Right, well, like I was *tryin'* to say, you had just called me. I couldn't very well knock people down to get here now, could I?"

He squinched his eyes tighter, if such a thing were possible. "There's that sass, young lady."

Jeannie prayed for patience. It would not do to start off at odds with one of her law professors.

"Sorry Sir, I mean, Professor Meyers. What did ya need to see me for?"

He glared at her a couple of seconds longer before he responded, "Are you sure you want to be a lawyer? You'll not teach?"

Confused, she replied, "Yes, I wanna be a lawyer. I *will* be one. I don't really know about teaching, to be honest. If I did do that it probably wouldn't be till later on in my career."

"Ah, I see. Well, I must say it is good that you don't really want to teach."

"And why is that Professor?"

"Professor Meyers," he corrected.

Through clenched teeth she responded, "Professor Meyers."

"No," he barked. "Say it in a *complete sentence.*"

Briefly wondering what she had done to deserve such a Professor, Jeannie bit the bullet and responded, "And why is that, Professor Meyer?"

"Because you speak like a guttersnipe. You need to work on your diction and you don't like adhering to authority, not to mention your lack of control over your emotions. You can clearly see them written on your face and in your body language. I wouldn't want you teaching law to my grandchildren."

Jeannie was so taken aback, for a second she didn't respond, couldn't respond. Who in the hell did this old geezer think he was? If Vette were here she would be rollin' (as disrespectful as that would be) about Jeannie's present predicament.

"Soooo, because I don't want to disrespect you *Professor Meyer,* I'm going to go ahead and leave now."

"Oh, I see, you can't handle constructive criticism."

"I really don't know if you can even call what ya just said constructive Sir, I mean Professor Meyers. And those are *your* opinions. They don't have to be mine."

"You silly little henwit. I'm trying to help you."

"I don't think I like your kinda help."

"Nevertheless, you will need it. "

Jeannie couldn't hold back a moment longer, "Now you listen to me *Greybrow*. I don't need nothin' you got."

"*Anything.* So why are you in *my* class then, oh know it all?"

"Ya know, I don't know anymore."

"Hmph. I knew it. A little adversity and you go running off with your tail tucked between your legs. How will you ever be a lawyer? You have to have nerves and focus of steel, Miss Jeannie Derit."

Jeannie felt the blood in her head rushing. She so wanted to explode. So wanted to, but then she thought about Sara and her Momma. She thought about Vette and Eric and even the gorgeous ass Officer Suggs. She had people counting on her and she had plans for herself as well. And damn it all, she would be a lawyer if it was the last thing she did. She loved the law and wanted to play her part. So, her response was a lot more tame than she had thought it would initially be.

"I don't appreciate how you're saying what you're saying to me, but I want to be a lawyer more than I don't wanna have to deal with your rudeness. So, I'm gonna *ace* your class, *Professor Meyers*. You- just- watch."

She quickly hiked her purse up on her shoulder, turned around and started walking back up the way she came. She did not look back.

Professor Meyers watched her until she was gone, smiling all the while.

Jeannie muttered to herself irritably while she stacked up some oranges Sara had knocked down while she hadn't been paying attention. Sara loved to grab stuff at grocery stores especially. And Sara was suffering from a real bad case of the grabbies. Sara squeaked with excitement when another orange tumbled from the pile, fell and hit Jeannie on her back as she was getting up from the floor.

"Shit!"

"*Tsk tsk tsk.*"

Jeannie hurriedly straightened herself, looked up and stared straight into the gorgeous eyes, face, smile, *everything*, that was Officer T.J. Suggs. Well, hello, she thought dreamily.

"You're always cussin', gorgeous. What're you gonna do when you're in the courtroom Jeannie, cause you sure can't curse in there."

Waspishly, she replied, "I know what I can and can't do in a courtroom Officer Suggs, so I don't need you tryin' to school me." As much as she was so giddy on the inside *and* he smelled so good, she still frowned at him cause she was gonna be damned if he knew about her stupid fascination with him. She was about to speak when she happened to notice Sara staring up at him with fascination.

"I wish you wouldn't do that to my baby girl."

"What'd I do, Jeannie?"

"Oh, you know. All that male potency and stuff. And she should be too young to even respond to that, but there she goes again moonin' all over you."

He kissed Sara on one of her cheeks, causing an excited squeal to come from the little one.

Suggs caught Jeannie's eye and smiled flirtatiously at her, "I sure wish I could get her mama to moon after me too."

Jeannie gulped with nervousness. She started to feel a little flushed. God, what this man did to her. Against her will, her expression softened and she was going to say something really weak and stupid. And he was obviously gearing for some action too as he quietly moved his buggy and then hers to the Apple section right next to them.

"Suggs! I found them!"

Jeannie's eyes liked to pop out of her head when a drop dead gorgeous Latino woman rushed up to Suggs with Star fruit in her hand.

It was so unexpected. And, honestly, she didn't know why what with Suggs being as good lookin' as he was and also on account of her sayin' she wanted nothin' to do with'im. But she was genuinely stuck for a moment. When she noticed that the woman was finally registering that she had interrupted something, Jeannie snapped out of it. The woman was just apologizing, when Jeannie interrupted, "No, no. *I'm* sorry, Mam. My daughter and I are in your way. We'll just be goin'."

If she weren't surprisingly hurt by what was obviously going on between the two, the look on Sugg's face would be humorous. He simultaneously looked ill, irritated, sexy and dare she say, wistful.

Jeannie reached out and grabbed Sara and the buggy. She moved through the tight space between her buggy and his when he caught her hand. Against her will, the touch of his hand made her falter. She looked up into his eyes and momentarily forgot about the other woman.

"I want to see you again Jeannie and not just in passing. How can we make that happen?"

Torres chose that moment to speak. "Uh, Suggs, I hate to interrupt, but we need to get going or we're gonna be late."

"Yeah, yeah. I got it Torres."

When he called the woman by her last name she realized the woman must also be a cop. Damning herself for even doing it, she asked, "So you two work together?"

Torres' manner had changed a little bit. Her eyes were hard and she smirked a little at her. "Yeah, I *guess* you could say that."

Suggs was looking at Jeannie so he didn't see Torres. He heard the suggestive tone of her voice though. "Jeannie, Torres is a cop. We're at the same precinct. She used to work with Ranald, too."

"Oh. Well, uh, I guess it's great you both obviously get along so well.

Suggs choked a little and then seemed to not know what to say. Jeannie couldn't resist needling him before she left him in the hands of the delectable *Torres*. Life was so not fair.

"I can't believe you're at a loss for words. Big bad, T.J. Suggs. What you gonna do now?" Needling him further she said quietly, "Tsk, tsk, tsk." With that, she hurriedly walked away, pushing a giggling Sara in the buggy. She felt T.J.'s eyes on her as she walked off. She didn't

think so, but she wondered painfully if he was in love with *Torres*.

A week and a half later Jeannie was doing some research for a 25 page essay when she

was interrupted by someone knocking on the kitchen door. Jeannie ran to the kitchen door as fast

as she could without falling down the 2nd level of the great stairs. She was muttering to herself

irritably when she opened the door.

Suggs stared at Jeannie intently, ravenously soaking up her appearance and trying to not

feel like a stalker at the same time.

Jeannie knew she looked like a retarded fish as her mouth dropped open at the sight of a

man that shouldn't be as gorgeous as he was. Life was not fair.

"Hello, Beautiful."

Feeling horribly flushed and anxious, a bright red blush crept up her neck and temporarily

stained her cheeks. She really hoped it didn't show too much at least and before she could

respond, he spoke again.

Smiling, he reached towards her and lightly ran his hand down the inside of her arm. "So

that blush, it's just for me, huh? I make you blush, Sprite?"

So easily seduced by him and not knowing what else to say, she blurted out, "I really like

it when you call me beautiful and, uh, gorgeous."

"Oh, you do. Finally, I'm saying something right to you."

Suddenly realizing that Suggs was just randomly at the mansion door, the side kitchen

door at that, Jeannie's treacherous, elated feelings started to sink.

"What's going on? Why are you at the kitchen door?"

Suggs light-hearted smile died as well. His voice was suddenly brisk and professional as he responded, "I have some news *and* Eric wanted me to do a perimeter check on the mansion. In fact, I'll be here for a while and another uniform will be patrolling as well."

Jeannie's eyes widened with distress. Suddenly, remembering her manners, Jeannie stepped back from the door.

"Come in, Officer Suggs."

He smiled at her, but his smile was now strained. Jeannie's heart sunk further.

"Thank you Jeannie." He followed her as she walked through the massive kitchen into the Sunroom that was attached to it. She noticed Suggs was very quiet and observing everything in his surroundings. She showed him to a wicker couch while she sat in a matching chair across from him. Knowing she wasn't going to like this *news,* she sighed and looked into his eyes. His eyes were tender as he gazed at her. He spoke first.

"This place is huge, huh?"

"It sure is.... *So*, I know this must be bad cause you called me *Jeannie*."

He looked surprised for a moment. "I guess I did. I'm in cop mode, *Jeannie*."

Taking a deep breath, she asked shakily, "Is Vette alright?"

He nodded his head slowly. "Vette's fine, Jeannie. I mean, this is about Vette, yes, but also *you* and also The Hammer."

Jeannie gasped. *Her and The Hammer?*

"What do ya mean, me? *And* the *Hammer*. I know who that is. I know what he tried to do to Vette's mom. What does *he* have to do wit' *me*?"

"Okay, so Eric received some intel on Russini-,"

"Wait!" Jeannie interrupted throwing her hands in the air. "Who the hell is Russini?"

"Oh. The Hammer's name is Russini."

"Mm. Okay. Go on."

"Alright. So the Hammer has put a hit on the mansion. Well, on the occupants of the mansion. Lopez has a snitch-."

"And Lopez is?"

He smiled wanly. "I guess you wouldn't know'im. Lopez is a Fed, like Ranald used to be. Anyway, his snitch was placed in Russini's prison to get some info they needed from the Hammer. The Hammer had the snitch keeping watch while he arranged the hit with some Columbians that also want to take out Ricardo." He paused for a moment preparing to explain who Ricardo was, when Jeannie beat him to the punch.

"*Him,* I know about. He killed Pogo."

"Yeah, he did and he's also a sadist, sociopath and soon to be a dead mother fucker."

Jeannie gasped in confusion and surprise. "What do ya mean? Vette said he's a high ranked Columbian drug lord; that he's almost untouchable."

Suggs grimaced in distaste at her last statement. "There was a time that, yes, we couldn't fucking touch'im. Actually, we still can't."

"What?" Jeannie immediately questioned. "What do you mean? I'm confused."

"He's finally stepped on the wrong toes, Sprite."

"Ah, I see. Other bad fuckers want to get him now."

"Yes mam. And Russini is one of those bad ass mother fuckers who want him dead. Now, he's also surrounded by other people who want him dead. Ricardo set up a lot of his so called friends to get *their* deals with the heavy-weight suppliers. Those bastards all want him cut up into little pieces."

"Jesus! And to think Max Bates was involved in all this as well. This is crazy, Suggs."

Suggs grimaced again. "Welcome to our world, Jeannie. Anyway, so Russini has this hit out on the mansion, namely Vette I think, as she was married to Max, but of course he would want no witnesses. Everyone would be executed. He also has a strike team assembled to take out Ricardo. They just wait on word from him, through whomever he has handle it on the outside."

Jeannie was sure she looked as ill as she felt. "This can't be happenin', T.J. He's sending people to kill us? Oh God and Sylvette gets in soon! She's in danger as well, even though she doesn't live here anymore. Oh my God! Moran and the staff! Sara!"

Suggs stood up and walked towards the now panicked Jeannie. She was still rambling and intermittently whispering, *Oh God,* when he leaned down and grabbed both of her arms. He stood her up and tipped her face up to his. She looked at him with her vivid green eyes that were slanted like a cats. He looked at her freckles that dusted her nose and cheeks. She rambled and he stared. A moment later he leaned down and smiled when her eyes belatedly focused on his, read his intent and then panic clouded them. He met his lips to hers and tasted her sweet nectar as she slowly and hesitantly brought her arms up and wrapped them around the back of his neck. He pulled her closer and lightly bit her bottom lip. When she gasped, he slid his tongue inside her warm mouth. She tasted so sweet. He made love to her mouth over and over. His dick was rock hard when he vaguely heard voices coming from what he assumed was a hallway outside of the kitchen. Reluctantly, he stopped having his way with her mouth and slowly pulled away from her. Before he completely pulled away he leaned forward and pressed a soft kiss on her kiss-swollen lips.

Jeannie shook her head to get a hold of her passion for Officer T.J. Suggs. Lord, she had forgotten where she was! She could clearly hear the voices headed towards them now. Suddenly, a thought hit her.

"Oh no, *Suggs*! Do I look like I just, well, was just-," she faltered with embarrassment.

"Being kissed?"

Blushing scarlet, she responded quietly, "I think it was a little more than kissin'."

"I think you're right Jeannie. But later. We still need to go over some serious things. I shouldn't have done that while I'm on duty, but you tempt me beyond belief, Sprite. And you look fine." Jeannie was still beet red when he grabbed her hand and continued, "Let's go see what the noise is all about so we can get back to the business at hand."

"Where're Jeannie and Moran? Sara?"

Jeannie was surprised to hear Sylvette's voice and the scared and frantic tone of her voice as well.

Suggs turned back to look at her. "Good. Ranald's back. We can really tackle this now."

"Yeah, and now not only are we easy pickin', but Vette and Ranald are too. And he really wants them, right?"

"Yes, he does, but there's still more I have to tell you Jeannie that is just about *you*."

He didn't explain. An odd look came across his face and then he abruptly turned back around and continued walking towards Vette and Ranald.

If possible, Jeannie's heart sunk even further.

Later on that afternoon, Vette and Moran were sitting on Jeannie's bed. Jeannie was very pensive. So were Vette and Moran. Little Sara was with Jeannie's mom for the next couple of days. Jeannie had just seen them off. Thank God for that at least. Sara had a cozy little room in Sally's double wide.

Vette spoke into the charged silence. "This is all my fault. This is all my fault."

Jeannie opened her mouth to speak, but Moran beat her to the punch.

"What in the hell you talkin' bout girl? This isn't your fault, Sylvette. It's just the devil's luck is all baby." Moran's voice softened and she reached over and rubbed Vette's shoulder. "Please don't blame yourself."

Jeannie thought of something and smiled at Vette suddenly, with mischief clearly evident on her face.

"Really, what we need to do is learn how to kick some ass."

Vette had been somber since she and Ranald had come back. Their honeymoon had been cut short from the news about Russini's hit. But a small smile showed as she responded, "Ya know Jeannie, I think I like that idea."

"Yeah!" Jeannie exclaimed. "Then we could protect ourselves and beat some Russian ass too!"

Sylvette burst into laughter and looked at Moran. "So whaddya say, Auntie? You wanna learn how to be bad asses with me and Jeannie?"

Moran stuck her tongue out at them. "Why tease an old lady, you young *She-Ra's*? *I'm* not about to make a fool of myself. I'm made for pampering and spendin' money, honey's."

Jeannie really felt like hell on the inside, but Moran was so funny. She broke into laughter and *Vette* was laughing so hard she had tears coming out of her eyes. Jeannie secretly wondered if they might not all be a bit hysterical.

<u>Chapter 4</u>

Ranald and Suggs were walking down the hallway that led to Jeannie's room, when loud peals of laughter broke the silence that cloaked the huge mansion. On edge, both of them instinctively went for their guns.

Ranald grimaced as he realized it was just laughter. He looked at Suggs. Suggs was looking at him with a wry smile on his face.

"We're like two old, dusted ass cops right now. *Really* jumpy man."

"I wish you weren't right, Suggs. Although I can say I'm glad they can find something to laugh about."

"It's gonna stop as soon as we walk in there."

Eric frowned in response. "Okay. No more comments from you. Damn, Suggs."

Suggs pushed Ranald on the shoulder. "Aw, come on. They may stop laughing, but they know we're the best mother fuckas around to protect'em."

"So says your cocky ass, Suggs. How you know Jeannie feels like you can protect 'er?"

Suggs put his hands up. "Wait, wait, wait man. I meant collectively, not just Jeannie. Ya know, I meant *all* of'em should know that we're on the job."

Ranald stopped walking and looked at Suggs. He smirked, "Your, *I'll never just want one woman or have a fuckin complainin' ass female giving me grief,* bullshit. You *like* Jeannie, Suggs. A *lot,* if you couldn't tell your damn self."

Suggs was openly glaring at Ranald and quipped back,

"Okay. I know you're all domesticated and shit now. But don't confuse me with you. I ain't lookin' for a female. In case you haven't noticed *bitches* never run out. They're every fuckin' where."

Ranald wasn't impressed by Suggs response.

"Whatever, man. You still didn't deny that you like 'er man."

Suggs eyes narrowed dangerously. "You should come to the gym at the precinct so I can kick your ass, Ranald. It's been a long time."

Ranald didn't even bother to respond to Suggs taunt. He smiled to himself though and just started walking again. They reached Jeannie's door and heard Moran yelling, "Whoo hoo, Jeannie! Kick some ass girl!"

Suggs grinned and Eric just shook his head. Eric opened the door and stopped abruptly at the site that greeted him. He was stunned into silence. Suggs, however, choked from trying to hold back laughter.

"Uh, charming, beautiful, *graceful* Ladies, what in the hell are yawl doin'?" The laughter could clearly be heard in Ranald's voice.

Jeannie knew a blush had to be appearing on her somewhere. Her embarrassment at that moment knew no bounds. She quickly stole a look at Suggs and was dismayed to see a devilish grin on his face as he openly stared at her. Oh the fates were cruel.

Jeannie was at that moment looking up at Suggs while her teeth were stilled wrapped around a big chunk of Vette's calf. Vette was caught mid snarl with one of her hands wrapped in Jeannie's red curls. Moran was standing over them with a horrifyingly mortified look on her face as she had been shamelessly cheering them on.

Eric, eventually breaking the awkward silence, cleared his throat while trying to gather his own composure. He didn't know whether to laugh, help them up or stay clear away from the madwomen.

"Mm hmm. So, do yawl need help, um, untangling yourselves?"

After he spoke there was a brief moment of charged silence. And then Suggs cracked. He started laughing and it felt good to laugh. Then *all* of them did...and couldn't stop for a long time.

About two hours later they were all sitting in the formal dining room at the opulent and ostentatious table waiting for dinner to be brought to them. Their hilarity had died a while ago. They were all engaging in quiet polite conversation when the doorbell intruded the quiet of the mansion. Vette and Jeannie jumped. Moran giggled hysterically and hiccuped. She held her hand to her chest in obvious nervousness.

"Jesus!" Moran rushed out. "I didn't think about how nerve-wracking this whole situation was going to be." She turned towards the guys, who were leaving the table to get the door.

"No one would just walk up to our door, ring it and then come in and kill us would they? I mean, that would be ludicrous, right?"

Suggs grimaced and silently walked away.

Eric turned to Moran and said, "Don't worry, Ms. Moran. It'll all be okay. Don't worry."

She smiled gratefully in return and then Eric followed Suggs. Turning to Jeannie and Moran she smiled encouragingly and said, "See girls, there's nothing to worry about."

Jeannie narrowed her eyes and felt deep in her heart that was not going to be the truth in this situation. The Hammer would exact his revenge and so would Max Bates. Jeannie was more scared of the mess they were in now then when Jed used to wig out on her.

"Moran, I hope you're right."

"So do I baby."

Vette suddenly raised her hand and whispered loudly, "I can hear talking. It doesn't sound like anything bad is going on."

Jeannie jumped up and slowly walked towards the hallway that led to the massive foyer. Jeannie listened hard and swore she heard laughter, short masculine laughter.

"Moran! I think Vette is right."

"Well get closer, Jeannie. Ya know they not gon' tell us everything. See if they're talkin' bout what's goin' on."

"Okay." Jeannie turned back around and started to walk cautiously forward when she sensed Vette come up behind her. Without turning around, she whispered, "Glad you comin' girl. We cain't let'em hear us. Moran's right. We might be able to find out some shit."

"Hey! What the fuck?," Vette whispered loudly. "How'd you know I was behind you. I was loud?"

Jeannie's heart stopped momentarily and even in the situation they were in, she thought about Jed. She turned to Vette and smiled a brief ghost of a humorless smile. "I had to learn to be...aware, if ya will. I never knew what direction *he'd* be comin' from."

Jeannie and Vette shared a strong bond, so Vette knew who Jeannie meant and shared her pain. Vette smiled gently and put her hand on Jeannie's shoulder, "You never have to see *him* again. *Thank God.*"

Jeannie and Vette stopped at an alcove indented in the wall of the hallway. From the direction they were coming from it was on the right side of the hallway. They leaned forward and could barely make out two male figures to the left and they could clearly hear a *third* male voice on the same side they were on. Him, they couldn't even begin to see through all the tropical plants blocking their view. They could hear the three quite clearly though.

Suggs leaned against the stair bannister and nodded his head, yes, *again* after Ranald's younger brother, Kameron, asked him the same question for the third time.

"I mean, this is unbelievable! And protecting the women in *this* situation," he paused to throw his hands wide. "This situation is full of faults. The bad guys can get in by so many ways. Since *we'd* just be protecting them we're unable to protect *all* entry points. And no one knows about this? No one in the department?"

Ranald responded tersely, "Come on, Kameron. Of course Lopez and Willis know. How else could we have what we need to handle this. Besides, they're still prepping the route to the safehouse."

"Okay. But you know we have to move them out of here anyway, right?"

Suggs spoke up. "Why move them? Isn't that what they'd expect?"

Kameron glared, "I guess you didn't hear what I said earlier."

"I'm with Kameron on this one, Suggs. How can we defend such a great fuckin' space? It's gonna be just us. And Lopez feels it'll stay viable longer that way. The more people who know, I guarantee it'll get to the cops on Russini's payroll."

"Yeah, I get that Ranald," Suggs responded. "But there's gotta be a way we can defend this space. And, ok, so we don't have but the three of us. We can still man the entry points by blocking them and booby trapping them. That'll throw the bastards off guard. See, they'll expect our natural instinct to be to run. We stay here they'll figure we're stupid, naive, ya know, unprepared. They would underestimate us. We'd have the advantage and we could keep'em out."

Kameron seemed to be thinking about what Suggs suggested and Ranald was pacing back and forth.

Kameron broke the silence. "Okay… I can see benefits to your idea, but we still can't keep them here for a long time. Eventually, we'd have to move man."

Ranald stopped and looked at Suggs. "Yeah, we will need to move'em eventually cause he'll just take the risk and blow us up once it becomes too much of a chore. But I guess it makes sense to decimate'em and give'em hell first."

Suggs felt a heavy weight lift off of his chest. Finally, a plan. He hated to be idle and especially in a situation like this. Besides, he *did* want Jeannie to know she could trust in him and he would protect her. Why it mattered to him so much, he really wasn't quite sure. He just knew he wanted to keep her safe. He wanted her safe and with *him*. He'd be damned if he'd ever admit that shit to Ranald though.

Kameron nodded his head with a sense of finality and then remembered something. "So, what about the other shit that's supposed to be going on? There's another player, right? A different threat?"

Ranald's eyes met Suggs'. Suggs was worried about this upcoming well..battle, but it also excited him. But what Kameron was asking him about now filled him with nothing but two things, fear and dread. And he resented like hell that he felt that way.

Ranald waited a moment and when it became apparent that Suggs wasn't going to talk, he stated calmly, "Yeah, so Jeannie's ex-husband broke outta jail with a couple of guys, not sure if they're all together, but he broke out. The most disturbing thing about it is that in his cell Jeannie's name was written everywhere and everywhere her name was written there was dried semen *and* blood, Jed's blood. He had a solitary cell and obviously the warden never reported it or they never checked on'im, I don't know. Anyhow, he's loose and I'd be willing to bet he's gonna come after her. He's obsessed with'er. I let Suggs know as soon as I was aware. He broke out late last night."

Kameron was clearly disturbed as he frowned and haltingly asked, "A-and, I'm assuming he used to, well, be-."

Suggs broke in, "Yeah, he used to beat her. And she's so small Kam, so small. Yeah, he beat'er. I did the first report on their domestic violence case, I didn't know who Jeannie was then though. I held her file in my hand tellin' me he was hurtin' her, but we treated it just like every other domestic violence case that doesn't involve kids, we push it to the end of the pile because the women, the women they always seem to go back or get killed by the man they keep runnin' back to. And that report was from when she was 19."

Kameron looked at his older brother questioningly. Suggs obviously was not taking this news well and something deeper seemed to be going on.

"Suggs," Ranald began. "I know you don't wanna admit you dig Jeannie, but let's just pretend like you're okay with admitting it. You don't have to worry about it. It's not like he can just walk up in the house and then just as easily get through all of us. And *she's* changed Suggs. She ain't gone let him just get her either."

"He'll come after her, Eric. You're right about that."

Kameron chimed in with a look of steel on his face, "Like Eric said he'll have to get through all of us and our fun toys. No way it's happening."

Suggs nodded his head. "Alright. Well, I guess the only thing to do now is prepare the house- in and out. And before you ask Kam, we have more than enough toys. You Navy Seals are so fucking paranoid."

Kam laughed and walked over and pushed Suggs lightly on the shoulder, "Whatever, man. Paranoid or not, a Seal can kick a cop's ass anyday."

Suggs raised a brow and smirked. "Oh you want a lesson, young one? Cause I'll happily oblige. It's been a while since I've had a chance to whoop your cheeky ass."

"That's real funny Suggs, especially since your *old* ass is only 4 years older than me. And I accept your challenge. When all this is over I'll give you a lesson so you don't get taken down again by a big badass Russian."

"Whoa!" Ranald interrupted. "That's hitting below the belt Kam, even for you."

Suggs tried hard to control the rush of fury that came with the reference to him and the big Russian who liked men, namely him. He knew Kam didn't know that detail though. Now that Ranald had opened his damn mouth, Kam was looking at him oddly. Trying to play it off, he smiled and shook his head.

"Kam, it was just that the guy got me down, ya know. I was helpless, he could've taken me out and I wouldn't have been able to stop'im."

"Well, yeah, whoa. I can see why it's a sensitive subject. I'm still surprised you admitted that to me though, man."

"Well," Suggs responded wryly, "Your brother kinda let the cat outta the bag, didn't he."

Kam smiled mischievously and turned to Eric. "Eric, you're a bad friend."

Ranald put his hands in the air in the don't shoot poise. "Hey man. I was tryin' to be a friend by advising *you* to stop talking about it."

Kam smiled mischievously again and turned back to Suggs. "You know I'm never gonna stop teasin' ya about that. Damn! I've never been able to put your ass down."

Suggs saw Ranald mouth, *I'm sorry*, from the corner he had moved to. Inwardly sighing, he quipped back to Kam, "Huh, I'm surprised *you* admitted that, fool."

Kam threw back his head and laughed. "Well, guys, at least this'll be interesting."

Jeannie and Sylvette looked at each other when they stopped talking. Both of their eyes spoke volumes to each other.

Vette whispered loudly to Jeannie, "I don't wanna hear anymore, do you?"

Jeannie's head was still spinning from everything they had heard. Considering how Jeannie felt now, maybe they shouldn't have eavesdropped.

"Naw, Vette. I cain't really say I wanna hear anymore. Let's just go."

Vette had tears in her eyes when she responded simply, "Alright."

They hurried back to the dining room, each wrapped up in their own thoughts. Moran quickly stood when they came back in the room. Her anxiousness was clearly written on her face. Before Jeannie could even sit down and process what the hell they had heard, Moran grilled them.

"So, what'd you two find out? What happened?"

Sylvette sat down and pushed Jeannie's chair out so she could do the same and looked up at Moran. "It's kinda bad, Auntie. Kinda bad."

Moran's face fell and she said quietly, "Oh." She sat in her chair and closed her eyes. "I was hoping you wouldn't say that." She opened her eyes and pierced the two of them with her gaze. "Tell me."

Jeannie heard the two of them talking, but could barely focus on what they were saying. Jed was coming for her? Russini was sending people to kill them. She was a danger to her baby.

Thank God she hadn't stayed with them. She had thought she was being paranoid. She could not help her 'what the fuck' that escaped her lips.

Moran stopped what she was about to say. "Jeannie, did you say, what the fuck?"

Jeannie looked at Moran and honestly, at that moment, did not know what she was talking about. "I-I'm sorry Moran. I ai-I mean, I'm not sure what you're talkin' bout." The haze in her head was growing and she was starting to feel nauseous and weak, like the energy was bleeding from her body.

Sylvette looked at Jeannie and she looked really pale, paler than usual. "Auntie, we're gonna have to talk later. She's gonna need some time. Trust me." Sylvette stopped talking because she thought she heard voices not far off and listening hard she heard what she thought she had heard again. She looked at Moran. "They're coming back."

"Okay," Moran whispered loudly. "Later, then." She looked over at Jeannie. "She looks like she's gonna be sick. Jeannie, you might wanna go lay down child."

Jeannie was afraid she was about to pass out. She could barely gather the energy to speak. She was so scared, so scared. Scared for her baby and her momma, her friends and everyone that worked here, she was scared for their men, she was scared for herself. Her vision began to dim, she spaced out for what seemed like minutes and then she felt a dull sting to her shoulder. She felt another and it stung a lot more. The fog that was in her mind began to clear and she lifted her head, shaken that she hadn't realized it had fallen. It took effort to lift her head because it felt as if it weighed a ton.

Sylvette shook Jeannie's shoulder this time and whispered loudly in her ear, "Jeannie. Don't pass out on me girl."

Jeannie's vision blurred briefly again and her head just felt so heavy. She was fading again. She was so weak she couldn't even stop her head from hitting the table...but Suggs did. His hand broke her contact with the table just before her head would have smashed into it. Her face was laying in his hand and she felt so woozy; she didn't even care. He was behind her and he lifted her head all the way up and back a little, leaning her against his arm. He put his hand on her shoulder to steady her and for her to lean on.

"Take deep breaths, Jeannie. Just lean on me and take deep breaths." Over her head Suggs glared at Sylvette and Moran. "What happened to her? Why is she over here passin' out? She looked fine enough when we left the room. What happened?"

Ranald went and stood by Sylvette while she was getting up from her seat. "Be easy, Suggs. They didn't do anything to Jeannie. Maybe she just got sick."

Jeannie heard them though they sounded far away. She started trying to do breathing exercises that Vette had told her about but it only made her want to cough. Sluggishly, Jeannie talked to herself in her mind. She told herself to shake it off, get up. They had to fight. Had to fight. They had to fight. She had to be awake to fight.

Jeannie was slowly becoming more aware and her chest didn't feel as heavy. She kept breathing as deeply as she could, without coughing, and then the conversation they had heard flooded her mind again. T.J. was still rubbing her hair and she was leaning on him. God, it felt so good to lean on him. And, even in her sluggish state, as soon as she felt that feeling she knew that she still hadn't changed. She was just as weak now as she had been when she had been married to Jed. Still lookin' to lean on some man. Her mind screamed to her, never again! She had to get up and shake it off. She had to not be afraid, but she didn't know how to not be. She wished she could lean on T.J. and it would be okay, but she had done that bullshit enough. She didn't need to start liking being around him and feeling comfortable enough to lean on him, touch him..know him. She had promised herself she would never give a man that kind of power again. Never let a man drop her on her ass and then kick her while she was down ever again. *Never.*

Suggs felt her stir and looked down at her. His heart ached as he saw how pale she was. He wanted to bear her pain for her it hurt him so much to see her hurting. What had happened? She slowly sat up fully and she turned to look up at him. Her sparkle was gone from her green eyes.

"Thank you for bein' my leanin' post, T.J." Her voice was threadbare and strained.

He looked down at her and didn't even notice he was smiling tenderly at her. "What got you so upset Sprite?"

Jeannie loved his smile *and* his lips. She wanted to run her fingers over his lips and then reach up and… Suggs interrupted her thoughts, thankfully.

"What is that face, Sprite? I've never seen it before."

Trying to play it off, Jeannie blinked her eyes rapidly. "I just went off somewhere. And I guess I just was sitting down an' thinkin' and talkin' bout things and it just seems like so much, ya know."

Suggs sighed and grimaced. "Well, I need you to be your normal spitfire self Jeannie. Remember, I have something else to tell you. It's gonna be ok, but we gotta discuss the threats that are comin' for us so we can effectively fight them."

"Threats?"

"Yeah, threats." Suggs looked at her and narrowed his eyes. "Ya know, on second thought, you don't look too good. Maybe you should go lay down." He stopped briefly and looked around as if looking for someone. "Wait, Sara's not here? She's still with your Mom?"

Jeannie's heart fluttered dangerously. He was asking about Sara and he looked genuinely concerned. Jeannie couldn't help it when a weak, but warm smile spread across her face. "She's with my Mom. And after while they're going to Florida to stay with my Mom's family for a little while. A-a-and I'm okay. Just worried, but okay."

Suggs looked relieved. "Okay. Good. Okay." He looked over at Ranald and Kam and slowly nodded his head.

"Ok," Ranald began. "Ladies, this is my brother Kameron. He's a Navy Seal, amongst other things. He's gonna help out with a problem we're gonna have."

Moran was openly ogling Kameron. "The problem is this Russian man, right?"

"Yes, Moran."

"Hmm," she responded. Then she turned her gaze directly to Kameron. She stared into his gorgeous browns and asked coyly, "And, young man, what is your rank amongst the Seals?"

Kameron smiled, showing his dimple in his right cheek and winked at Moran, "Now if I told you that, *Moran*, I'd have to give you a sweet death."

Her eyes sparkled as she simply responded, "Mm."

Eric cleared his throat and continued, "Yeah, so, the issue is that his men are going to attack the mansion in an attempt to kill us. The Hammer wants everyone in this house dead as a way to retaliate against Max Bates and to destroy any records on him that may be hidden in this mansion. He's trying to erase all of his connections to Bates."

"My God!" Moran quietly exclaimed, horror clearly evident on her face.

Ranald smiled firmly, but gently in Moran's direction while he was rubbing an equally distressed Sylvette's shoulders. "I want to be as real as possible with yawl. This ain't gonna be easy. I have intel that states there'll be lots of assholes trying to get in here. Try not to worry though. Respect the situation, yeah, but we've got a plan for this. If all goes well, we'll be moving you out of the mansion soon. We'll also need to round up the staff as well. It's not safe to leave anymore. People leave, then they're wide open. And one of Russini's snitches has already been seen near the premises. I'm sorry to spring this on yawl, but we really just found out ourselves and Russini ain't wastin' no time. We expect they'll attack tomorrow evening."

Vette looked up at Eric. "Why are there no other cops here? It's just us, the people in this damned house, isn't it?"

Eric looked out at all of them apprehensively. "Okay. Well, yeah, it's just us."

Moran's face fell. "Wait, you mean there's no help comin'?"

"Well, no Moran, there isn't. But we're trained very well in what we do, so as I said before, we've got a plan. They won't be expecting it and that will be our trump card. We're also gonna rig all the hot spots in this mansion."

"Hot spots?" Moran asked.

"Yeah," Kameron answered. "He just means points of entry."

"Oh," she responded. "Well, I think there's a lot of hot spots in this place."

Kameron sighed and replied simply, "I know."

Ranald added, "Yeah, we looked at a schematic of this place. There's a lot, yeah, but most of the hot spots are hidden. Anyway, it would be great if you ladies and some of the staff would help place the traps. We'll show you what to do."

Moran sighed. "This sure is a lot to take in guys. Are we gonna be handlin' guns and such Eric?"

"Yeah, Moran, you will be. You'll be handling explosives, different types of knives, crossbows and such."

Her beautiful eyes large as saucers, she looked down at her long, midnight purple lacquered nails with regret and she replied simply, "Oh."

Sylvette felt a hysterical giggle escape from her lips and she blurted out, "Wow, Ranald, you're really in cop mode now." She promptly dissolved into a fit of laughter. "This whole situation is crazy. Crazy!" Her voice started to become shrill. "We should have help here or leave now and you can protect us while we're going to a safe house or whatever, so the damn snitches won't even matter!" Sylvette hiccupped and slowly her laughter dissipated.

"Vette," Eric began quietly. " I know it's a lot to take in, but believe me when I say at this moment in time it would be so much easier to defend you in this house. This area can be controlled. Out there we'd be sitting ducks. I'm talking snipers too, Vette. This is the Russian mob we're dealin' with. There's too many ways they can get you guys out there and all together there are 13 people in this mansion, not including Kam, Suggs and I. That's a lot of people to protect in *open* dangerous territory."

"But still, you could try to move us tonight. You said yourself the threat is more likely to be an issue tomorrow night."

Jeannie had been listening carefully to the conversation. Finally, what had been nagging her became clear. "Ranald, can I ask you a question?"

"Course Jeannie, shoot."

Ignoring T.J.'s exaggerated sigh, she responded, "We're bait, aren't we? You and the bureau are using this to charge him with something that you would have undeniable proof for and he wouldn't be able to get out of jail. He'd be deported and tried in Russia where they would essentially bury'im. Then, poof, Russini issue gone and Ricardo's gone cause The Hammer woulda already taken care of him."

T.J. started to choke with inappropriate laughter and Jeannie sat full up, now able to ignore her waning wooziness a little bit. She lifted her head up and looked at him, openly glaring, "You fuckin' asshole. That's it, ain't it."

Suggs wiped his streaming eyes and tried to catch his breath. That Jeannie boy. She truly threw him off. His voice was strained as he answered, "What the fuck, Jeannie. Why you didn't pat my back or somethin'?"

"Are you serious?' She responded incredulously. "It's sad ya didn't choke longer!"

Moran intervened, "Now Jeannie child, calm down. They'll explain." She looked at the 3 men. "Okay, so, who's gonna answer Jeannie's question?"

Kam spoke up. "Well, I guess I'll answer as both my compadres are being paralyzed by death stares." He smirked a little and then continued, "Ok... Jeannie, you're right." Kam then stopped talking and had apparently said all he was going to say. He looked wonderingly out at his audience as they all stared at him for a couple of seconds, obviously waiting for more of an explanation. Kam threw his hands in the air as if pleading innocence. "Hey, *I* don't need any death stares. I just answered the question."

"As fine as you may be, young man," Moran began, "it distresses me to find out that your intellect is not of the same caliber as your looks. It's a shame."

Jeannie couldn't help but smile. Moran was a saucy one. Jeannie looked at Ranald, "Are we bait, Eric?"

Eric looked down at Vette with what could only be called resigned apprehension before he responded, "Well, yeah, we all kinda are. The Hammer wants Suggs and I somethin' bad also. We fucked up a lotta his business for him and we took out a lot of his men, too. The thing is, he won't be able to resist this opportunity to get us all at once and he'll figure that we're unaware about the attack. Oh, sure, he figures we'd be expecting a couple of minor attempts, but nothing like what he's planning. And that's where he's wrong and we'll show 'im just how wrong. He will, *is*, underestimating us."

Vette sighed and looked over at Jeannie. Jeannie read her eyes and understood. She nodded her head in understanding and Vette's expression changed to one of resolve.

Jeannie took a deep breath and asked quietly, "What else do we need to know guys, cause we sure didn't hear that bit and we assumed we had heard it all."

Suggs sat down in the chair on Jeannie's right and grabbed her hand. She looked at him and he asked, "What're you talkin' bout? What've you heard?"

Vette spoke out, "We listened to some of yawl's conversation cause we figured you'd leave us out and we wouldn't know anything."

Eric responded, "But we did, we *have* told you."

Vette rolled her eyes exasperatedly, "Duh, that's how we thought you guys were *gonna* handle it. It's obvious you're telling us, Eric. What Jeannie is asking is what else do we need to know cause we thought we had heard everything. We didn't hear anything about all of us being used as bait."

Suggs stood up and walked over to the archway that lead into the dining room and leaned against the wall. He casually pulled a cigarette from his pack in his back pocket and lit it slowly.

Jeannie watched him and was surprised as she hadn't known he smoked.

Suggs looked at her and then Vette. Casually he asked, "So all 3 of you ladies listened in or just you and Jeannie?"

Vette sighed, "It was me and Jeannie."

"Hmm." He smiled mirthlessly and looked at Jeannie. "So you also know then about your ex."

Wondering where he was going with this and if he was mad right now, Jeannie responded cautiously, "Yeah. I heard bout it."

Suggs abruptly stood straight and barked out, "What the fuck, Jeannie? What if we had said things in there that you really didn't need to know? You're not a fuckin' cop! You have to learn how to fuckin' do what you're told, Jeannie. We do things for good reason, even if the *great Jeannie* isn't privy to'em."

Ranald opened his mouth to speak, but Suggs continued, cutting him off. "I mean, Jesus, how're we sposed to know we can trust you to do what you're told? How can we keep you ladies safe?"

Jeannie responded, "Look, I know ya feel we shouldn't have listened in but there's nothin' wrong with wantin' to know about somethin' you're involved in! Vette and I needed to know. And since I'm gonna be a lawyer-."

"Well", Suggs interrupted, cutting Jeannie off, "you ain't no lawyer yet, Sprite!"

Jeannie's temper erupted and she stood up and turned towards Suggs. "You fuckin bastard! I'll do what I please to protect me and mine! And knowin' information cain't hurt us, you lying fuck. That don't even make any dang sense."

Suggs eyes narrowed dangerously and he responded through clenched teeth, "So help me God Jeannie, you say one more disrespectful word I'm gonna have to rinse your damn mouth out with soap *and* alcohol. Then, I'm gonna turn your foul mouthed ass over my knee!"

Moran looked back and forth between the two. The passion and angst flowing between them was almost palpable. Hmm, Moran thought to herself. Interesting. This was the man who was the cause of all Jeannie's erratic behavior of late. Now, she was sure of it.

Kam threw in, "I don't know if I would threaten a woman who called you a *fuck* like that's your given name. She's scary." He winked quickly at Jeannie and then quickly smiled innocently to Suggs.

Suggs knew Kam too well. "Very funny, ass. For real man, what if what they know hurts them if something were to happen or go wrong."

Kam threw his hands up again. "Hey! Hey! Peace brother. I feel ya. Honestly though, I don't think it's that big of a deal. They're already involved up the ass, ya know. I just think lil ole Suggs might be a little more anxious than usual due to his little re-, mm mm, uh due to all the ladies we have to protect."

Suggs narrowed his eyes dangerously and took a step towards Kam, "You cheeky bastard."

Ranald spoke up, "Calm down you two. Suggs, be easy. At this point it doesn't matter that they overheard us cause we told'em everything anyway. Look...ladies, yes, this set-up is a good way to flush out Russini because it gives us a better chance to provide supporting evidence that he's a murderer and a menace. And, you're right, Jeannie. Even if he is deported there's no way he wouldn't get the death penalty in Russia for his crimes. So, either way, justice is served."

"Yeah," Vette muttered quietly, "As long as we don't get killed in the process."

Jeannie looked at Vette and saw the worry in her eyes. It mirrored her own, but she did feel that this would probably be the best way to tackle their current issue.

"Vette, I don't know...maybe this is the best way to move forward. How would they protect us adequately from here to a safehouse if there's so much wide open space and we don't know what kind of artillery they have?"

Ranald looked at Jeannie and nodded his head in her direction. His hands were still massaging Vette's tense shoulders when he stated, "Jeannie, you've got it. It's not pretty, but you've got it."

"Yeah," Kam piped in. "And when you say artillery, you're using the right word. For The Hammer to be making a move like this means that he has a lot staked in it. He'll have oozies- machine guns, automatic and sniper rifles and I would imagine a Bazooka or RPG would be included as well."

Moran gulped loudly and couldn't help a whimper of distress that escaped her lips. "Y-you mean things that blow up stuff, right?"

"Yes," Kam answered. "But like my brother said, for this mansion I think that would be a last resort. If we had tried to mobilize you then those kind of toys might definitely have come into play."

Moran listened to him intently and frowning, responded, "What if they attempt to blow up the mansion unexpectedly? What then?"

Ranald answered her as plain spokenly as possible because the women needed to know what they were up against. "We die."

"Oh my God. Oh my God."

Jeannie called out to Moran, "Hey. It'll be ok Moran. We just won't let'em blow us up."

"That's right, we won't," Suggs seconded.

Moran was slowly losing her composure. "How can you all sit here so calmly? Hello people! You're telling me we're about to face a large number of mercenaries coming to kill us and possibly blow us up and we're stuck here just waitin' for something like that to occur? What's wrong with you guys? We need to get the hell outta here!" Moran quickly stood and pushed her chair back. "I'm leaving this crazy place and Jeannie and Sylvette I suggest you come along."

Jeannie opened her mouth to speak to Moran at the same time that Vette stood and pushed her chair back to leave the table. Ranald was trying to grab Vette's arm to stop her from leaving, while Suggs hurried to get to the side where Moran was, gathering her purse and intermittently wiping tears.

"Wait, Moran! Wait." He reached Moran and lightly touched her shoulder. "Moran, it would be dangerous for you to leave. It would."

Moran scoffed at him. "It would be dangerous to stay as well. It sounds to me like we just need to take our chances." She brushed his arm off and determinedly walked around him.

Suggs rushed after her. "Come on, Moran. Trust us."

Vette looked over at them and stepped away from her husband. "You can't make her stay Suggs. I'm not comfortable staying either."

<u>Chapter 5</u>

Jeannie watched everything unfold and was suddenly very unsure of what to do. She looked over at Kam, who had been very quiet through this latest development. He was leaning against the wall by the archway. He happened to start looking around just as she looked at him. They met eyes and he suddenly grinned at her and shrugged his shoulders. He mouthed, holy fuck, and shrugged his shoulders again. Jeannie shrugged her shoulders back to let him know she didn't know what to do as well. Ranald was going back and forth with Vette and she kept slapping away his hands when he reached out to touch her. Moran was waiting off to the side for Vette while Suggs was still trying to convince her to go along with the plan. All Jeannie knew was that something needed to be done. She wondered if it might not be a good idea for Moran to leave. Moran could go upstairs and she and Vette could go with her. Maybe then they could talk to each other and come up with a common plan of action amongst the three of them that they were comfortable with. Of course, she didn't see how what they came up with could be that much different than what the guys had come up with. Jeannie felt like Ranald was right in that they would be more vulnerable to attack outside of the house and then, on top of that, the safehouse location was 38 miles away and the route still being figured out. Yeah, she thought to herself, they needed to dip off so Vette and Moran could be easy and they could all talk rationally. Taking a deep breath, Jeannie jumped in.

"Hey!" When the commotion didn't stop, Jeannie yelled louder, "Hey!"

All of them stopped abruptly and their eyes turned to her. Jeannie felt herself blushing at all the attention. Clearing her throat, she advised the men, "Gentlemen, I think it would be best if you gave us some time to process everythin' and discuss this amongst ourselves."

Suggs barked out, "No, Jeannie! Absolutely not. You guys could try and sneak out or anything."

"Oh, so we're prisoners. Is that what T.J. is saying Eric?"

Vette looked at Eric and glared at him as she waited for his response. To his credit, Ranald was very affected by his wife's current state of irritation with him. He cleared his throat a couple of times before he responded slowly, obviously carefully choosing his words.

"Of course you're not prisoners Vette, Jeannie." He cleared his throat again. "I think Suggs was just trying to say that we need to trust that you'll stay in the house."

Vette responded tersely, repeating what Jeannie had said. "So, then you're saying we're prisoners."

Kam suddenly started coughing and it sounded suspiciously like a cough that was covering laughter.

Suggs looked over at him and narrowed his eyes warningly. Kam coughed again, but nodded his head in amused understanding to Suggs.

Ranald responded cautiously, "Not exactly, baby. It's just that we really feel that it would be dangerous for you out there. I promise you Vette that we're gonna do everything within our power to protect all o' you. Oh and what we didn't say before is that we're also gonna do some ground reconnaissance once the smoke clears a little and take out whatever big toys they may be hiding as a surprise. So, see, it'll be ok."

Vette slowly backed up until she stood on the other side of Moran. Her eyes were cold when she responded, "Eric, you don't know if you'll even be able to do that and you're nervous about the whole thing as well. *I* can tell." She cut her eyes at him and then looked at Jeannie. "Come on Jeannie. Let's go upstairs with Auntie."

Jeannie nodded her head and couldn't help but look at Suggs, who was on the other side of Moran. He was looking at her as well. His expression was hard to read, but he openly eyed her from head to toe. His gaze, as always, had her transfixed and she jumped when Vette called her name again.

"Coming now."

Kam walked to Ranald and pushed him a little on the back. "Just let'em go, Eric. They need some time I bet. We can start talking to the staff and briefing them. Then, we can get this shit started."

Ranald nodded his agreement and watched as Jeannie met up with Vette and Moran. Vette wouldn't spare him a second glance. Jeannie hugged a very distraught Moran and then they disappeared as they rounded the corner by the main stairs.

Suggs was highly irritated and glared in the direction of the main stairs or *Great* Stairs as he waited for Ranald to finish his spiel with the staff. His thoughts were firmly centered on Jeannie. He wished he could go and talk to her about her ex. He didn't really know how to be there for a woman though and honestly, he had never had the urge. He never had relationships. His mom hadn't wanted him and had left him with his Stepdad. He had never known any of his family on his mom or biological dad's side, so he really had no reference, but he *knew* she had to be thinking about it. He remembered that report he had worked for her case from when she had been 19. Her husband, Jed, had burned the inside of her hands with a curling iron and had fractured two of her ribs. He remembered because she had gone to the hospital for skin grafts. It had all been in the report. Jed should have been locked away then and he wasn't sure why he hadn't been. He really wished he could kill that man with his bare hands, he really did. Suggs' phone rang suddenly and it was jarringly loud as it had just fallen silent while Ranald drank some water. He snatched it out of his back pocket and saw it was Torres. "It's Torres, man. I'm gonna dip out for a second, alright?"

Ranald nodded his head and turned back towards the staff to finish answering their questions.

Suggs nodded at Kam on his way out and Kam appropriately and promptly flicked him off. Shaking his head at the young fuck, he went around the corner and down the hall to one of the restrooms. The sitting area of the bathroom had a Divan couch in it. He sat down and dialed Torres back.

Torres saw who it was calling and as eager as she had been to talk to him just moments ago, now she was a little unsure. She knew he would think it was odd for her to just be checkin' up on him. That wasn't their MO. And it wasn't like T.J. was rude with it, it was just understood that all he offered was a good time. A problem had surfaced though because against her fuckin' will, she had fallen in love with him. Torres had never loved a man before, not really. The job had always been her passion, but the more she had spent time with him, the more she had fallen for him. Now, she knew without a doubt she loved him. She wanted to know more about him. In the four years she had known him and in the two years she had been messing around with him, she hadn't learned much except he avoided getting too close to someone like the plague. Torres was really conflicted because she was taking a big risk by exposing herself to him. She knew that if she could be cool with him just being her friend with *great* benefits, they would continue to see each other indefinitely. After all, she was sure she was probably the only woman he saw regularly. But how could she do that anymore? She had seen his reaction to the pretty little redhead at the grocery store. Torres had been surprised by the ferocity of her dislike for the redhead. She had wanted to choke the life outta the little green-eyed bitch. She really didn't know how to proceed with him now. Everything had changed for her. Figuring she oughta just handle it head on and at least try to tell'im, she took a deep breath and answered the phone.

"Hey, Suggs."

Her low, throaty voice slid through him and he found himself wanting to leave out for a bit and drown in the ever luscious Marcella Torres. Drowning in her was pleasure to the tip of his toes and a way to escape from the fucked up situation they were in right now.

"Hey yourself, Torres. Thank you for callin'. You're really saving my ass here. Preciate ya. So, what's going on?"

Her heart beat furiously at the sound of his voice. Damn, she really hoped he would give them a chance and not walk out on her forever. She started to tell him how she felt, but it stuck in her throat, so she hurriedly improvised.

"Well, I was calling about...the sting."

"Sting? There's no sting. You weren't briefed?"

"Yeah, but we were told it's a sting. Maybe they don't want us to know what it really is."

"Yeah, but you're a Fed."

"Mm hmm, but you don't think there are also some of mine on Russini and others' payrolls?"

"Yeah, you're right, you're right. High connections. Mm, well on the low Torres, I'm at the Bates mansion."

"Isn't the mansion *under contract?*"

"It is. We've taken up the contract unbeknownst to our impending guests. We relocate after the contract has been either exhausted or decimated."

Torres' mind ran amuck with the new intel. Suggs could be a sitting duck out there! The Hammer wasn't gonna come light. They all knew that his intention would ultimately be to burn the mansion to the ground, just to make sure all his connections with Bates were eradicated. And The Hammer was also known for hunting down anyone for even thinking about starting some shit with him. She tried to think about why they just didn't move the occupants of the mansion to a safe house. Then it hit her; the nearest one was about 40 miles from the mansion and they would *have* to put those people at a far out location because Russini would never have his men stop looking. That would be a long distance to cover while trying to protect the occupants of the mansion *and* not blow cover for the safehouse location. Suggs probably figures after the attack, as long as they can put a serious hurtin' on Russini's men, it would be safer to move everybody then. She could see that, but how were they gonna stop all the men Russini would send? How would they be able to do that? I mean how many men did Suggs even have?

"Suggs, are you gonna need another gun? It sounds a little..risky."

Suggs chuckled wryly into the phone. "Yeah man, you said it. But...I really think for right now, it's the best option. And we know what's comin'. Have a little faith Torres. And shit, here I was hoping you was callin' to tell me you miss me."

Torres' heart sped up almost immediately at his last statement. He had said that to her before in the past and she had thought nothing of it. Now, she found herself feeling wistful and wishing he really did want her to miss him *and* that he would miss her.

"Actually, I do miss you Suggs. I guess...I..kinda miss you alot."

Suggs really wished he could leave and go drown in Torres for a while. Being around Jeannie always made him horny as hell, but he damn sure couldn't slide in between Jeannie's sweet thighs. But Torres was a different story. She was safe. She was just like him and he loved that about her and their situation. She demanded nothing from him so there was no pressure, thank God. They could just fuck and have fun.

"I miss you, too, Torres. Besides a couple of days ago, I really haven't been stoppin' by as much and I need to correct that. I just think I'm kinda goin' through some changes, ya know. It's just got me a little off."

"You're so sweet, Suggs." Trying to say what she really wanted to say and failing dismally, again, she continued, "So, yeah..uh, I wanted to talk to you about that."

"About what?"

"What? Oh, yeah-um, I was talking about what you said; how you've been a little off. I noticed some things, Suggs. You seem a little burnt out, maybe jaded a little."

"Burnt out, Torres? Damn." Suggs voice trailed off as he really thought about what she said. Was he burnt out? If he was, cause he had also had his doubts, what the fuck would he do with himself? He ultimately had always wanted to be a cop and that was all he had ever been. Not liking the current direction of the conversation, Suggs quickly thought of a different subject. He wasn't about to discuss this type of shit with Torres. She was cool and all and he enjoyed her. Suggs just hoped she would get the hint that he wasn't gonna talk about that kinda shit with her.

"Anyway," he continued. "Naw, Torres, come on. I'm not burnt out, but I'll tell you what I *am*; fucking horned out and bored as fuck. Instead of being between your creamy thighs, I'm here with fuckin' Kam's punk ass."

As he expected, she laughed quietly. "Oh wow. Suggs, I didn't know he was there. I bet that fool is buggin' the hell outta ya, huh?"

"Of course he is. I know what the problem is, I haven't beat his ass lately. His cheeky ass is overdue."

"Well, I'm sorry you're being tortured. Tell'im I said hey, though, when you see'im. I-I just really hope that you're safe and I wish you would let me come. I could help."

"I know you could, honey. I know. I just don't know who's out there watching this mansion and I don't want trouble for you. Besides, I'm *sure* there're mother fucker's posted around so they can report what they see back to that Russian fuck. It's a liability, Torres."

Sighing because she was fucking wussing out and she knew she would have to hang up soon, she responded with disappointment in her voice. "Yeah, I hear ya, Suggs. You're right."

Suggs picked up that something was wrong and hoped she was alright. "Torres, you good? You sounded, I don't know, like...disappointed or somethin'."

She knew his question was her chance. She was so fuckin' scared to bring it up though. Suddenly, an image of the redhead from the grocery store flooded her mind. And that redhead was there with him right now at that mansion. Deciding, fuck it, she should just do it, she opened her mouth and plunged in.

"I actually do have something on my mind, Suggs."

"Alright, spill it. What's good?"

"Well, I don't think you're gonna like what I wanna say to you."

Suggs was confused. What could she possibly want to say that would piss him off or whatever? "Just say it Torres. I can't see what you would say that would cause a problem or anything."

Knowing she just needed to quit stalling and get it out because she was a fucking grown-up, she said simply, "I would like to know you more, Suggs."

Suggs immediately was uncomfortable. What did Marcella have going on? She wanted to know him more as in officially date him? All he could think was, wow.

"Know me more than you *already* do? I think you *know* me pretty well and I *know* every part of you." Purposely trying to shift the conversation from where she seemed to be heading, he continued before she could respond. "Like I said before, I wish I was with you right now showing you what I *know*."

Torres listened to him and damned herself for being weak. She knew he was changing the subject, but his voice slid through her and unbidden images of their recent loveplay flooded her vision. Her body started to get all tingly at the thought of tumbling around with him on her bed.

"Suggs, I want you so much. I...I think I might be developing feelings for you, Suggs. I know you don't do relationships, but I at least wanted to let you know how I feel about you."

Suggs groaned internally with frustrated disappointment at her words. The stupid ass woman was fuckin' it all up! Damn Torres for catching feelings. They had been going on strong for a while. He truly had not expected to hear that declaration from her. Not Torres. *Fuck*!

"Torres, what did I tell you from the beginning?"

Torres heard the frustration in his voice and knew she had made a mistake. Her heart sinking, she responded tonelessly, "You told me that you wasn't gone ever be tied to a woman and no woman should ever want to be tied to you."

At that moment, as he listened to her, he knew what Ranald had meant about feeling guilt. Torres actually sounded like she was about to cry. He could *hear* the pain in her voice. He should have said something else to her, but she had caught him off guard. Truly. And he was honestly a little pissed. He had liked messing around with Torres. He had gotten used to having comfortable pussy on deck and she was cool with it or had seemed like she was. She had always known that he wasn't committed to her, but he knew she also was aware she was the only one he fucked with consistently. Because of that, at least, he should've taken better care of her feelings.

Besides, she knew him fairly well and she had to have known she would be taking a risk to spill how she was really feeling. Yeah, he felt bad. He was pretty irritated with her because of what would happen now, but he did feel bad. And now, he felt a little awkward; an emotion he didn't often feel and had never felt with Torres.

"Look..uh..Torres. Honestly, my first thought is to not see you like that anymore. Ya know, to avoid any fuckin' complications. But...I mean, when you say *feelings*, what do you mean?" He made himself exercise patience while he waited for her response.

Torres thought hard about how to answer him and because she knew the cat was already out, she figured she might as well be real with him. Praying silently that somehow they could work, she confessed her feelings.

"So, *honestly*, I *know* I have feelings for you, Suggs. I'm in love with you and I *didn't* plan on it to happen, Suggs. I *really* didn't. It just really kinda hit me when I saw you with the *redhead* at the grocery store." She opened her mouth to continue, but Suggs interrupted.

"Wait. You mean..Jeannie?"

On her end, rolling her eyes hard, Torres replied, "Yeah. *Jeannie.* Anyway, what I'm tryin' to say is, when I saw you with her and you seemed interested in her, it kinda, I don't know, felt wrong. I- I mean... I was hurt. I was a little peeved too. I just, I just realized what I'd been fighting for a long time. Everyone knows you're a *bad boy* and you like it being that way. I *knew* never to fall for you, Suggs. But, I have and I want to know you more. I would love for us to try it out, ya know. Just try. We've already had a relationship of sorts anyway. I...I just felt like I should be real with you." She paused and took a deep breath. "So, go ahead. Rip me a new one Suggs. I'll be ready this time."

Suggs gripped the phone so hard, his hands had started to ache. *What the fuck,* kept running through his mind. Torres was *in love* with him? *Him?* He didn't even *really* spend time with her. He enjoyed fucking Torres, so that's what he did. Occasionally, they'd work on a case together or go have lunch with a bunch of other co-workers. How could she have fallen in love? He was never with her on holidays and purposely never spent her birthday with her. He didn't want to set up the wrong expectations. *Damn!* Now, he had to let Torres go and he surprisingly, albeit briefly, found himself wishing he were different. Torres was not a bad catch. She really wasn't, but he didn't love her. He just didn't. For him it was truly a physical thing and it was convenient because they were both cops and good friends. God, he felt like a douche because he knew this would hurt her and he truly had no wish to hurt Marcella. Marcella was a good woman, a good person. Sighing and not hiding it, Suggs groaned loudly in frustration before he responded.

"I'm sorry I was, mm mm, a little cold at first. You just kinda sprung this on me though. Shit, I thought we were in a good, mutual place, Torres. I'm really sorry that you developed feelings for me. And, besides that, I don't deserve you. There's got to be a man better for you out there than me." He had started to ramble so he paused abruptly to gather himself. All he wanted to do now though was hang up the fucking phone.

"Look, what *I'm* saying very fucking badly is that I think you're fuckin awesome, Torres. You're fuckin' intelligent and have many natural talents that piss everybody off. You already know you're fucking gorgeous. And stupid me...stupid me, but I don't want a relationship, Torres. I don't believe in that shit, not for myself at least. I guess what I'm saying is that I can't ever give you what you want. It probably *is* best for us to just be friends from here on out Torres. You feel me?"

Torres felt numb. She just felt numb. She had known. Yeah, she had known. But had she really and truly believed he would cut them off, no. No, she hadn't. She thought he viewed her differently, but he really hadn't; not when it mattered. All she wanted to do was go home, get in her bed with her gun and teddy bear and go to sleep. Talk about letdown of the century.

"Suggs, I hear you. I..I don't agree with some things, but that doesn't matter, does it." She hurried on before he tried to answer. "I'm just gonna go and I hope everyone is safe. Just...be careful Suggs. Don't underestimate R-R-Russini." Her voice broke as she tried to contain her tears. Not able to say anymore, she quickly hung up the phone.

Suggs listened to the dialtone a moment before he clicked it off. He still couldn't wrap his head around what had just happened. He was so preoccupied that he didn't hear Ranald come in and walk up on'im.

"Hey man. Why you chillin in the bathroom?" He looked around the bathroom quickly and continued, "Correction, I see why you're chillin in the *super playa* bathroom. This shit is nice!"

Suggs wryly responded, "It's still a *bathroom,* Ranald. You're right, I probably shouldn't just be chillin in a bathroom. I just dipped off into the first room I saw so I could take the call. Shit, for a moment, I forgot I was in the bathroom."

"And what I'm sayin is, with all a this, that is very understandable."

"Oh, yeah, yeah."

Ranald moved through a second set of doors that led to the toilets and showers. He went to a stall and called out to Suggs. "Was Torres good?"

Suggs waited for Ranald to come back. "I guess she is man." Suggs stood up to follow Ranald out, but then he called out, "Wait, man. I gotta tell you what Torres told me. You're not gone believe it bruh."

"Damn, Suggs. I thought you said she was good."

"Naw, naw. It's not like that. She called me to tell me somethin' about her...and me."

Ranald's eyes opened wide and he looked at Suggs harder. "She's *pregnant*, Suggs?"

"No! God, no! Why you such a woman all the time, man? Why's that gotta be the first thing that comes to your fuckin' head? Don't put that on me, man. Damn! She's...she's in love with me man. She wants to be official. She, she saw me and Jeannie, she said, at the grocery store and was jealous, I guess. Anyway, she said she tried not to be, but she is."

"Oh. Wow, bruh. I mean, Torres *is* a hard ass, *but* she's still a woman. A damn beautiful woman at that."

Suggs couldn't help a frustrated groan at Ranald's last comment. "I know, man! That's what *I'm* sayin, right. But, wait...what do you mean she's still a woman? What's that supposed to mean?"

"I mean, come on, it was never *official*, but everyone knows you and Torres have been fuckin' around for a while. It was probably just natural for her to develop feelings, ya know."

"Naw man, I don't know. I try to avoid women who seem like they're commitment bound or clingy, so I can avoid situations like this. I *told* her man. I let her know from the beginning."

"Well, I've heard Vette say this crap all the time; *there comes a time when a woman needs more, Eric. It's just natural.* Anyway, that's probably what it is. Ay man, and then you know women are competitive about men. She didn't like whatever she saw between you and Jeannie, man. And, if you didn't know, *everyone* can see there's somethin' between you and Miss Jeannie."

"You're such an old busybody, Ranald. Come on man. Let's go and find the girls."

"Yeah, loverboy. Hmm, I wonder if that had been Jeannie-."

"*Shut up*, Ranald."

<u>Chapter 6</u>

Jeannie and Sylvette were folding laundry in Moran's room while Moran was lounging on her chaise with a cocktail in her hand and a cold rag on her forehead.

Jeannie was thinking about Suggs. She had run into Eric in one of the hallways while she was going to get the laundry basket. She had attempted to ask about Suggs whereabouts offhandedly, but wasn't really sure if she had succeeded. Anyhow, Ranald had obligingly advised that Suggs had taken a call from a colleague, Torres, and had dipped off somewhere. Even though her heart had sunk immediately at his words, she had managed to thank him without croaking. Now, lost in her sad and jealous thoughts, she grew a little more somber when she also began thinking of their current situation and how they were all going to be involved in a mini *war*. So glad that she had gotten Sara out in time, she silently prayed for the Lord's protection over all of them. She knew they would all need it.

Moran grunted a little as she tried to sit up from an awkward position and hold the rag on her forehead as well. Thankfully, she had laid her cocktail on her night stand.

"Girls, do you think Eric will have gloves to protect our hands and nails when we have to shoot those awful guns?"

Vette laughed and answered, "Right, Auntie Moran, they're men. Yeah right, they would think about that."

Moran frowned. "Well, damn. Now, I'm really pissed off."

Jeannie added, "Well, hopefully, Miss Moran, we won't need to be shootin' nothin."

"But you said you agreed with their plan."

"Well, yeah Moran, cause I couldn't think of nothin' better. Can you?"

"No. What do I know about this kind of stuff, child? I just know I trust yawl, so I just need for yawl to know what's the best thing to do."

Vette spoke, "I really think it's the most solid plan we have, Auntie. I don't like it..really don't, but I do."

Moran exhaled slowly. "Ok. Ok. Well, don't we have to start setting booby traps and learning how to use their, uh, police...weaponry?"

Jeannie couldn't help a quiet snigger, "*Weaponry*, Miss Moran?"

"Oh, shut your foul mouth, Jeannie. You know what I mean."

Vette laughed and said, "Auntie, seein' as how we might actually have to use some *weaponry*, we might need to educate you first on what you're gonna be fuckin' people up with."

"Vette! Your mouth. Why, you sound just like Jeannie!" Moran whipped around and glared at Jeannie. "Now what do have to say for yourself Jeannie?"

Jeannie looked at Vette and Moran waiting for her response expectantly. Trying not to laugh, she responded jovially, with a big, broad smile on her face, "Well, hot damn! Sounds fuckin' alright to me!

Moran's lips suddenly started trembling and she could see Vette's shoulder's twitching suspiciously. Vette broke first as she couldn't contain her hilarity any longer. Vette howled she was laughing so hard. Moran was not that strong either. Tears of mirth fell down her face and laughter sprang from her lips. Moran laughed and laughed. Jeannie was rollin', sitting on the couch leaning over trying to catch her breath. She was red as a radish and that only sent Moran off again.

Suggs and Ranald stopped at the door and listened to the loud and raucous laughter coming from the women. Suggs shook his head in bemusement. How did they do it, he wondered?

Ranald looked at Suggs with a perplexed look on his face. "Suggs, what I wanna know is, I mean, what I don't get is, they were *upset* just like last time. Upset, man. Now the little weirdos are in there fuckin' rollin'. Not that it's a bad thing, but I don't get it."

Suggs responded back quietly, as the girls hilarity seemed to be dieing down, "I really think it's like, histrionics man. I think they're hysterical, shock, ya know."

Ranald seemed to consider what Suggs said as he quickly turned to look at the door. Still looking at the door as if he could see the women on the other side, Ranald sighed.

"Suggs, Vette was right about one thing. What *if* this shit doesn't work? What if he does decide to just blow the mansion up and cut his losses?"

Suggs pushed Ranald's shoulder and turned away from the door. He started to walk back the way they came and motioned for Ranald to follow. They stopped at the top of the Great Stairs.

Suggs didn't want the girls, in no way, to overhear them. And Suggs knew Jeannie. If she picked up on one thing, she'd be trying to know all about what he and Ranald were talking about.

"Look, if this doesn't work, we're all dead. You know that, man. Kam knows that."

Ranald glared at Suggs briefly, "Fuck you, man. Maybe I just don't wanna consider that bein' a possibility with Vette being here. If you *loved* a woman how I love Vette than you would understand that no matter the odds, man, I can't allow myself to consider the possibility that we die."

"So what do you want me to say then? I guess we would just try and move everybody out the house. Right?"

Ranald rubbed his face with his hands and responded wearily, "Yeah, yeah. That'd probably be the only other option. I guess...well, we could use the tunnels."

"Yeah! I forgot about those! The tunnels lead directly to the waterpark."

"Why the waterpark?" When Suggs shrugged his shoulders, Ranald continued, "Okay, so...we use the tunnels that lead to this waterpark and that area is fairly lit up, right?"

"Yeah. If we have to take that route we can call the boys en route to meet us."

"Got it. Okay. Look, thank you for humoring me. I'm a little worried."

"I feel you, Ranald. We should have worked out a backup plan anyway and this one is good. We just need to study the schematics so we can know exactly where to go. Some of the tunnels go to sewage pits under the city."

"Ok. Let's get to the girls. I'm gonna take Vette to the South Wing for a while before we get started. Barius is working with the staff, right?"

"Yeah, they started in the east wing."

"Good. Let's go."

"Bye, Moran. Get some rest for a couple a hours. We're gonna need it."

"She's right, Moran. Rest." Suggs smiled at her and ducked his head back out the room.

Jeannie winked at Moran and watched as Moran smiled and settled back against her pillows and closed her eyes. Jeannie quietly closed her door and turned to Suggs. He was so close to her and Lord, but she immediately felt hot and feverish. She was embarrassed by how she turned to mush from just being in his presence. Because he was so much taller than she was and as close as he was to her, she found it difficult to not feel overwhelmed by him. But, surprisingly, not in a bad way. When he looked down to meet eyes with her, she was already gazing up at him. She melted when he smoothly slid his arm around her waist and pulled her even closer to him.

"I've waited all day for this," he whispered as he lifted her onto his feet. "Sweet Jeannie." He ran his hand over her ass and cupped her bottom. He lifted her up again and her legs wrapped around his waist. He looked into her mossy green eyes that were limpid with desire. They met at the same time and Suggs tasted the sweetness of Jeannie's lips. She moaned into his mouth and he attacked her lips with burning passion. He opened her mouth and slid his tongue into her warmth. He sipped the moisture from her tongue and she moaned again, grinding herself on his dick. With one of his hands, he reached up and grabbed her hair, pulling it; stroking it sensuously.

Suggs dick was so hard and he wanted to be in her so badly, he was having trouble standing up straight. He staggered backwards and Jeannie's back hit the wall beside Moran's door, making a soft thud.

Immediately, Suggs let Jeannie go and she slid down. He leaned her up against the wall quickly and looked at her with his finger to his mouth, letting her know to be quiet and still. Jeannie was super flushed from their encounter, but she quieted her breathing and winked back at

Suggs. Man, she hoped Moran did not open her door. Like they were some horny ass high school kids afraid of getting caught for messing around, they both tensed when they heard Moran shuffling through her bedroom. She was muttering something to herself. Jeannie listened with bated breath as they heard her walk towards her bedroom door. They heard her reach the door and then they waited, but not too much later they heard her turn away and walk deeper into her bedroom.

Suggs quietly exhaled. "Damn," he whispered. "That was close."

"Yeah, it was spiderman. Come on. Let's go to my room."

Suggs couldn't believe his ears. Go to Jeannie's room. He had never expected an invitation to her bedroom. Oh, how he had dreamed though.

"Are you sure? I mean, no pressure."

Jeannie narrowed her eyes at him. "Oh, I get it. You're just assumin' that because a what just went on, when we go to my room you're *gettin' some booty*, as Vette says."

Suggs was never not amazed by her wit and ferociousness. While he answered her, he motioned for her to lead the way. "Look," he whispered back. "I had no expectations, Sprite. I just didn't want you to think you needed to be obliged, ya know."

She looked over at him, peering at him with caution written all over her. "Mm hmm." When they reached her door she opened it with a flourish and declared in a loud whisper, "Here we be laddie, at the cave of wonders."

Suggs smiled at her terrible Irish accent and walked into Jeannie's room. Immediately, his eyes were bombarded by the color green. Green was everywhere. She had even made Sara's obvious area of her huge room green. Somehow, though, it wasn't overkill and now that he really was looking he could see a lot of earthy brown and deep purple colors in the room as well. The blinds were rather wide and a honey-tannish type of color. They had sparkly green beaded curtains that came together at the ends, like a toga, covering them. It was very 'I Dream of Genie-ish'. It suited her as she looked like a fairy. She had books thrown everywhere. And Suggs also noticed she didn't have a traditional bed. Honestly, it was like a harem style bed, for lack of a better description. The bed, divan thing had a sort of tent around it with deep purple and lush green throws draping over the bed as well. It was very interesting and sort of *hot* actually. He could bet it would feel really awesome to roll around with Jeannie on those satin sheets and velvety throw looking things.

Jeannie openly shook her head at Suggs cause he was so not paying attention at that moment. He had openly eyed everything he could in her room. When he walked further into the room, into the suite area and saw her bed, he had stopped to look at it and dazed off, she guessed.

"Suggs!"

Suggs jumped as her voice startled him out of his fantasy. "What! Shit!"

Jeannie cheesed at him and told him innocently, "I was trying to help you."

Suggs looked at her disbelievingly. "Jeannie, rest assured, I know you're the most beautiful *enemy* I will ever have."

"Why, Suggs, I mean, T.J., what ever could you mean?" She coyly batted her eyelashes at him. She wanted him so much. It was if a fever were starting to grip her. And the tension in the room was definitely starting to build. *Sexual* tension.

Suggs eyed her with his desire clearly evident, as it always threatened to rob him of his sense when he was around her. She was playing with him and clearly enjoying herself. He watched, with full attention, as she suddenly grabbed his hand and led him to the sitting area of her bedroom. Then, catching him off guard, she pushed him on his chest and he lost his balance and fell back on one of her large, overstuffed ottomans. She waited until he had straightened himself and then, surprising him further, slowly slid her body onto his lap, straddling him. He naturally adjusted for her even though uncertainty on his part was obvious, *just like other ways he was feeling.* He could feel her body quivering with desire at the closeness of their bodies. His head swam as she pressed her body even closer to him and looked into his eyes.

"What could you mean T.J.?" She smiled impishly at him. She held his eyes and leaned away from him. His hands were immediately on her back to hold her. She slowly unzipped her shirt and felt his bulge in his pants throb. He looked into her eyes and she licked her bottom lip, biting it. Then, she wiggled her shoulders, let the shirt fall and her full breasts sprang free. She cupped her luscious breasts in her hands, flooding his vision with her hard dusky nipples.

"Am I really your enemy, T.J.?"

Suggs couldn't believe what was happening. His dick was happy with the current direction of things, yeah, but his mind was a little wary. Jeannie just randomly being sexy and stripping for him, he doubted it. He wanted to suck her hard nipples and feel her skin against his, God knows he did. All she had on at this point was a black mini skirt, black lace tights and black boots. Her red hair tumbled over her shoulders, brushing the tops of her breasts. Suggs honestly felt she was the most beautiful woman in the world. How could he resist her power over him? Even if she were the enemy, he would gladly walk into her trap. *Damn...*he needed to call a halt to the playing shit. He was gonna do something they would both regret before long.

"Jeannie," he started in a strained voice, "Uh, we need to stop playin' now. I'm only a man, honey."

Jeannie was currently screaming at herself for the hundredth time, what the fuck're you doing? Jeannie had never been so bold before with a man, but Vette had given her some tips and if they were gonna die, she might as well get as close as she could to Suggs and practice her wiles. Besides, she knew, just like he did, that they would never work and she knew he would soon be snatched up by the luscious and bad ass Marcella Torres. And that hurt her more than she cared to admit. It shouldn't, she admitted to herself, but it did. She wished she had let her guard down with him before and gone on a date. Now, in the face of this dangerous situation they were facing, she could admit that to herself. T.J. Suggs was the only other man besides her ex to ever strike her fancy and she intended to go and get something *she* wanted for a change. And what; *who* she wanted, was *him.*

"Oh, Suggs...I *know* what you are. *You're* just what I want and *you* have what I need."

Suggs pulled at his uniform collar as he suddenly felt overly fuckin hot. She was slowly grinding herself against him, driving him crazy. Suggs knew he was in fuckin' trouble. For whatever reason, she seemed to have decided she wanted him. What the fuck?

"What do you mean, Sprite? What do I have that you need?"

She smiled mysteriously at him, slid back away from his lap and dropped to her knees in front him, her heart pounding deeply. She looked up at him as he stared into her eyes. "I'll show you," she whispered softly. She lowered her eyes and undid his shoes. She pulled them off and laid them neatly on the carpet on the side of the ottoman. She peeled off his socks and looked up at him as he started unbuttoning his belt and pants. His eyes met hers again and she helped him pull his pants off, the air between and around them charged with their angst and lust. She eased forward, between his legs. His boxers were black and his dick was out the slit, brown steel, hard and engorged, straining against its own skin. It throbbed and a clear fluid started seeping from the tip of it.

"Oh, *really*, T.J."

"Jeannie, you had to know how bad I've been wanting you."

She smiled into his eyes, "I'm glad you want me like I want you. I wanna show you how much I want you T.J. And I won't ask you for nothin' in return. I don't *want* nothin' in return. Just now, this moment."

Suggs could barely think as she blew lightly on his tip. All he heard was that she wanted *it*. "Okay, Sprite. Whatever you want. *Whatever*. Just put'im in your mouth. I'm bout to fuckin' flip out Jeannie if I don't feel your lips on me."

Jeannie had secretly hoped for a different response from him in her heart of hearts, but she ruthlessly pushed that out of her mind. All that mattered was now. Now, right now, she would have him.

She smiled at him naughtily and leaned down. She swiftly brought her mouth down over his throbbing dick and sucked his plump tip into her mouth. She stroked his dick with her hand while she lightly sucked his tip. She slid her tongue teasingly over the tip while she sucked and stroked him. Suggs' hips were jerking and he moaned through clenched teeth as she brought her mouth further down and began sucking harder, licking his tip as she came up... over and over.

"Aw...shit," he groaned. "F-fuuuuck."

He grabbed her head and pulled at her hair while she took him deeper and sucked him like she was dying of thirst. And, oh, he definitely wanted to give her something to swallow...but not right then. No, he needed to feel the inside of her, to know what her walls felt like, how they would grip his dick. He already knew how sweet her mouth was.

Trying to control his urge to cum all over her sweet lips, Suggs lightly pulled her hair.

"J-Jea...nnie," he called out, obviously straining to maintain his composure. "Slow down baby. Baby-Sprite, please. Oh. Oh...yeah."

She wouldn't stop. Sweet Jesus, the woman wouldn't stop her exquisite torture. Suggs finally knew he was gonna have to manhandle her. He wanted to feel her..needed to feel her. He swiftly pulled her hair and lifted her head up. Her eyes were dark and cloudy with passion. She had a bemused look on her face and then Suggs quickly sat up as far as he could, grabbed her shoulders and lifted her onto his lap. Her wild hair was just settling in around her face when he brought her face to his and he said, "My turn."

Jeannie's heart beat frantically in her chest. Oh God, she thought. His turn? What was he going to do to her? She stopped thinking a moment later. Suggs started kissing her. He made love to her mouth until she was dripping with need and unconsciously winding her hips and grinding against his dick again. Already nearing his limit due to her vigorous mouth play, Suggs stood up with her still clinging to him, stroking his tongue with her own. He didn't even think she had noticed that he had stood. He stumbled his way over to her bed.

Jeannie was sucking on Suggs tongue when she felt him bump into her bed. She couldn't help a small squeal as she hadn't even realized he had picked her up. He teetered precariously and then winked at her playfully. They fell into her bed. Immediately, they sunk into the throws. Suggs was almost on top of her and he looked down into Jeannie's vivid green eyes that were crinkled at the edges because she was still giggling and playing with him. He had never seen anything so beautiful in his life. God, when had he become so fuckin' fanciful?

Jeannie stared up at Suggs with all the desire she felt for him shining in her eyes. Her mirth slowly died away as his gaze grew purposeful and determined. He sat up a little and put his hand under her back. He smoothly scooted and arranged her so that she lay directly beneath him. She could do nothing but watch with delicious nervousness as he leaned down to taste her lips yet again. While she could still think, she briefly wondered how she was ever going to let him go.

Suggs rubbed her thighs lightly, driving her wild with sensation.

"Let me help you with these baby." He slowly unzipped her thigh high boots, kissing her as he exposed her legs. He smiled knowingly as Jeannie moaned and squirmed beneath him. He slid his hands up her stocking clad legs and when he reached the top of them, he leaned down and kissed her most sensitive part through her tights.

"I love the way ya smell, Sprite. Mm, so sweet."

Already out of her mind, Suggs was making her body hypersensitive. Jeannie could only moan in reply.

Suggs slowly began to pull off her lace tights. He couldn't help but lean down and kiss her pretty pussy as he pulled them down. He wanted to make her wet with desire for him. So, pulling them off completely, he sent her tights flying across the room.

He quickly got rid of his boxers and settled himself in between her warm thighs. He heard her gasp as his head probed the entrance to her pussy. Suggs eyes rolled back in his head. She was so tight and dripping with the wetness he had caused. When he felt her hands settle on his back and her thighs quiver, he couldn't help it. He pushed into her swift and hard, his control almost gone. When he was deep inside her and he felt her soft walls throb, he couldn't help the moan that escaped his lips.

Jeannie felt she had died and gone to heaven. Just *him* heavy and thick inside her made her body spasm. Tears leaked from her eyes as she felt herself begin to throb on the inside and then the force of her orgasm was so strong and it was so exquisite that it was almost pain. Then, she felt him move inside of her. He was already so deep inside of her. Her back arched uncontrollably as he moved in and out of her. He sucked hard on her neck while he started circling his hips, grinding his dick deeper into her warmth. Jeannie felt like she was going to pass out from the ferocity of his loveplay. Her body was so taut with the need to cum all over him again. The tension kept rising and rising inside of her.

"Suggs!"

"I know baby. I'm almost there too..baby." He finished unintelligibly, "Oh baby...Jeannie..don't wanna stop baby. Inside you. Mmm. Wanna stay in."

His fevered whispering against her neck drove her crazy. His warm breath caused her body to twitch and throb.

Suddenly, Suggs loud groan happened at the same time that he thrust into her, touching her so deeply she came again. She mewled with anguished sensation. Her walls throbbed and contracted on his swollen dick. She felt it all the way to her toes every time his hips thrust forward from the force of his ejaculation. Good God, she hadn't known that it could be like this. She felt loved and beautiful. Her whole body felt deliciously abused as they both lay there, spent and drenched with passion. Suggs laboriously lifted his head up and looked deeply into her eyes. Jeannie could barely focus on his expression as she still trembled with pleasure. Her heart, that was now his, melted even further when he whispered "Sprite" against her lips and then kissed her again as if he were just discovering her warmth, her taste. Oh, the pleasure…and he gave more again and helpless against his ardor, she just hung on for the ride.

An hour later, Suggs looked back at the still sleeping Jeannie. His gorgeous green-eyed fairy. He confessed to himself, couldn't deny, as foreign a feeling as it was to him, how much she moved him..how much he cared about her and her little cutey, Sara. Shaking himself because he needed to focus on the shit situation they were in and he needed to get going and catch up with Ranald. He had taken far too long with *his Jeannie.*

<u>Chapter 7</u>

"Fuck! What does the intel say again? Dammit, are you sure?"

"Suggs, here. Look at it yourself, man. Kam just looked at it too."

Kam looked over at Suggs, uncharacteristically somber. "Yeah man. It's not good. Just read it."

Suggs heart sank as he read the missive. My God, he thought. As he continued to read, he realized they were only going to have one viable option left to them.

"All the ways in are blocked, right?"

"Blocked and booby trapped, my friend. Those mother fuckers'll get sliced and diced." Kam winked at Suggs for good measure.

"You're a fuckin' idiot, Kam. This isn't a game, ya know. *Fuck*!"

"What? I don't get a fucking pat on the back, nutfuzz? While yawl were in their *havin' the time of your lives*-", he stopped to purse his lips and blink his eyes really fast, trying hard not to laugh. "I was out here gettin' to work. So, yawl cain't say shit about shit."

Ranald sighed and shrugged his shoulders. "Man, whatever. Both of yawl are trippin'. *Nutfuzz*? Wow, Kam. We need to get movin'." Ranald started to walk away and then abruptly turned around like he forgot something. He continued belatedly as if an aside, "Oh, but Kam, I wanted to correct your dumb ass. *I'm* the only one that was puttin' it down. Vette *did* have the time of her life." Winking and smirking at them, he turned around and started walking away.

Immediately Kam and Suggs started guffawing and laughing after Ranald to shut up with the bullshit. Ranald shrugged his shoulders and threw over his shoulder, "I'm heading to the east wing, fools. Come on. And... don't be mad Suggs."

Jeannie ran the brush through her curly hair and probably should have done it again, but she already had a feeling she had missed something. She had learned to trust her intuition and she needed to get to the guys like pronto to see what was going on. She looked at the brush with disgust, threw it on her dresser and ran out of her room.

Suggs was bent over a bench set up in front of a large bay window. He was working on modifying a cross-bow when he heard the rapid patter of feet running down the hallway above him and then running, half tripping down the great stairs. When he heard a *whimsical* voice yell out 'fuckin' shit' he knew for sure his sprite was coming. Shaking his head at himself and that damned Jeannie, he tried to brace himself for his first view of her since he had loved her to sleep earlier. She came barreling around the corner all of a sudden and it was no use. Damn, he had it bad. At the sight of all that red hair flying all over the place and her vivid green eyes, his heart beat so fast he had to calm himself down. This situation was crazy. That he, T.J. Suggs, should fall for a Jeannie type, was fuckin' unbelievable. Shit, to prove that he really was in the *Twilight Zone* right now, Torres fuckin' declared *her* love for *him*. *Women.*

At the determined look on Jeannie's face, Suggs knew he was in for some bullshit. Was she upset about earlier? He hoped not. Cause *damn*. Jeannie had off the charts good pussy. The purely male part of him wanted that good stuff all to himself. Course, he knew that would mean commitment and shit like that.

"T.J." Jeannie rushed out when she stood in front of him. She looked up and into his gorgeous eyes and much to her embarrassment her vision was flooded with memories of their loveplay.

Suggs waited for Jeannie to finish what she was going to say, but damned if her whole demeanor didn't just change. She was staring up at him now with soft, limpid eyes. What was going on in that crazy mind of hers now, he wondered?

Jeannie's heart pounded harder as her gaze dropped down to his sexy ass lips. She flushed as she remembered those hot, *thorough* lips on her body and damn if she couldn't help but stand up on her tiptoes, put her hands on his hard chest and meet her lips to his.

Suggs realized her intent and happily leaned down to kiss her soft lips. He hadn't expected this kind of greeting from little tempestuous Jeannie. She was constantly surprising him. And damned if she didn't taste just as sweet as he remembered.

"Mm Mm." Moran had just walked into the room and truly felt like an intruder while Jeannie and Suggs tried to swallow each other's faces. Moran was tickled pink to see it. Jeannie was obviously in love. And shaking her head to herself, Moran also thought to herself that Officer T.J. Suggs must be a very brave man to take on a little tank like Jeannie. Moran wondered again how the Jeannie she knew had ever lived in a situation where her husband was beatin' her ass.

When they heard the voice clearing, Jeannie jumped back from Suggs at the same time that he jumped back from her. Like two naughty children they looked everywhere but at each other or Moran.

Moran couldn't help it. At the mortified looks on the two youngsters faces, she burst into laughter. She held up her hand in supplication as she registered the mortified looks on their faces.

"I'm sorry. I'm sorry, you two. Don't mean to laugh. It's just your expressions! Anyway, no worries. I just didn't want to seem like a peeping Tom and I gotta get through here to get to the formal dining room." When they still stood there looking awkwardly around, Moran felt kindda bad for her teasing. "Oh, come on you two! Don't be shamed on my account. I think it's sweet *and* about time. Anyway, I just didn't want to intrude, but I need to get to the kitchen and the other hallway is blocked with all kinds of knives or machetes or somethin'."

Suggs took a deep steadying breath and prayed his woody was not showing. Go down, go down, he chanted to himself on the inside. Please, go down.

He cleared his throat and briefly glanced at Jeannie's red face. "Sorry bout that Moran. Uh, it was, uh, unplanned. Anyhow, I need to catch up with Ranald and help. Later we'll need to talk with you ladies as well. The plan has changed and we'll be movin' out in a couple of hours."

Moran immediately questioned, "Movin' out? Movin' outta the house?"

"Just you wait a minute, Miss Moran. I'll tell you everything in a bit. I just need to catch up with the guys and confirm everything. Just wait on me, alright?" He flashed her one of his killer smiles and thanked God when it obviously mellowed her out. Miss Moran loved her some men and Suggs knew how to ooze on the charm.

Moran felt her heart flutter when Officer T.J. Suggs threw one of his lady-killer smiles at her and looked into her eyes with his beautiful grey ones. Whew! She thought to herself. She understood how Jeannie had lost herself to that one. There was a part of him that was very hard, but he still was able to exude a sensuality that was palpable and he was just gorgeous on top of that.

"Alright then, Officer Suggs. Of course I'll wait on ya. Just don't leave us waitin' too long."

"Yes Mam." He tilted his Stetson toward her and then turned to look at Jeannie. They caught eyes and he slowly smiled, showing his dimples. "You, I will *definitely* talk to later."

Vette rolled her eyes exasperatedly. "They are really startin' to piss me off. Jeannie, what do you think is goin' on?"

Jeannie was watching Vette do her nails (why she was doing'em right then, at that moment, what with all that was going on, she didn't know) and asked out of context, "Why are ya doin' your nails right now? They're pretty, but now?

Vette smiled at Jeannie. "You talkin' bout me girl?"

Jeannie started laughing. "Hell yeah,Vette. What's that about?"

"It calms me."

"Okay, it calms ya Vette, but they gonna get messed up. Did you think about that?"

Vette's face screwed up with displeasure. "Actually, I didn't. And I'm not thanking you for tellin' me neither." She stuck her tongue out at Jeannie and glared at her Aunt because she was laughing like the shit was funny.

Vette growled in frustration and threw the fingernail polish down on the table. The top wasn't on, so a lot of the nail polish flew out of the bottle and splattered all over her table top. Vette jumped up, cursing, and flung her chair back, obviously about to wig out. She whipped around to glare at them both.

"Fuck-you-both!" With that, Vette stomped out of the room with her head high and let the door slam behind her. Laughing so hard they could barely walk straight, Jeannie and Moran hurried after Vette and closed the door behind them.

"Okay..mm mm...Ladies. Our situation has changed and so has our time frame." Ranald paused and looked at his watch. "We actually got the intel a couple of hours ago, but we just needed to make sure that all the known entrances and exits were blocked off and booby trapped. I'm glad also to say that we still have a lot of weapons left, which is good cause we'll need'em."

Suggs then began, "So, this is the deal. We're not going to engage them. We're gonna fool them." When Jeannie, Moran and Vette started shifting in their seats and looking at each other uncomfortably, Suggs hurried out, "Be easy, Ladies. Be easy. Let me explain. We're not going to directly engage them, but that doesn't mean we may not have to fight them. We received word that The Hammer plans to have the mansion blown up at sun-up tomorrow."

Jeannie's heart pounded with renewed dread, "You mean, like.. dawn?"

Suggs responded plainly, "Yes."

"Oh," was all Jeannie could utter.

"So," Suggs continued, "We're going to move you guys and the staff out of here and we're gonna be leaving within the next 2 hours."

"Wait, wait!" Moran jumped up out of her seat. "You guys said it was too dangerous to leave the mansion right now. Not that I want to fight them off, but you did say that going outside was bad too."

Ranald responded, "You're right, Moran. You're right, but with this new intel our plans had to change. What if he's really gonna have this place blown up before dawn? See, we can't take that risk. So, we're moving you out through the underground tunnels which I am pretty sure Russini knows nothing about. They go all the way to an abandoned theme park and some uniform cops and Detectives are going to meet us there. From there, we should be able to have you moved to a secure location, without fear of being followed."

Jeannie, shrewd as always, asked, "And there's no but?"

Vette smacked her lips and seconded the question with, *mm hmm.*

Ranald looked over at Vette. "Thanks for that, hon."

Smiling cheekily at her husband, Vette replied, "Anytime, babes. Anytime."

Kam walked forward and smiled admiringly at Jeannie. "Cain't get nothin' pass you Jeannie, huh?"

Suggs pushed Kam on the shoulder lightly. "Man, that's Jeannie all day. Always thinkin' bout somethin' and puttin' her nose into somethin' too."

Kam snickered and antagonized the situation even more. "If I were you I wouldn't take that Miss Jeannie. You cain't let him be talkin' bout you like that."

Suggs pushed him again. Harder this time. "Shut up Kam and let me just tell the sprite about the but." Suggs rolled his eyes exasperatedly and turned to the three pairs of eyes focused on him. "So, on the off chance that The Hammer does know about the tunnels we'll be pursued possibly the whole way there, but even with that if we get a good head start we can be at our rondevu point before they get to us. If need be we just need to be prepared to hold them off, back them off, whatever."

"Ok. So, how long are the tunnels? Are they, what's that damn word, inchikit?"

Kam couldn't help but smile and advised, "It's *intricate.*"

"Sprite, how the hell you gonna know how to use intricate in a sentence, but don't know how to say it?"

Jeannie scowled at Suggs fiercely, "You shut up, Officer nitwit!" All her softer feelings from earlier evaporating rapidly, she continued, "I'm not stupid. I just didn't know how to say it. I guess I should be burned at the stake now!"

"Jeannie, Jeannie. Calm down," Ranald broke in. "Don't listen to Suggs, Jeannie. I ain't never been good at sayin' certain words or spellin'em. So never you mind Suggs. Ok?"

"I was just playin' with ya anyway, Sprite. You're sooo easy."

"Whatever," Jeannie grudgingly mumbled.

Vette broke in. "Ok, guys. Can we please get off this now? Focus. We have to get movin', don't we?"

The time had come and Jeannie was trembling on the inside. There was so much to think about, so much to consider. And after this ordeal, if they made it, she still had to deal with Jed. *Jed.* The shit-stain of her past.

Moran and Sylvette both held small 9's in their hands and were looking as ill as they come. All three women had been practicing in the back of the mansion where the auditorium was as it was soundproof. Jeannie had handled guns before so she did pretty well. Vette actually was pretty alright too as Ranald had bought her a small Smith and Wesson pistol a while ago and frequently had her at the range practicing. Moran had the most difficulty as she had never handled a gun before and didn't have a large amount of strength in her arms. She had a difficult time dealing with the recoil and holding the gun steady.

Jeannie was standing against the wall in the back of the Great room kind of fading out of notice for a moment, watching the other people in the room. She was terrified on the inside, yes, but she also felt so alive. Her feelings were conflicting, but there was no denying that no matter what, they could not fail. An image of Sara and her mother flashed before her eyes and she felt her determination increase tenfold through her fear. She would see her mother and Sara again. She would.

About a half an hour later they stopped shooting. That was all the time they could afford to spare.

"Ok. Ladies, to answer Jeannie's question from earlier...6.58 miles." Kam stopped talking and looked pleasantly about him. Again, obviously done with what he had to say.

"*Kam*!" Moran barked out, startling everyone. "You're not *finished*."

Kam had the nerve to look genuinely bemused, "I'm not?"

Moran rolled her eyes and ran her hand down her face, obviously exasperated. "Never mind."

Ranald pushed Kam out of the way and finished where his brother left off, "The tunnels stretch for a little over 6 ½ miles."

"That's far, Ranald! Like really far to go to be getting away from guys with guns."

"Jeannie, I completely agree. That's part of the reason we didn't consider this at first. At this point, we really have no choice though. You feel me?"

"I don't like it, but, yeah, I guess I do."

"Ok. We're gonna be going through tunnels and they will shift. It will be dark, but I am going to give you all a flashlight and a copy of the map. You will only be able to use the flashlight sparingly and if you're told not to turn it on, you need to listen because you may expose our position." He paused while one of the maids passed out the maps. "Now take a couple of moments to look over the map and commit as much to memory as possible."

Kam stood up and ambled over to Ranald. "Hey brother, I'm going to go and do a perimeter check. I'll take the gardener and Mr. Sams."

"Okay. Be careful. Wait, who's Mr. Sams?"

"He's one of the drivers, honey." Sylvette rolled her eyes and mouthed, *what the fuck does it matter*, to Jeannie.

Kam set off and the others that were left tried to memorize as much as they could of the map. Eventually Suggs and Ranald headed to the front to start a perimeter check from the inside. Sylvette and Moran went to go around the mansion checking on last minute details with some of the staff.

Jeannie studied the map thoroughly and tried to notice the tricky points where it might be easy to get confused and then get lost. In Jeannie's mind, to lose the group probably meant sure death. God, it was gonna be so dark in the tunnels. She prayed that they all made it through what was coming. It was gonna be a lot more difficult than what she knew the men were saying. A few moments later Jeannie was still studying the map in one of the sunrooms when the air was suddenly rent with what sounded like *gunshots* coming from right outside the mansion. It sounded so close that Jeannie jumped up, startled and her map slid to the floor. Her heart thudding furiously and painfully, Jeannie set off running to the front of the mansion where she could now hear the guys and Moran shouting and talking at once.

"Jeannie! Jeannie!"

Jeannie's stomach dipped with dread as she heard the fear and panic in Vette's voice.

"Vette, I'm coming! I'm coming!"

Jeannie rounded the corner and ran smack dab into Vette. Vette and Jeannie hit really hard and fell haphazardly against a closet door. Vette's head flew back, hitting a tall lamp that stood in the hallway by the door and promptly started to teeter sideways precariously, while Jeannie's head knocked into the door. Jeannie barely had time to catch her breath, but reached out to catch Vette's hand that was flailing around trying to find something to grab onto. Vette yelped a little, prepared to fall back on the lamp and floor, but Jeannie grabbed her and pulled her up. Vette righted herself and they both fell back against the door and just leaned against it, panting and trying to get it together.

"Are you alright Vette? I-I didn't...mean.to hit you. Damn!"

Before Vette could answer Ranald came running into the hallway from the dining room. He looked left and saw them leaning against the door and the lamp shattered on the floor. Panic entered his eyes and yelling Vette's name, he ran towards them. Suggs and Kam followed him.

Ranald reached Vette and grabbed her, pulling her into his arms. His eyes were continuously scanning the area around him. Suggs and Kam ran up behind him and pulled out their guns.

"Jeannie, you alright? What happened? Someone in here?"

Jeannie noticed Ranald never really looked at her when he shot the questions at her as he was still constantly surveying the area. He had placed himself almost in front of Jeannie as a shield while he simultaneously let go of Vette and gently pushed her behind him as well. As Suggs placed himself to their right and let Kam have the left, Jeannie noticed Sugg's shirt was covered in blood and he had a smeared bloody handprint on his left cheek. She quickly looked him up and down and didn't see any noticeable injuries and he seemed sharp and not in pain. His expression was disturbed, yes, but he seemed otherwise alright. So it was someone else's blood then. Guilty relief flooded her veins and she said a quick prayer for whomever's blood covered T.J.'s shirt. What in the hell had just happened out there, she wondered?

"Jeannie!" Ranald whispered harshly. "Are ya alright?"

Jeannie snapped to and realized she had never answered Ranald. "Yes," she called out weakly. She answered him again, this time clearing her throat and speaking pass the big lump of dread in her throat, "I'm good, Ranald. We're good. Just ran into each other and knocked over the...the lamp over there. That's all... .all. We didn't see anybody." Suddenly feeling nauseous and unintentionally making a liar of herself, Jeannie thought she must have hit her head harder than she thought and bent over to keep from passing out. Weakly, she reached up her hand and reached out to touch Suggs. "Suggs," she called out weakly.

T.J. thought he felt something tug his shirt and looked back. Quickly taking in Jeannie's predicament, he put his gun away and turned to Jeannie. "Ranald!"

Ranald relaxed his guard and turned towards the girls. He saw Suggs lifting Jeannie in his arms and Vette standing next to them holding herself, looking distraught.

"What happened Suggs? She was just talkin' to me, man."

"I just think she's in a little bit of shock. They did just knock into each other too."

Vette looked at Ranald. "Where's Moran? What were those gunshots and then I heard you guys yelling and the door opened and it just sounded like-."

"Wait, Vette, wait. Let's get Jeannie and everybody else into the auditorium first. We've got to move in the next 15 mins and sooner if we can."

Vette couldn't disguise the panic in her voice. "Why? Why! What happened out there, Eric? Do they know about our plan? Are they trying to come in?"

Seeing his wife wasn't going to let up, Ranald turned to Suggs. "Suggs, you go on ahead and take Jeannie into the auditorium. Kam, make sure everyone else gets there too. The equipment is already over there. Sylvette can help me and Moran in the Great Room and we'll be right behind you."

"Check," Suggs replied and nodded to Kam.

Jeannie lifted her head and caught Vette's eye. *Be careful*, they mouthed to each other at the same time. Jeannie watched Ranald and Vette until Suggs rounded the corner, walking quietly and briskly to the auditorium.

Jeannie was sitting in a chair next to the door that led to the stone stairs descending into the corridors of the underground tunnels. Her brief bout of exhilaration that she had felt earlier was unfortunately gone. God, now she felt tired and downright afraid. So many what-ifs were running through her mind. Jeannie had just really began to focus on the fact that they would be in the dark and it *bothered* her so much that they would be in *complete* darkness for more than *6* miles. Complete darkness terrified her. Shit, she was more afraid of the phantoms that waited for you in the dark than the men that were coming to hunt them down. She silently began doing the only thing that she believed could ultimately help them. She closed her eyes, bowed her head and prayed earnestly to God.

Suggs stopped at the door to the auditorium. He had just left her a handful of minutes ago and now he was coming back with a whole new..*situation*. He wondered how Jeannie would react or if she would even care.

Torres looked up at Suggs. "What is it, Suggs? You need to put me down?"

Vette glared at Suggs back while Ranald tried to ignore the fact that his wife was squeezing the hell out of his hand. Ranald sighed and shook his head. He knew why Suggs was stalling, even if Suggs couldn't figure it out.

"Suggs. Ain't no help for it brother. We gotta get movin'."

Ranald watched Suggs shift Torres, take a deep breath and reach out to open the door.

"Yeah."

Jeannie heard the doorknob rattling open across the floor and jumped up eagerly. She was tired of sitting. She might be afraid, but she figured it was better to just go ahead and get it started. She kept repeating to herself over and over again in her head; *we cannot fail, we cannot fail*. Running, she got to the door just as Suggs was wal-. Jeannie could not complete her thought, couldn't even remember if she had been thinking. All that was running through her mind was, *what was Agent Torres doing here and in Suggs arms no fuckin' less?* Completely unaware that she stood there with her mouth agape and Suggs equally stood stock still directly in front of the door, blocking Ranald, Vette and Moran from coming in behind him. Jeannie and Suggs stared at each other, each trying to read the other.

Muffled grumbling could be heard as Vette pushed her way through the door causing Jeannie and Suggs to break eye contact. Vette rushed to Jeannie's side. Even though Jeannie stood alarmingly still, Vette threw her arms around her and hugged her.

"Girl, you're okay. I was worried about you!"

Jeannie heard Vette as if she were talking to her through a long tunnel. Trying to clear her mind of all the things she was feeling; none the least, unhappy shock, she focused on her friend.

"Uh, yeah. Yeah, I'm good Vette. It was just that I hit my head, I think."

Ranald squeezed through and stepped through the door and seconded Vette. "Yeah, Jeannie. You're our little tough one. Don't scare us like that okay."

"Um, yeah. Yeah, I got it. Thanks, Ranald."

After that, there was an awkward moment of silence. Just when Suggs was sure that this situation couldn't get any worse, Marcella attempted to re-introduce herself to Jeannie.

"Suggs," Torres murmured, looking up at him again. Her murmur could have been a yell as quiet as it was in the auditorium. Even the staff picked up on the tension in the group and were appropriately quiet. Vette openly glared at Torres and Jeannie was beet red from anger, hurt and most of all jealousy. Vicious, painful jealousy. Torres rested in Suggs arms so familiarly. They were obviously comfortable together as Jeannie noticed Torres had also not stopped rubbing his arms as he held her. Jeannie felt herself beginning to fume on the inside! The fucking bitch!

"You can put me down. I can hobble around and I'll let you know if I need help."

Jeannie watched as Suggs didn't say anything. He just put her down and Jeannie noticed that his face was now carefully blank. As Torres painfully walked towards her, Jeannie saw she had been shot in her upper left thigh. Now she knew what all the commotion had been about and whose blood was all over T.J.. Moran must have been taking care of her wound as her pants leg had been split up the middle and her thigh was wrapped up. Jeannie watched her walk up to her with confusion. Why was she approaching *her*?

Torres extended her hand to Jeannie. "I just wanted to formally introduce myself to you, Jeannie. I'm Marcella Torres and I've been T.J.'s *steady*, if you will, for years now." Marcella's lovely eyes suddenly hardened and grew brittle. Narrowing those eyes, she continued, "I just thought you should know from our last meeting. You seemed *confused*. But now you understand, *don't you.*"

When Jeannie didn't accept Torres' hand, nor answer right away, Vette growled out, "Why you bit-."

"No, Vette."

Vette turned to look at Jeannie in surprise. Jeannie smiled at Vette hollowly. *Thank you,* she mouthed to her. Then, she turned her gaze back to the bitchy Marcella Torres. Unfortunately, she was so pissed off that she blurted out the first thing she thought, "I'm glad your punk ass got shot."

Jeannie heard Moran gasp and then almost everyone started talking at once.

"Jeannie! Torres!" Ranald barked over the commotion. When it grew quiet, Ranald turned to Suggs. "No disrespect man, but control your bitch."

Suggs glared at him, but Ranald shrugged it off, obviously beyond the point of caring. Turning to Torres he said, "And Torres *you're being a bitch.* Why the fuck are you here? Don't tell me it's to see Suggs. Don't tell me no lame shit like that Torres cause we're in the middle of a gotdamn operation that you may have fucking compromised! You are a fucking... federal agent, Torres!"

Torres turned towards Ranald and snapped back, "Fuck you, Eric! I know what the fuck I am."

"Well then fuckin act like it, Marcella."

That quiet statement had everyone stop what they were doing and look at Suggs. Suggs sighed and said wearily, "Look, all of this is ridiculous right now. If you guys'll just head on over to the door and get geared up, Torres and I will be right along. We still need to stay focused on the mission at hand guys." Suggs paused and searched out the only pair of eyes he cared about.

When he looked into Jeannie's vivid green eyes, he continued, "And I'm sorry, Sprite. This whole situation was news to me."

Jeannie's eyes opened wide with shock and hope at his words. Maybe what Torres had said wasn't true. Trying to ignore the tears in her heart, she nodded briefly to him, turned around and left the man that she now knew she loved, with another woman who knew him as Jeannie now did as well.

<u>Chapter 8</u>

Suggs and Torres were outside the door of the auditorium, arguing heatedly.

"Ranald is right, Torres! I mean, come on. What the fuck did you come here for? I know it wasn't on orders."

Torres' head was spinning. All she could think was had she done all of this and he was still going to reject her?

"Look, I know what I admitted to you earlier was a shock, but I wanted to come here and see if you had reconsidered. I-I, I just don't want to believe we're over. Just like that. I-I'd even just take back what I said. I'll stick to our original arrangement. I'll take you whatever way I can get you, Suggs." When he just stood there staring at her for what seemed like a long time, her hopeful smile began to falter and she felt herself start to tremble from nervousness. "Come on, Suggs. I mean, *damn*, do I have to beg here? I'm telling you, you can have me any way you want. I won't push for nothing else."

Suggs heard her words, but couldn't believe them. Was this woman *serious*? And why now? She knew how wrong it was for her to be here right now. Torres was as bright as they come. "Torres, you know what, I just *don't* have time for this right now. *None* of us do. Since they saw you come in, I'm betting they'll make their move even sooner just to be safe. And we have more than 6 pitch black miles to walk until we're *hopefully* home fuckin' free. *You get me, Torres*? You see what we're dealing with?"

Torres listened to him and knew he was right, but she was just feeling so much panic on the inside right now. Was she really going to lose him? Trying to not focus on it, trying to have hope, she asked, "Can we talk about it later? I mean, I know you're right about all of this, but about *us*, after all of this, you'll talk about it with me?"

Suggs tried to brush aside his irritation. He really tried, but he honestly didn't care about anything Torres was saying. He needed to get to the team and *Jeannie*. Sparing her a short glance as he started to go back to the door, he answered, "Whatever, Torres. I really do hope *this* has been worth it for you." He looked down pointedly at her thigh. Luckily, the bullet had gone right through. "Do you need my support?" He offered grudgingly. He didn't think it was going to be good for Jeannie to see him carrying Torres again. He had seen the anxiety in Jeannie's eyes and had perversely been happy to see it. If Jeannie *was* falling for him, she would never admit it though. And surprisingly enough, he found that he hoped she was falling for him.

"It'll go faster if you carry me, Suggs, until you can't anymore and then I'll just use you for support, okay?"

Suggs mumbled, yeah, but couldn't believe his fucking luck. Now he was gonna be stuck with Torres. He wouldn't be able to stick as close to Jeannie. Maybe he could get Kam to stay with Torres. After all, she was definitely Kam's type.

Ranald held up his flashlight. All together, there were 16 people remaining in the mansion. Ranald confirmed his headcount and then advised, "Okay, folks. It's time. We're going to use the buddy system. Everyone will be paired with someone else. When you hear your name just get with your person. Each group will have one flashlight. Those with crossbows, remember to keep them steady and watch that trigger finger. No one wants an arrow up there ass. Okay! Here we go; Kam and Jeannie, Sylvette and me, Arlisa and Moran, etc."

Jeannie had finished suiting herself up and was surprised at how easily she was functioning when on the inside she was screaming inside herself. Just...screaming. She looked around at everyone in the room. The staff all wore their vests and had their various weapons. Moran was shaking like a leaf, smoking a cigarette. Jeannie had never seen her smoke before. Cigarettes were so not Moran. Yet, she puffed away, her other hand holding her machete limply at her side. Sylvette had her vest on and stood staring off into space next to Ranald who was methodically studying the map. She looked to the left and saw Suggs walking up with a very obviously disgruntled Marcella Torres in his arms. Jeannie looked up and was caught in T.J.'s gaze. Even under the circumstances she could not help but admire the male beauty of him. And against her will, her heart softened under the pleading for understanding in his gaze. Besides, it was apparent their conversation hadn't gone the way Agent Torres had wanted it to go.

"Okay folks! Everyone's here now. I'll lead the way and Jeannie and Kam will take up the rear. Remember the plan everyone. Here we-."

Abruptly, a loud popping sound rent the air and then the group began to hunch their shoulders and cover their ears with pain as a loud whining sound was heard and it steadily was getting louder.

Ranald and Suggs eyes widened at the same time with shared realization. "Everyone down! RPG! RPG!" Suggs tossed Torres down and she rolled towards the group, grunting in pain. Suggs heard everyone screaming and grunted as he hit the ground and rolled towards the tunnel door and the group. They all huddled together, their eyes wide with with shocked fear, as the air was unnaturally still for just a half a moment and then a wave of heat and then hot wind seemed to smack the group with its force and for a moment all Suggs knew was he couldn't breathe.   Then his ears, that he hadn't realized had gone deaf for a moment, became clear and the sound of the blast was like what he thought the roaring of a volcano might sound like. It sounded like everything around them had exploded or imploded and then the ground began to shake as they could hear another explosion of a large part of the mansion thundering through everything that stood in its way. Suggs could hear Moran screaming, *Oh God, Oh God,* over and over. Suggs could barely move his head the force of the blast was so strong, but he had to see Jeannie. His eyes watered from ash and fire-stained wind as he looked to his right. He saw Jeannie huddled against the door, her face covered in ash. Her green eyes were wide and filled with shock. They both looked up as quickly as they could as a terrible creaking could be heard above them and then, loud cracking.

"Oh, *fuck*! Now the roof! Everyone get into the tunnels now!" Ranald looked at Jeannie.

"Get that door open Jeannie and keep it open till everyone gets through!"

Jeannie's heart raced as she turned and stumbled towards the door and fumbled with the handle, cursing viciously under her breath. She groaned in frustration and coughed as ash clogged her throat. Finally, getting the knob open, she fell through the door. She stumbled over her feet and quickly opened the door all the way, the dim light from the auditorium leaking into the pitch black behind Jeannie. Roaring over the roaring in her ears, not sure whether the blast had actually stopped or not, Jeannie yelled frantically, "Come on guys! Come on!" Jeannie watched as a couple of the staff members came running through, their footsteps echoing in the cavernous tunnel. Jeannie breathed a sigh of relief when Moran rushed through the door.

"Jeannie!" Moran called out in the ash thick air, relief bringing tears to her eyes. "I could barely see in there and the ceiling shit was falling all over me, gettin' into my eyes. I- I didn't know..didn't know if you were alright." She stood next to Jeannie and rubbed Jeannie's arm. Moran didn't seem surprised when Jeannie didn't say anything back. What could be said anyway? All they could do now was keep moving.

Suggs waited for Torres to crawl through the door and then slip down through the opening. He heard Kam follow him. With the dim light that was provided, he immediately tried to find Jeannie.

"Suggs. Suggs!"

Suggs jumped as he heard Marcella almost yell his name and the ensuing echo that occurred as a result. He stopped looking for Jeannie and looked down at Torres.

"Help me up, will ya?"

Suggs groaned on the inside, but knew they had to get moving. They had been very lucky that blast had not directly penetrated the auditorium. While he helped Torres up, he looked around into the tunnel as best he could. The tunnel seemed wide enough for them to get through, but he had hoped it would be a little wider. The ground was hard stone and he could see nothing in the stillness of the tunnel that the dim light from the door did not touch. He stood to his full height, Torres leaning against him and looked behind him. There was Jeannie, getting ready to close the door after one of the staff. He felt tension that he had not realized had been there release from his chest. Thank God she was safe. Focusing in on the darkness of their surroundings, he quickly turned on his flashlight. When the last light from the door was snuffed out, Suggs could hear one of the women whimper in fear.

"Listen up!" Ranald whispered loudly in the dark. "Turn on your flashlights and get with your buddy and get in position. We *need* to *move*. Soon they'll come in to do a sweep of the area. Kam you get moving with the dynamite."

"What's the dynamite for Ranald?"

Ranald didn't even look over in Jeannie's direction when he answered, "Jeannie, I knew that question was coming and I was just about to get to ya. Kam is your partner so you hang back just a bit behind, but keep movin'. Kam'll catch up. Kam's gonna make the damage in the auditorium around the door look like it was damaged in the blast as well. With the structure compromised, it'll work in our favor. We don't need them to find that door."

Jeannie was scared shitless, but she made herself buck up. "Alright Ranald. You can count on me."

"Jeannie!" Suggs called out in a low voice. He waited until she whipped around and didn't give her a chance to speak. "You be careful now, Sprite. I want you back just as ya are."

Jeannie was glad he couldn't see her blush. *Everybody* had heard him. But boy was she secretly jumping and whooping for joy on the inside. Take that Agent Smarty Pants, she thought happily to herself. Jeannie kept her flashlight on him as he turned around with Torres limping next to him, moving to their position. Happy that he had eased some of the anxiety in her heart, she made herself turn around and locate Kam. Spotting him close to the door, bent down on one knee looking through his bag, Jeannie hurried over to him.

"Kam, I'm scared shitless, but can I help?"

Kam chuckled dryly. "Jeannie, you're so fuckin' cool." Shaking his head ruefully, he lifted his ash streaked face up and looked at her. "You can definitely help. Here. Hold these and remember that mostly we have a 45 second delay and then *boom*!." He handed her four sticks of dynamite. "Okay, so I've got four here, too. Twist the ends like this." He stopped for a second to show her how to do it. It took them about four minutes to complete the job. "We're gonna light them, open the door, and toss them out. Don't throw too far."

Jeannie's heart raced as Kam eased open the door. Cautiously, he peered through the murky ash and satisfied he didn't see any muted glow from a flashlight in his immediate sight, he reached behind him and signalled her to come up. She hurried to the door, lit the fuses and they both tossed them out at the same time. Kam wasted no time, slammed the door and grabbed Jeannie's hand. "Let's go!" he yelled.

Jeannie ran beside Kam, knowing they only had about 45 secs to get away from the blast radius, their flashlights guiding their path and then they heard the blasts. A moment later a shockwave or tremor rent the air and the tunnels walls began to groan and then the ground started to shake violently. Jeannie couldn't help letting out a terrified scream as both of them were thrown off their feet and Kam's hand was ripped from hers. Jeannie hit the ground hard, the breath being knocked from her. She gasped and coughed as clouds of dust enveloped her. Jeannie could hear nothing, nor see anything. Beneath her she heard a terrifying cracking and then she felt the ground slowly giving away. She felt herself falling..falling. Broken sediment and rocks pounded into her arms and legs...pain and then, nothing.

The group gasped collectively as the ground suddenly started to quake beneath their feet. The beams of their flashlights immediately were directed to the ground.

"Detective Ranald! It's coming from the ceiling, too."

Ranald peered into the now dusty air around him. He could barely make out where people were. He heard a lot of coughing though. He blanched as little fragments of rock and dust fell from the ceiling. What the fuck had just happened?

"*Suggs*! Hey man, flicker your flashlight, so I know it's you."

"Ranald, we gotta keep moving, but I think that might've been from dynamite."

Ranald heard Suggs behind him and turned around. He waited for Suggs to come into eyesight and then as if appearing from nowhere, Suggs and Torres were right there. Suggs wiped around his eyes and Ranald did the same.

"Ranald, I wanna go check on Jeannie and Kam. Did you expect that aftershock?"

Ranald sighed wearily. "Naw, I didn't. But, really, it was all speculation anyway. We didn't have time to test the integrity of this shit. It-It didn't sound good though. I'm sure the door is blocked, but with the blast being so strong…."

Sylvette hit Ranald in his arm. "You better shut up with that, Eric!" Tears fell down her dusty face. "Jeannie is *fine*! She *is* alive! K-Kam i-is..*alive*, dammit!"

Suggs listened to Vette and started to feel ill. He was worried, dammit. But they needed Sylvette to be calm and focused. It wouldn't take long before Russini's idiots began to look for another possible exit for them when they realized that there were no bodies. He didn't know how they would get in, but he didn't want to assume they wouldn't find the tunnels either. Suggs looked out at everybody all huddled together, as much as they could be, looking scared shitless. Torres was leaning on him, trying to catch her breath.

"Hey, Vette." He reached out and lightly touched her arm. "Ranald didn't mean nothin'. Course they're alright. Kam's dumb-ass is a Navy Seal and as good as they come. He's makin' sure they're alright, ok. And, just to be sure, I'm gonna head back to see if they need any help. Yawl need to keep movin'. And *you* gotta make sure Moran is alright. Now I need you to help Eric get these people out. We still got a long ways to go." Vette still looked scared and a little dubious, but a bit more determined. "And don't worry. Kam and I got Jeannie."

Suggs ran as swiftly as he could through the fallen rock and dust. He had to hurry! God, he prayed Jeannie was alright.

"Jeannie! *Jeannie*! Are you alright down there? I can't see you! *Jeannie*! Jeannie, talk to me! Fuck! *Jeannie!*"

Jeannie heard something...something from far, far away. It started to fade and she began to drift off again, but then, there it was again. The sound. A sound. It was too far away. Too far away.

"Jeannie! Jeannie! Jeannie!"

Jeannie heard it again. Yes, it *was* there. Only louder this time. Closer. She heard it again and began to discern a name. It was...yes, *her* name! Suddenly, everything rushed into the darkness that invaded her mind all at once, illuminating her sight and gasping for air, her eyes popped open. The pain from her fall she felt all at once and couldn't help but groan.

"*Jeannie*! Is that you? Jeannie?"

Kam's voice sounded like a blow horn in the cavernous tunnels and it echoed as well. Blanching from the onslaught of pain in her ears, she opened her mouth to tell him to shut up, but then was silenced by the stinging of her cracked and dry lips. Whimpering with pain and discomfort, she licked her lips with her dry tongue and was able to soften them a little. Her voice sounding strained and weak, she called out as loud as she could.

"Kam...mm mm, I'm here!"

"Jeannie! Jeannie, oh man! Thank God, Pippi Longstocking! I thought you had, well, you know what I thought."

"It's okay, Kam. Let me..let me look at my situation real quick. Can you see me?"

"That's a negative, Jeannie. I don't have a visual, but you don't sound too far away."

Jeannie grunted with pain, but pushed the slate rock that had fallen on her legs. She screamed with surprised pain as the rock slid further down into what looked like a mini cave from the level below the one she was on. The rock scraped against a deep gouge in her calf that still had a shard of what looked like quartz rock sticking out of it.

"Jeannie, what happened? Is it collapsing?"

Her teeth chattering with pain, she tried to ignore it and called out, "K-Kam... Did yawl know there were levels?"

"*Levels*?" he repeated. "Hell naw. So you fell through to another level? Are you hurt? Are you okay to walk?"

Panting with exertion, Jeannie tried to pull herself up out of the rubble that still covered most of her body. Behind her was the part of the floor that had broken off, crumbled and slid down one level due to dynamite. In front of her there were a lot of holes in the floor, not to mention the massive one above her. She could see rubble that had fallen down to a third level. If she was careful she might be able use the rubble behind her to climb up to the level she needed to be on.

"I can see three levels. I'm on the second. I can walk, but I think I might have somethin' fucked up stuck in my leg."

"*Shit!* Do you see a way I can get down to you?"

Suggs stopped right in front of a massive sloping wall of rubble and dust. He waved his hand in front of him to try and clear the air and to make sure he was seeing right.. *Fuck,* he thought to himself. How was he going to get through *that*? On top of that, how would Kam and Jeannie be able to get on his side?

"Fuck!" he whispered furiously. Knowing he needed to chill and think about the situation with a cool mind, he relaxed his breathing. He couldn't get pissed, he needed to get to them cause one thing he knew, they *were* on the other side. Suggs walked up to the wall and looked at it closely. On the left of the wall the rubble was more shallow, not by much, but it was. He had no choice but to try and dig through. He didn't think the wall would be that thick, it would just take fucking time and that he didn't have.

Kam jumped and looked up and around him. He had heard something. He was sure of it. He really hoped the ceiling wasn't giving way. He hadn't reached Jeannie yet. To be sure, he listened some more, but heard nothing else. Ignoring whatever it had been, he got back to it. He knew one thing, they needed to hurry the fuck up before something *did* give way. They might not be as lucky next time.

"Okay, Jeannie! I see your little dusty hand."

Against herself and through the pain, she couldn't help but smile at Kam's antics. He was probably the only guy who could make her smile at a time like this. So, gathering all her strength, she pulled herself up again, using her right leg to help. She gripped the edge of the rock so hard

she was sure she was bleeding. Grunting with effort, she tried to pull her body, that suddenly

weighed a ton, up.

"Come on Jeannie! Just a little further. My rock is starting to tip."

"Wait!" she called out desperately. "Don't come down any further Kam. You'll fall and

all that shit'll give, too." She stopped to brace herself and rest her arms. "Just gimme a minute

Kam. I'm easin' my way up and then you can just pull me the rest of the way."

"Well, come on, fireball, we need to tend to your leg."

Muttering to herself, *like I don't know that,* Jeannie reached back up and started workin'

on gettin' up the rock she was on and then to the rock that led to the top.

Suggs moved the last small boulder that was in his way. Walking up to the hole, he got on

all fours and crawled to the entrance. He leaned through and from his position he saw the

massive hole in the floor, but he couldn't see through the dust to the bottom.

"Jeannie! Kam! Can yawl hear me?"

Kam was just hauling Jeannie up the rest of the long slab of rock when he heard Suggs

yell out there names. "Hot damn!" He grinned down into Jeannie's strained face. "Your *lover*

boy is *here!*" Then Kam took a deep breath and pulled Jeannie all the way up, ignoring his sore

muscles. They both collapsed on a bit of rock by the wall, breathing hard from exertion and

relief.

Suggs thought he heard someone saying something, but he couldn't quite make it out.

"Jeannie, Suggs, is that you?"

Kam heard Suggs and he was sure Jeannie had too, but they were both panting so hard from pain and exertion, all he could do was lightly beat on the long concrete plank that they laid on.

Everything on Jeannie ached and she didn't even want to focus on her leg. Still, knowing that Suggs had come for them..her, made her smile on the inside. She loved him so much and the realization of that wasn't so hard to take like she had thought it would be. Yes, she did love her some T.J. Suggs.

"Jeannie! Kam! I'm coming. I hear you!" Suggs eased carefully around the huge crater in the floor. His heart pounded heavily as he continued to ease his way down the narrow bit of floor left by the wall. When he cleared the jagged ledge, he jumped over a huge crack in the floor and to save time, he didn't continue to try and work his way around, he began to climb down. Suggs realized this was a bit more precarious than rock climbing, but it was almost the same. He just had to make sure his hands were holding rock that was secure. Suggs climbed over the ledge and fit his hands in a crevice that was in the large boulder he hung from. Relaxing himself, he hung on and looked around. His drop would be about 6 feet if he let go, but the rubble underneath him didn't look secure and he looked harder at the rubble. Were there different levels to this damn thing, he wondered? It looked like the level below him, if that's what it was, had also been affected by the blast. He looked to his right and left and still couldn't see Kam and Jeannie. He knew they had to be close though. He had heard them. He just hoped they weren't on the level below the one he was on. It wouldn't be easy to get down to that third level or whatever it was. Suggs hands were starting to ache so he knew he had surveyed long enough. There were a couple of boulders and slate rock piled up on each other to his right. He would just have to swing a bit to get there. Grunting with effort, Suggs tightened his grip and swung his body out, preparing for his jump. After his third swing, he leapt out towards his destination and after a moment he landed in the middle of a long piece of slate rock. Standing to his full height, he tried to see through all the dust.

"Jeannie! Kam! I can't see you through all this shit! Where are you?" He waited and then he heard the knocking again. It was coming from in front of him somewhere and it sounded like it was above, on the upper level. Easing his way through the rubble he jumped from rock to rock until he reached a massive piece of slate rock that had broken off and now rested at the edge of the level they had been on and that extended all the way down to the third level. Suggs bet the slate was what Jeannie and Kam had been forced to tackle as well. He hoped they would be on the other side of the massive hole in the floor. And knowing the only way to know if that's where they were was to get up it, he got started. When he reached the middle of the slate, it started to creak. Suggs stilled immediately. "Fuck!" He whispered furiously under his breath. He probably had about 14 feet to go. His mind racing furiously, he tried to think of a way to still get up there without dying first. Then it hit him. He just needed to keep his weight off the slate as much as possible. He was gonna leap his way up. Crouching low and taking a deep breath, Suggs shot forward off his feet. He landed in a crouch and before the slate had time to register his weight, he leaped forward again. Breathing hard, after he landed again, he gritted his teeth and leapt forward one more time.

Jeannie, with Kam's help had moved back further into the tunnel, where the massive hole began, sitting up against the wall.

"I don't think I can do this Kam. That shit," she pointed to the shard of rock protruding from her calf, "Is gonna hurt. It hurts like hell now!"

"Jeannie, if we don't get this out, you're not going anywhere. And we need to get fucking going. Ya feel me, Pippi?"

Jeannie was so scared of the pain that was coming and she didn't even feel ashamed of showing it. Oh God, she thought to herself, how am I gonna get through this? And where was Suggs?

"Is T.J. comin', Kam? Do ya think s-somethin' happened to his dumb...ass?"

Kam looked at Jeannie and hid his worry from her. She was pale, her eyes were dull and droopy. Her body had the shakes too and she had lost a lot of blood...shock. Kam was further worried because she didn't seem to notice at all. They needed to hurry and get her leg together and wrapped up so they could head back. He did know if the explosion had slowed them down it had to have also slown down Russini's men, but it also could have tipped them off that something was going on down here. Shit, not to mention, by now they would have also recognized there were no bodies. Fuck, was all he could think to himself. He sure could use some help and Suggs was taking a long time.

"He's coming, Jeannie. I heard him and so did you. He just has to make his way through all the mess we were in, that's all." Kam knew what he was going to say next would upset her so he eased his tall self down and sat next to her. Grabbing her hand, he continued, "We can't wait for him, Jeannie." When she immediately tensed and tried to snatch her hand away, he gripped her hand all the harder. "Listen, Pippi, he'll catch up. You know he will, but he won't want me to keep you here in this precarious situation. We have the floor to worry about and the men The Hammer hired to take us out. We *have* to move, but first...that leg, okay."

Jeannie closed her eyes against the terrifying image of Suggs lying hurt or dead somewhere. "Kam, I'm not gonna do it. I'm not leavin' him."

"Huh, Kam shouldn't be surprised. You never listen, Sprite."

Jeannie gasped as Suggs casually walked out of the dusty gloom like he had always been there. Jeannie began to lift herself to get up to run to him as relief poured over her in waves and then was stopped short by a brutal reminder. White hot pain shot up from her leg and she screamed hoarsely in pain. Suggs rushed over to her, sat on the floor and then shifted her top half into his lap.

Jeannie stared up into his eyes and tried to calm her breathing. The sharp pain was subsiding but the ache and throbbing was almost just as bad. Unbidden tears fell down her cheeks and she saw Suggs look down at her injury and pass some sort of silent communication with Kam as he turned his gaze in Kam's direction. Jeannie watched Kam's face and wondered at his apprehensive look. She had never seen him look that way before. Trying to speak past the pain, Jeannie opened her mouth to ask what was going on, but shut it back immediately and almost bit her tongue off. Her teeth clacked together and her brain seemed to stutter for a moment. Her vision was flooded with white and the white grew steadily hotter, steadily hotter, until waves of red overtook the white, suffusing her body in an agony of pain. She tried to escape it, tried to twist away from it, but she was being held.

"Stop it, damn you! Stop! Please! I can't take any more." They had snuck her, set her up! They were trying to distract her, the bastards.

Kam reached out to lay his hand on her hip. "It's almost out, Jeannie. It had almost went through, from an angle. Just hold on a little longer. I have to keep pulling it out." He looked up over her head at Suggs. Suggs nodded and then Suggs closed his eyes against her pain that he knew was coming. He leaned down to her face and met his lips to hers.

Jeannie felt a moment of numbed pain as T.J. met his lips to hers. She felt a moment of cooling relief and then just as quickly it was wrent away from her. She screamed with agony into his mouth.

Her hot, fat tears fell from her eyes and landed on his lips and he had to fight the urge to cry with her. When Kam had it pulled out, he held her as she whimpered with pain and exhaustion.

"Kam, get us some cloth. We can't wait too much longer here. She needs to be wrapped up so we can move."

"Yeah. Only, as you can see my shirt is almost non-existent." He smiled ruefully. "Too bad your other baby momma, *Torres*, couldn't be here. Mm mm mm."

Suggs glared at Kam warningly. Through gritted teeth, he responded, "Shut your blow hole, Kam. It's too bad a boulder didn't take your ass out. And, never mind, I got it." Suggs ripped a bit off his shirt and eased from beneath Jeannie. He helped sit her up against the wall and carefully arranged her bad leg. Her calf was leaking badly.

"This'll hurt for a moment, Sprite. But nothin' like before, ok."

"Alright, T.J. Hold still, right?"

"Yep. Here we go." Suggs fit the cloth carefully under her leg. Swiftly, he lifted it up and over and then tied it tightly over her wound. Jeannie grunted with pain but other than that she seemed to be controlling it. Satisfied, Suggs stood up and helped Jeannie rise to her feet.

Kam and Suggs both stood in front of her and she knew one of them would end up carrying her at some point, for necessities sake. Inappropriately, she hoped it would be Suggs. She was so glad to see him alive and well. She wished they could be alone for just a moment, but she knew that was impossible.

"Jeannie, are you there? Hey!"

Snapping to, realizing she had faded away for a moment, she could feel a blush spreading. Kam was openly amused by her and Suggs had grown irritated.

"Come on Jeannie. I need you to stay with us. We *have* to get with the rest of the group."

"You're right. Mm mm. I'm ready."

Suggs grabbed her face quickly and kissed her hard on the lips. "Put your weight on Kam and I. We'll carry you when needed."

Quickly and carefully Kam and Suggs led her through the rubble and carried her across the narrow ledge that was left of the level that they were on. Suggs had told her that it was intact on the other side of the rubble wall. When they reached the wall, Jeannie was all but spent. Her leg was on fire and she was losing strength in her limbs.

Suggs panted with exertion as he looked up at the wall. It would still take a good amount of energy to climb the sloping wall to the minute hole he had created. He looked over to check on Jeannie and she looked exhausted. Even her fire red hair was limp and dull. He watched her limp closer to the wall and then rest on it, leaning with obvious relief.

"It's my turn to carry 'er, Suggs."

Suggs didn't think twice before he responded, "No. I got it. Just get me back by bein' Torres' anchor when we meet up with everybody."

Kam's face lit up with glee. "Riiiiight. I like the sound of that Suggs. Maybe I'll get that chance after all. You got a bet, old man."

<u>Chapter 9</u>

Ranald held up his hand and then stopped. Turning around, he waited for the group to stop and then he tried to see behind the group as far as he could with his flashlight. Where were they, he wondered? They were taking too long. He prayed they were alright.

"Do any of you see or hear anything back there?"

Moran called out quietly, "If somethin' or someone is back there, they're too far back for us to see'em. Do ya think my Jeannie is alright, Eric?"

Ranald smiled in the eerily illuminated murkiness for Moran and Vette's sake. "She's got Kam and Suggs with her. They'll all protect each other. Okay... Well, let's keep moving and we'll check again in another half a mile. We still have three miles to go folks. Let's move."

Vette squeezed his hand and looked up at him with watery eyes. "They'll make it Vette. They'll make it."

Ranald and his group had moved forward about a 1/4th of a mile when the ground beneath their feet started to tremble. Immediately, the people in the group began to huddle together and gasp in fear. Ranald waited with bated breath for *what* he wasn't sure, but something to happen.

He whispered loudly, "Brace yourselves whatever way you can and start moving quickly forward. No matter what, move forward, but don't run. We must keep our sound down."

He turned around and rushed forward, further into the darkness and everyone followed suit. More tremors could be felt but not as strong as the initial one they had felt. They kept moving and the tremors began to become lighter and lighter until they could no longer feel any.

"Has it been a quarter of a mile yet, Eric?"

"I think it has Vette. I think it has." He checked his watch and indeed they had just gone beyond a quarter of a mile. He stopped and held his hand up. When they were all huddled together, he spoke, "After this we'll stop and talk to each other even less. I think that back there was Russini's men trying to either bury us or figure a way in to get us. Either way, we don't need to lead them to our rondevu spot, so we gotta move swiftly, but as quietly as possible. We all should hold on to each other as well because we can't use our flashlight's anymore unless needed."

"What about Jeannie, Kam and T.J? What about them, Eric?"

"Moran, now that *they* are back there, we can't take anymore risks. We can't afford to stop. My brother and Suggs...and Jeannie, are on their own."

Vette snatched her hand from her husband's viciously. "You monster!" she sneered at him. "We're not leaving them!"

Ranald felt his heart rent in two from the look on his wife's face. "You hate me, Vette? It's the same thing I would expect them to do if they were in this situation right now and we were where they are. Kam and Suggs were prepared for that possibility. Have a little more faith in them...and me. Please, Vette."

Vette felt terror clutching at her heart and she didn't know what to do. She looked out over the faces that seemed to be multiplying, obscuring her sight and finally found Moran. Moran was pushing her way to her and Vette threw herself into her Aunties arms, sobbing into her chest.

"Oh God, Auntie. Jeannie...J-Jean-nie."

"I know. I know, Vette. But you know that stubborn little Jeannie and if there's a way, she'll sniff it out. She'll come back to us. They *all* will."

Kam ran ahead to scout the area in front of the wall. Suggs doubted the bad guys were in the tunnels, but better safe than sorry. That damned Ranald was always pumping that into his head. Speaking of Ranald, he hoped they were all alright. Suggs leaned against the wall with Jeannie and rubbed her soft hair.

"When Kam comes back, we'll need to move Sprite. You can lean on me. Have you had enough rest?"

"Ya know what I've had enough of, T.J.? I've had enough of this God-forsaken place. I just can't wait till we're all outta here. A-and, I've been thinkin' of school. I even miss my evil professor."

Suggs listened to her ramble and smiled in spite of himself. Leave it to Jeannie to be talkin' about such things at a rotten time like this. Suggs found himself suddenly wishing he was as idealistic as she was. Not even this reality could dim her ideals, hopes. After so many years on the force and growing up with an alcoholic father, Suggs didn't have any more hopes or ideals, or at least none that he recognized. He had just been living until the day he was going to die, until he met Jeannie, in a hospital room of all places. From there, she had turned his world upside down.

Suddenly, Suggs heard a sound in the space in front of them and he moved swiftly in front of Jeannie. She grabbed the back of his shirt and held on tight. Suggs was tense and ready until he began to discern that the sound was footsteps. Waiting before he relaxed his guard, he knew he needed to confirm it was Kam. He turned around and put his finger on his lips, telling her to not make a sound. Suggs eased forward and then swiftly ran into the dark, bracing himself against the wall. He heard the footsteps much clearer now and eased forward. He tried in vain to see in front of him, but he still couldn't. *Fuck*, he thought furiously. *Was* that Kam? Suggs ears pricked of a sudden as the sound coming towards him suddenly changed. It was as if the person had started running. Startled, unsure of what was happening due to the dark, Suggs cautiously began to back up. Jeannie was back there and he didn't know for sure that whoever was running towards him was Kam.

"Hey! Suggs!"

Suggs felt Kam fly by him through the darkness. Relief flooded his heart and he turned around, using the wall for guidance and trotted back to the crumbled rock wall. Knowing he neared the wall, Suggs turned on his flashlight so as not to startle Jeannie.

Kam whirled around, startled. "I just got here. I was just calling you. How are you behind me?"

Jeannie stood just in front of him, her eyes wide and relieved. Suggs couldn't hide his relief either.

"So, I saw something strange and from the tracks I could see it may have affected our group."

"Explain Kam. Quickly and quietly."

Jeannie stood between them, walking and half-leaning on Suggs. They were slowly moving forward because soon there would be an area that might be unstable.

"A few clicks ahead now, the ceiling and floor are really cracked. There's recent dust and scattered footprints leading away from the area. I don't think whatever happened was an accident. Why would there be cracks in the foundation in just that spot and not close to the blast sight?"

"You think it was Russini's men," Jeannie surmised. "That's a shitstorm waiting to happen."

"Hmm, it sounds like whatever happened, happened and they moved on. So maybe they still haven't found a way in yet. That's good. I just hope nothing happened to the group."

"Yeah. Hope they're alright."

"Me, too, Kam. Me too."

Ranald wanted to stop and look for them, but he knew he couldn't. Especially if Russini's men were now aware of these tunnels. He was unconsciously squeezing the hell out of Sylvette's hand and he started when she pulled her hand from his again. Still walking, he turned on his flashlight and turned it towards her. He wasn't surprised to see beams of light from the rest of the group start popping up, their lights glaring in the dark.

"What happened, Vette?"

"Nothing!" she whispered back furiously. "Except for you crushing my hand. I should be asking you what happened. Are *you* okay?"

Moran moved up towards them. "What's goin' on? Is somethin' wrong? Did they find us?"

Ranald held up his hand in supplication. "Wait, Moran. Calm down. Nothing's wrong. I just, I'm just a little worried about my brother and Jeannie and Suggs. I had hoped they would be caught up by now. We have 2 miles to go. I just hope they make it in time." Moran looked at him with despair clearly etched onto her beautiful face.

"Will we survive this, Eric Ranald?"

"Of course we will, Moran. Don't give up."

"I'm not a fanciful woman, well not all the time, but I swear there are phantoms in this dark." She shivered with apprehension and looked around her. "It's almost like it's *breathing*."

Ranald felt a chill go up his spine at her words. "Don't say that, Moran. You're scaring other people. We just have to keep going, Moran. Just keep going."

Moran wiped at the tears falling from her eyes and nodded her head in understanding.

"Well, *Nephew*, let's get movin'."

They had walked about a fourth of a mile more, when another tremor came, the ground shaking under their feet. They all huddled together and held on until the trembling stopped. Ranald looked out at all of them and put his fingers to his lips. Now he knew it was Russini's men. It had to be. And Ranald bet Russini's men knew where they were going. Fuck!

"Ok guys. Let's move. Quiet." Ranald barely spoke the words aloud, but they understood. They swiftly and quietly walked forward, arms out to stop them from scraping the wall. Ranald didn't know if those bastards could hear them or not or even how, but they knew *something* and he needed to get these people out of here so he could go back for the others. He just hoped Russini's men weren't waiting for them at the end of the tunnel. Suddenly, there was a loud booming sound, the sound echoing through the tunnels. Many of the people gasped and yelped as the ground beneath them shook with such force, a housemaid was thrown off her feet.

Ranald steadied Vette and turned around swiftly. He turned on his flashlight and pointed it directly into the group. "We still have to move as quietly as possible. We *need* to get to the park. Hold on as well as you can if there is another blast. I'm going to keep my flashlight on so we can move faster. Let's go!"

Suggs grabbed Jeannie and held her close when another tremor shook the ground beneath their feet. "What the fuck, Kam?"

Kam looked unusually disturbed and said simply, "We need to move faster."

He looked eerie in the flat yellow glow of her flashlight as he looked at her intently. "And you, Jeannie?"

Jeannie's leg was almost numb. She didn't know whether that was bad or good, but she would move as fast as she could. "Let's move, Kam. Let's get to'em."

They had moved swiftly through the tunnels for another mile when they heard the echoes of a blast. Then the ground began to shake again. This time, Jeannie lost her balance and fell back, into the wall. Jeannie felt the wind get knocked out of her and before she could catch her breath Suggs snatched her away from the wall and heaved her over his shoulder. Dust and sediment began to fall from the ceiling and it pelted their heads painfully. "Let's move, Kam!"

Kam moved in front of Suggs and led the way to run through the falling debris. They moved as one and Suggs adrenaline was pumping so hard he barely felt Jeannie on his shoulder. As long as they didn't encounter any more tremors Suggs found himself believing they might make it to the rest of the group. Kam continued to lead the way even when they got away and no more tremors hindered them. They ran for about ¾ of a mile when Kam finally slowed and eventually stopped. He stood in the middle of the passageway and threw his head back, his hands gripping either side of his face. He didn't make a sound, just stood that way. Suggs watched him with concern and gently let Jeannie down. Her legs seemed to be wobbly so Suggs lead her to the wall.

"Lean here, Jeannie. I'm gonna check on Kam for a moment."

Panting, he reached Kam and put his hand on Kam's shoulder. "Hey, idiot. You good, man?"

Kam righted himself and knocked Suggs hand off his shoulder. "Naw, super idiot, I'm not. You know what's waiting for us at the end of the tunnel, right? The Hammer's men. Yeah, *those* guys and we don't even have hardly any of our weapons anymore."

"Kam, your brother still has a bag full of bombs and another of semi-auto's. Naw, it ain't alot, but I'd say it's enough if they're out there. Besides, we have our men out there, too. What's wrong, Kam? You chickenin' out, Navy Seal."

"Naw, old man. I just thought you didn't realize what was going on. And I don't like that *we* don't have any weapons left. We might be coming into a hot ass situation with nothing or, rather, not much."

Suggs considered that and had to admit it wasn't good that they didn't have many weapons and the ones they did have had mostly been used to booby trap the mansion with, but they did still have what they had and as long as they didn't face an army they should be alright. They just needed to catch up with the group.

"You're right, Kam. So, let's giddy up and catch those bastards."

They had covered a lot of ground and it wasn't long before Suggs could see a faint, eerie yellow glow ahead of them. Suggs let Jeannie down. "I think we're on'em. You guys see it?"

Kam and Jeannie noticed it at the same time. "Yes!" Kam kept walking forward, cautiously moving towards it.

"Let's move faster!"

"Hah, easy for you to say, Sprite. That means carrying your sweet little ass." In a fluid motion, he bent down and when she straddled his back, he quickly rose and caught up to Kam.

"Kam, should we signal them?"

Kam rolled his eyes in disgust at himself. He should've thought of that a long time ago.

"Duh, of course we should. Since *you* have a *package*, I got this." Kam turned on his flashlight and gave Suggs his back. Kam put his hand over his flashlight and then lifted it off. He repeated that action a couple of times and then, suddenly, ahead of them the glowing from the group stopped.

"What the fuck?" Kam muttered.

"Just hold on. Ranald is probably trying to make sure we ain't bad guys. Just keep moving. We're almost to the rest of the group I bet and the exit."

Ranald's heart thumped heavily inside his chest. He had his gun out in front of him just in case, but he really was hopin' he was just gonna run into Suggs and 'em. He didn't want to have a gunfight in these rickety tunnels. Moments later, he was getting closer to the light and he noticed the stoccatto greeting. It had to be them! That was he, Kam and Suggs' code they used all the time.

"Kam! Suggs! Is that yawl?"

Ranald's voice washed over her like a healing balm. Finally, they had caught up with them. *Finally*. Jeannie couldn't contain herself and bopped Suggs on his shoulder. *"Hurry*, numbskull. I want to see everybody."

Suggs squinted from the little sting of pain she caused him. "Okay, okay, Miss Demanding."

Kam called back as quietly as possible, "We're coming, Eric!"

Ranald heard his brother and thanked God his idiot ass was alright. He had really begun to wonder. Now, they could all move out together. And Ranald knew he needed Kam and Suggs' expertise as well.

Forty-five minutes later, Jeannie was all bandaged up and had been given penicillin from the medical kit. Moran had deft hands and vast knowledge of natural medicine. Jeannie knew she probably would have never known that about Moran if they weren't in this situation. She wondered if Vette had known. Anyhow, Jeannie was glad she couldn't really feel much pain anymore. It seemed like soon they might all be in a *gunfight*. They had made it to the part of the tunnel that goes further underground, into the cave water ride at the amusement park. They *also* could hear what sounded like a mini-war going on outside the tunnel. They were all huddled around each other, sharing one light. They were at a junction point. To the right was the tunnel that led to the underground river, where they would exit the tunnel. Directly ahead of them the tunnel stretched for more than 14 more miles. The map didn't say where the tunnel to the left led to or how long it stretched. That tunnel ran off the map as well. Even though she knew what they were about to walk into was gonna be hell, it was creepy as fuck in the tunnels and she was glad to be getting out.

Sylvette's voice noticeably wavered when she whispered, "What the fuck, Eric? Oh my God, what the fuck?" The rapid gunfire and what sounded like an occasional explosion were even louder the closer they got to the cave entrance.

"Shhh. Calm down, Vette. They did find out about the tunnels and it was *them* I think trying to *stop* us before we got where they figured we were going. But, obviously, units, Detectives and possibly FBI are out there, especially with Torres here. We really don't know how bad it is. We're just gonna have to survey the scene." He met eyes with Torres. "I know you're hurt, but I'll need you to watch over them as well as you can while we do this. Suggs and Kam are gonna go with me."

Torres looked a little pale, but a determined look came over her features and she responded, "You know I got this, Ranald. I even have *Lucy*."

Ranald smiled, "Finally some good news from ya, Torres." He chuckled when she rolled her eyes at him.

Kam glared at his brother. "Hey, *Eric*. Don't go upsetting Marcella. She's already in a lot of pain."

Ranald raised a shocked and surprised brow. His little brother being concerned about a woman? The shit was becoming like a soap opera. "Oh, I see."

"What? That's it, brother?"

"Yeah, I'm pulling one of *your* moves." Shaking his head at his ridiculous brother, Ranald looked over at Suggs real quick and Suggs wasn't even paying attention. He was talking to Jeannie. And Torres' lovesick ass was staring at Suggs like she was gonna cry. Wow, was all he could think.

Ranald cleared his mind of all else but what they would soon face and spoke to the group, "Alright. Let's get going. Our boys might need some help out there. Oh! When we're able to move you safely, you're gonna be split up. 8 in one unmarked black SUV and 8 in another. We'll be going alternate, winding routes for as long as it takes to throw Russini's men off our trail. We also have the SUV's equipped with revolving plate numbers so they won't be able to track us easily. Now, when we get to the exit stay down until we come back for you. At that time, all of your weapons will need to be loaded and off safety. All I have to say is if you have to defend yourselves, do it smartly and with no hesitation because Russini and his men would not hesitate to end *your* life. We have about an 1/8th of a mile to go inside the cave. Let's move."

<u>Chapter 10</u>

If they weren't in such a perilous situation, Jeannie would really take the time to admire the scenery. They waited in a huge divot inside the cave wall, very close to the exit. A waterfall, not large, ran down over them. Warmish water intermittently sprayed or misted them. The limestone surrounding them was wet and gleaming with moss growing in different places. The area they were in *smelled* green. The colors of the plants were so lush and vibrant. It was such a terrible thing that this wonderful place was a battleground for their survival. Suddenly, Vette squeezed her hand. Jeannie snapped to and immediately whispered, "What is it? What's wrong?"

"Where were you, girl? You were miles away. How can you daydream with all this noise and yelling?"

"Shit, I don't know, Vette. I don't know. Anyhow, they've been gone a while now."

"Yeah, they have."

"Maybe we should go.. check it out?" Vette asked Jeannie hesitantly. Jeannie immediately looked at Moran, who was already glaring at them.

"Are you two crazy?" Moran hissed. "You two'll get in the damn way!"

Jeannie's mind whirled. Suggs sure would ream her ass if he saw her out there, but on the same hand what if something *had* happened to them. At the thought, her heart beat heavier and faster in her chest. It *had* been a while and, God Forbid, but what if something *was* wrong? At that thought, her resolve firmed.

"Moran," she began slowly, her words coming to her as she opened her mouth to speak, "I feel you. I understand, but what if something *is* wrong? I know we ain't no mercenaries, but at least we could help'em."

"Jeannie, no! I'm sure they're fine, honey. They're big, strappin', well-trained men..I mean, come on. They'll come back you two."

Vette cut in, speaking vehemently, "But what if they don't? We don't even know what's goin' on, except their still shootin' up each other. That's my *husband* out there, Auntie.

Torres was leaning back on the wall and chose that moment to speak up. "You guys know I hear you, right?"

Jeannie's blood began to boil as soon as Torres opened her mouth. Feeling herself about ready to say something smart to the bitch, she opened her mouth to speak, but was saved from acting like a cow by Moran's response.

"Excuse me, young lady. You're talkin' to us? Something wrong?" Moran didn't like Ms. Marcella Torres' tone. But.. maybe she had misheard her.

Torres narrowed her eyes and told them, "I'm in charge while the guys are gone. They didn't tell me it was okay for you guys to move. So, before you and your motley crew try your rescue attempt, remember, you can't. Ok?"

Moran felt her blood start to boil from miss high and mighties attitude. She put her hand up to Jeannie and Vette so they would know to be quiet. Moran would handle this hussy.

"Now, Agent Torres, while I agree that the girls shouldn't go out there, the guys have been longer than even *they* said they would be gone. Since *you're* in charge, tell us what we're gonna do about it because people *are* gettin' scared. Shouldn't we be coming up with a different plan or something? I'm only asking because I know *you'll* know what to do."

Torres visibly squirmed and then she quickly collected herself. Then her expression suddenly grew harsh again, marring her beautiful features. "I'm gonna go check on the guys. If something has happened *I'm* the only qualified person to do it. Yawl three can protect the ones remaining. Got that?"

Jeannie listened to her rivals words and as much as she didn't like the bitch, anyone could see she really was in pain and could use some medical help. She didn't want the woman to get worse. It had to be Vette and herself that went out to check on the guys. Torres wouldn't get very far without help and they all knew it.

Suddenly, her thoughts were interrupted abruptly by a loud explosion. The limestone walls around them groaned and the ground started to shake violently. Screaming rent through the cave, blending with the roaring of the explosion as people lost their footing and fell to the heaving ground. Jeannie saw Vette and Moran fall to the ground as big, jagged boulders came up and tore their way through the ground around them. Wild fear permeated her being and her heart was racing. What the fuck was going on? She screamed out as a huge tremor shook the ground again throwing her off balance. Not even thinking, she fell to the ground and rolled over little sharp pieces of rock to the side until her body smacked against the wall. Ignoring the immediate pain and grunting with effort, she found a furrow in the wall directly above her and dug her hand in, ignoring the jagged little bits of rock and quartz that were digging into her fingertips. The walls continued to shake. It seemed as if the whole structure was coming down around them and her ears rang painfully from a high pitched sound that had started she knew not when, but seemed to be increasing in volume...or getting closer. Jeannie felt terrible pressure build in her ears and it kept building. The aching in her ears was becoming unbearable and she closed her eyes to try and blot out the discomfort. It wasn't working. Cringing and crying from pain and rocks pelting her side, she was not prepared for another huge explosion that shook the cave again. Screaming wildly, now insane with fear, Jeannie screamed out Vette's name. "Vette! Vette!" Jeannie knew her screams were lost in the resounding echoes of the blast, just like the others would be. Fear for her life and her friends lives crippled her heart. Holding on and trying to stay as close to the wall as she could, she prayed her friend and everyone had been able to take cover.

A huge dust plume swept through the entrance of the cave and Jeannie could no longer see Torres or the gardener, Tom, who had been close to her. In fact, she hadn't been able to see a foot in front of her for a while. It was hazy in her mind but she thought she had seen Torres get hit by a boulder that had fallen from the cliff above them. She had definitely heard her hoarse scream and then, nothing at all.

The loud, roaring boom from the blast still reverberated through the cave and shook the walls. Due to the blasts, Jeannie's ears continued to ring. She felt dizzy and out of breath, but she knew she had to try and keep it together. Still, huge rocks fell from the top of the cave, crashing to the ground and into the water. The ground was shaking violently and Jeannie grimaced through the pain in her leg as soot and small rock pelted her everywhere that the wall didn't shield. Jeannie's head pounded violently and her eyes burned from the dust in the air. She could now hear faint screams and people calling out...maybe some whimpers, but they sounded so far away, even though she knew they couldn't be. She cried heaving sobs at the thought that something terrible was happening to them, but she could do nothing but pray and try to stay as close to the wall as she could while what now felt like an earthquake caused parts of the ground to crack and shift, more jagged boulders breaking through. Indeed, next to her the ground trembled violently and she screamed in terror from this new assault. Jeannie just prayed the ground would not give way like before in the tunnels. The ground shook again and it groaned and cracked.

Jeannie gasped with shock as water came up through a large crack in the ground. It shot up, roaring with its fury and then fell back to the ground like a waterfall, dousing Jeannie and slapping her face. The force of the water was so strong that it pressed her down, flattening her against the ground. Deluged with mass amounts of falling water, Jeannie gasped for air and then coughing and gagging as water filled her mouth, Jeannie began to lose strength in her hands and her hand slipped. The water pummeled down, battering the strength in her arms and she lost her hold on the wall. Her heart raced furiously and her lungs strained against her chest. Beginning to panic and accidently swallowing copious amounts of water, she tried to scoot forward on the ground while still trying to stay as close to the wall as possible. Unwittingly, she gulped in more water. Water flooded her face and she coughed in pain as water was sucked into her nasal cavity, burning furiously. Her heart raced furiously as she was unmercifully doused with the water that fell back to the ground as if in a fury. God, she couldn't breathe and she was losing strength in her aching limbs. She was barely able to keep pulling herself forward away from the deluge. She began to feel light headed and the muscles in her arms protested as her burned, cracked and cut hands continued to grip the dark mud, barely getting a good hold. Panicking, she tried to call out, but water filled up in her gaping mouth. She coughed violently, trying to keep the water from drowning her. She collapsed onto her stomach and cringed in pain as jagged rocks dug into her flesh. She quickly turned to her side, heaving up water. Preoccupied with violently throwing up water and facing the wall, she barely noticed that water wasn't streaming down her face, drowning her slowly anymore. It was there, but it seemed that the water was thinning or stopping. She frantically began to wipe at the water that was still lightly pouring down over her. It's fury was definitely calming down. Weak, grunting with effort she continued to pull herself along the wall away from the water. Jagged rock and sediment cut her arms and hands, but at least she was getting away from the water. Gasping for breath, she continued to pull herself out

of the water's way and when she felt like she could go no further, she realized only her feet were

still being hit by the *waterfall*. Coughing and tearing up from the stinging in her nasal cavity and

her chest, she still felt relieved. Jeannie wasn't trying to be fanciful but for a second there she had

thought she was going to drown. She pushed herself up and sat up, still breathing hard and

painfully. She scooted back and leaned against the hard wall, being careful not to jar her

throbbing leg. She vaguely noticed she had also pulled herself closer to the opening. Jeannie

groaned anew as she suddenly felt the sickening urge to vomit again and she curled into herself.

Sharp cramps of pain started to attack her and she moaned in agony. She started to feel really

warm and then she couldn't help but let it out and her body heaved painfully. Water spewed out

her mouth so violently, it also came out her nose. Her body heaved again and more water came

out, pouring out this time. Panting with exertion, she waited miserably for the next spasm that was

coming because she still felt queasy. She didn't wait long. She felt sharp cramps again and then

her body heaved and she threw up a little bit more water and bile. She felt small rocks still falling

and tried to ignore their sting. Jeannie had thought their situation could get no worse, but she had

been wrong. Her insides still quivered with terror. She pulled herself up and noticed the

trembling and groaning of the walls was lessening. Still breathing hard and intermittently

coughing, she knew she didn't have the strength or air to call out to someone through all the dust

and rushing water. Suddenly, she looked down and noticed that water was all around her, soaking

her bottom half. What the fuck, she thought to herself. Was this all from the cracks in the ground

or the waterfall? Knowing that whatever the cause, she needed to get her ass up. She needed to

assess her...their situation. But, her thinking was too sluggish. Her head felt like it was swarming

with a thousand small insect wings, beating incessantly. God, she was starting to feel dizzy again.

She had to get a grip. Not knowing what else to do she thought about her Mom. And her Momma would say, *just breathe child. Just breathe.* So, that's what she did. She closed her eyes and closed out the explosion, the guns, the rocks, the water, her discomfort and pain and she breathed. In and out. Slowly. In and out. And bit by bit, the haziness and most of the dizziness faded away. She just prayed that everyone would be okay. This was turning out to be hell. All she could see in her mind's eye now was Suggs, Vette, Moran, Ranald...everyone. She thanked God again Sara was safe and well with her Mom. She tried to give herself a pep talk, but she was so tired, still straining for breath and trying to ignore little spots of pain all over her body. Jeannie's neck ached and she knew that meant she was bone tired. God, she could still faintly hear whimpers and people calling out in the distance or at least she thought they were in the distance. Her eardrums had taken a beating and so had everyone else's, she imagined. She wondered again how Suggs and Ranald were doing out there. She prayed they were safe. She couldn't hear anymore gun shots. What was happening out there, she wondered?   She put her hand in the water, grimacing at the stinging pain from her cuts. She pushed herself up and trying to be careful of her leg, she laboriously stood and leaned against the wall, panting with exertion. Slowly and carefully, she limped back the other way, away from the entrance towards the waning waterfall. She had to find Vette and the others. And then, somehow, she and Vette needed to see what was happening with the guys.

Suggs woke abruptly, his eyes popping open, his breath caught in his chest. Previous situations had taught him to stay calm and assess his surroundings before he made any moves. His heart was racing and he was inadvertently gulping in air as fast as he could. Still, he tried to make himself continue to lay as still as possible and he closed his eyes most of the way. His mind was fuzzy, his head was spinning, his eyes stung. Where was he? Had he been thrown somewhere? Where was Ranald and why was everything covered in ash? He tried to see what was around him as much as he could, but there was so much dust and ash, he could barely see directly in front of himself. He started to smell burnt rubber and then suddenly, with no warning, his ears popped and a rush of sound invaded his senses. It was like..pain. Suggs was so caught off guard from the onslaught to his senses, without thinking he gasped in *pain* and rolled tightly into a ball, covering his ears in vain to try and shield the sounds. He heard choppie screams and muted yelling. He heard the pat, pat, pat of rapid semi-auto fire. He could hear the echoes of the blast reverberating around him. He even heard the wind whipping around him. His lungs started to burn and Suggs wildly wondered if he had died and was in hell. Then, through all the chaotic noise he somehow heard his name being called. The wind made it sound disjointed, but someone else that was out there was on his side and was calling him. He was fucking alive! Relief poured through him and he slowly straightened his body. Pain pierced his skull probably due to a head injury, but he grunted through it. He had already blown his cover and he was lucky that the air was so thick with smoke and ash. He would have been an easy target.

"Suggs!"

He clearly heard Kam this time calling his name and he sounded closer. Suggs didn't lift up all the way, but he positioned his arms and legs so that he could jump up quickly if he needed to. He couldn't be sure Kam wasn't being used as a trap. There was a moment of charged silence in the air around him as Suggs could tell both sides needed to reload. Suggs squinted his eyes, trying to see through the barely dissipating clouds of smoke. He heard a .9 crack off somewhere to his left not far off. Beginning to wonder if he should try and move, he cussed Kam out in his head (*Never on time ass nigga. Where the fuck are you?*). Suggs went rigid with tension when he heard someone stumbling towards him. He couldn't see a person yet, so he flattened himself back on the ground. Tense, but ready, he waited. His ears twitched as more shots were fired and he could hear more yells coming from the teams.

A few moments later, Kam appeared right in front of Suggs. It was as if he had appeared out of the thick, charred smoke like a blood-splattered wraithe.

"Fuck!"

Kam was bending low to the ground, looking alarmingly grey. "My bad, m-man. You probably couldn't even see me comin'. You good, T.J.?"

Suggs was relieved to see Kam, but he was worried about cover for both of them. Once the smoke cleared he was afraid they would be sitting ducks. Besides that, Kam didn't look too good. And where was Ranald? Suggs lifted up and ignoring his protesting aches, pains and burns, he stood to his full height and then immediately bent down.

"Never mind that, Kam. We need to take cover. What's the situation?"

Kam's teeth had started to chatter. "D-Don't know! Just wo-woke up not too far down from here. Was layin' almost under a car."

"Your brother?"

Kam's eyes dimmed even more as he shook his head, no.

Suggs heart dropped to the ground and he rushed out, "Not, not…?"

Kam shook his head, "Not that. Just haven't seen or… heard him. I-I called f-for both..of.. of you."

Suddenly, Kam seemed to lose himself. He shuddered and his eyes rolled back into his head. He started to fall over and Suggs lunged forward to grab him. Kam's bulk was not light so Suggs had to adjust Kam's weight and ease him down into a sitting position, leaning him on a fire hydrant. *That's* when he noticed *it*. Something had seemed not quite right with Kam, but Suggs couldn't see at that point why he hadn't looked well. So, now, holding Kam, he realized. He fucking realized and almost dropped Kam in shock. Kam's right arm, below the elbow, was *gone.*

Jed parked in one of the abandoned amusement park lots. It was huge, he noticed. His adrenaline was starting to go into overdrive with anticipation and he looked over at his companion, Sacha, and smiled widely. Then, he looked back out through his front windshield. The air was scorched and you could smell it. White and grey clouds of smoke and ash loomed over and out of the entranceway of the amusement park. Jed heard the intermittent gunfire in the distance. It was finally time. Nodding his head in satisfaction, he said aloud, "Hell yeah!"

A few minutes later Sacha walked next to Jed and ribbed him as they neared Russini's men and his cousin, Illir. "The little bitch has had many other men in her cunt since she left you rotting in prison, eh? Perhaps she thought of you while they were inside her...making her mewl like lamb."

Jed wanted to slice the stupid Russian's throat, but played along instead. Nothing could stop him from getting to her and he was close. So close to her.

"Fuck you, Sacha. *Fuck! That's* why I have to find 'er. I *will* find her."

"Dirty, sick American!" Sacha laughed and continued, "You want to fuck her to death. To remind her and then destroy her."

Jed didn't like Illir talking about Jeannie like he knew her. He also didn't like hearing about her letting other men touch her. But, again, Jed reminded himself of his goal. Jed then ignored him and continued to try and see through the thickening smoke and ash. Coughing lightly, he turned to Sacha.

"Look. We need to split up here. Your cousin said the people from the mansion are holed up in the cave ride. Where's your cousin now?"

"Checking, American. Checking"

Jed waited while Sacha called Illir. Sacha attempted radio contact three times and no one responded.

"Something must have happened, American. I leave you now and I tell Russini you kept your end. I go now to my cousin." Sacha straightened his vest, hoisted his M27 further up his shoulder, nodded briefly and disappeared to the left in a cloud of greyed smoke.

Jed waited a moment, savoring it, and then smiled. *Jeannie.*

<u>Chapter 11</u>

Jeannie looked out over everybody they had found, her heart heavy. There were still 4 people missing. Vette was tending to Marcella, who still hadn't woken up from a bad head injury. Moran had disinfected and wrapped Torres up as best she could with what little they could find. Moran was nursing a twisted ankle herself, but she continued to move from person to person tending to them the best way she could. Jeannie knew Vette was worried about her Auntie, but

Moran was determined. And Moran was worried about Torres and everyone else. Jeannie did hope that Torres woke up and she definitely didn't want anyone in the group to die. She just wished they didn't even have to be in this situation. God! What were they going to do? Suggs and Ranald had worked with them briefly on firearms and crossbows. Kam had even shown her and Vette how to hold a knife and the best places to hit quickly on a body, avoiding bone. But who were they kidding? None of them, except for Torres' beat up ass, really knew what the fuck they were doing. Jeannie felt so inadequate and she was scared, *damn it*! Where was Suggs? Where *were* their men?

Half an hour later, Jeannie leaned against a huge boulder, carefully sliding her good leg out in front of her and sank down to the wet ground. God, she was tired and she had been trying hard not to think about the guys, not to think about Suggs...T.J..

"Damn girl! I'm itchin' I'm so worried. How bout you?"

Jeannie scooted over to give Vette room and then looked over at her knowingly.

"You wanna go look for'em."

"I mean, yeah. Don't you? Don't you think we should? God, *Jeannie*, what if something happened to 'em?"

Jeannie's mind roared with all the concerns about going out to look for them and not going out to look for them...at least, not just yet. She didn't want to get in the guys' way, but there was definitely reason for concern. As bad off as they were in the cave, it had to be worse out there.

Jed ducked low behind the trees as a SWAT officer rushed by, swinging his gun left and right as he moved through the passageway between the trees and the entrance to the cave. Jed waited to make sure there were no more *pigs* running by. Quietly, carefully, he eased out from behind the trees. He leaned forward and looked around the trees to the left. There were fucking pigs everywhere. He could see that whatever blast had went off, had done some serious damage. Unmarked cop cars and patrol cars laid on their sides or were burned and beat up. There were bodies laying on the ground in different places too. From his vantage, he couldn't see any of Russini's men or Sacha and Illir. But he knew they were out there. Russini's men would never stop, not if they wanted to avoid the punishment the Russini family would have for them and their families if they failed. So, he needed the fucking pigs to move on before Russini's men finished making mincemeat of the cops. Cause, after that, they'd be sweeping through the cave ride, too. The Hammer explicitly told Illir, no fucking survivors. He had to hurry.

Twelve minutes later, Jed slipped inside the cave and flattened himself against the side of the cave wall. It was dark as hell in the entranceway to the cave. An ominous sound caused Jed to lean back from the wall with bemused alarm. The wall creaked alarmingly and groaned as if it were going to crumble and give way. What a creepy place, he thought to himself. He still couldn't see well in the darkness of the cave, but he heard echoes of noise from further inside the cave. And it felt like there was water everywhere. Why, he wondered to himself. What had happened in here? As he edged further along the shuddering wall, the water was steadily getting deeper. He was almost, now, calf deep in the warmish water. And, he knew, closer and closer to Jeannie.

✳✳✳✳✳✳✳✳✳✳✳✳✳✳✳✳✳✳✳✳✳

"Okay." Vette sat up straight abruptly and then stood up as quickly as she could. A resolved and determined look dominated her expression. "I'm ready, Jeannie."

Jeannie looked up at her friend and sighed. She had known if the guys continued to be gone too much longer, Vette would be right. They would have to go look for them. "Help me up, Vette."

Jeannie held up her arms and Sylette had tears in her eyes as she bent over to help her up. Jeannie straightened and then looked hard at Vette. "Ya know what can happen, right? You understand the risk?"

Jeannie's heart raced with building fear and adrenaline. They were really going to do this.

Vette wiped her tears off her face and then for a moment it looked as if she was going to tear up again, but she shook herself, squared her shoulders and looked Jeannie hard in the eye. Her eyes no longer watering, but glowing with determination, she responded, "Well, it is what it is. Are *you* ready to do this?"

Jeannie felt ashamed in the face of Vette's courage. And she knew Vette was right. It was what it was. They still needed to go out there. Jeannie tuned into the sounds of gunfire and yelling that were still going on and said a quick prayer for God's protection. Lord knew they were gonna need it.

"Well, I guess I am. We need to get some guns."

Smiling with relief because Jeannie was with her, Vette rushed out, "Oh, hell yeah! Hell *yeah* we're gonna need some of those. How many were you able to salvage?"

Jeannie thought about something super pertinent to their situation and rushed out in dismay, "The gunpowder in the weapons would be wet. We can't use'em then, can we?"

Vette cursed loudly. "Fuck!"

Moran hobbled over as gracefully as she could and stood right next to Jeannie. "I swear, child, you have truly been a terrible influence on my niece's vocabulary. Tsk, tsk."

Jeannie rolled her eyes in panicked exasperation. "Miss Moran, we have a real problem here. All the fuckin' gunpowder is *wet! Our weapons are fuckin' wet!"*

Moran looked between the two of them, perplexed now by Jeannie's manner and outburst about guns being wet. "What are you girls about?"

Jeannie flushed under Moran's piercing scrutiny. She felt like she was getting 'the look' from her Mama. Vette was in pretty much the same condition as she stated quietly, "We're, uh, going to get them, Aunty."

Moran's eyes narrowed with anger. "What in hell you mean talkin' bout goin' out there?"

Jeannie was worried. Moran hardly ever used poor grammar, southern belle that she was. Would Vette be able to get pass Moran? Would she? Moran could be pretty formidable, but she knew they had to try to at least see if they could find out where they were, what had happened to them.

Jeannie looked over at Moran, pleading with her eyes for understanding. "Don't get mad, Miss Moran. Please, don't. I'm sorry I yelled. Now, really, I don't think we can attempt quite what we thought, what with the guns and such being soaked. We're just gonna have to go out and do a lil spyin', I guess." Jeannie looked over to Vette for affirmation. "Cause if gunpowder is wet it won't work. Right, Vette?"

Vette still looked restless and was clearly not happy about not venturing out further to look for the guys, but Jeannie knew Vette knew without weapons, they really had little chance of success. Honestly, Jeannie wasn't so sure they would be safe, novices that they were, even with dry guns.

"I guess it's all we got, but it'll do for now. At least we can accurately assess our situation."

Moran shook her head, no, adamantly. "I don't agree with this girls. T.J., Eric, Kam, they would want yawl to stay right in here."

Vette replied impatiently, "Enough, Aunty. My husband's out there! Jeannie's man is out there! Kam...is out there. We have to at least try and see if we can see them..assess our situation. We're going."

A few moments later, Jeannie and Vette were getting what weapons they could take together. Jeannie reminded Vette they couldn't take anything too heavy.

"You're right, Jeannie. But that sucks ass."

A little hysterical giggle escaped her lips before she could stop it, but Jeannie just kept adjusting her knife belt as if she hadn't done it.

Vette practiced a couple of stab moves that Ranald had taught her. She stopped a moment and looked back at Jeannie. "Girl, I really do hope we do-."

Jeannie was listening to Vette, but her head was down. When Vette paused abruptly and then didn't finish what she was saying, Jeannie finally got the clasp latched on the belt and looked up with a half-hearted teasing smile on her face. Her intention was to tease Vette about her Tomb Raider thing she had going on. Instead, what she saw when she looked up *was* Vette...and the face of a jeering demon.

Jed stood on the edge of the shadows, directly behind *Vette*. He breathed deeply and rapidly, his eyes vibrant with purpose. He stared into *her* eyes. He absorbed her shock, panic, terror for her friend...terror for herself. He felt so complete at that moment. She was right here in front of him. The black bitch twitched and Jed pointed his knife further into her back so she could feel the tip of it pushing into her skin. He held Jeannie's eyes as he lowered his mouth to the trembling black bitch's ear.

"You don't wanna get fucked with my knife here, do ya?"

"Oh my God," Vette said shakily, tears starting to spill over from her terrified eyes onto her cheeks. "P-Please don't hurt me. What the fuck do you want?"

Jeannie saw what was happening as if through a long dark tunnel. Everyone, everything else in the background had faded away. There was only Vette, her and...*Jed.* Jed. Jed *was* there. He was there, right in front of her *and* he was hurting Vette. And his eyes, his eyes were burning into hers with hatred, satisfaction, anger, lust...they were just *wrong*. They had never been that wrong. Jeannie felt her soul quake she was so afraid. All of the old fears and insecurities came flooding back. She couldn't believe this was happening. *How* was this happening? He spoke first into the charged silence and she had no choice but to listen.

"What're you gonna do, Jeannie? I got your little friend here." He leaned down again and buried his face in the crook of Vette's neck, nuzzling her obscenely. Vette squealed with disgust and terror, but didn't move her body as he was digging the knife so far into her back she could feel the blade pricking her flesh.

"Oh my God. Oh my God. Please stop." Vette shied away as much as she could from him as tears continued to roll down her face. She whimpered in fear and called out for her friend. "Jeannie! Jeannie, oh my God. Help me. Help me."

Jeannie hobbled forward and Jed caught her eye. He smiled menacingly and said quietly, "Tsk, tsk. Stay where the fuck you are! I'll stick this bitch, Jeannie. I *remember* this bitch now. Yeah, huh, I remember her from the store that day. Well, now it's time for a little get back, Jeannie baby." He smiled evilly and lowered his head down to Sylvette's ear. He held Jeannie's eyes with his own as he swirled his tongue around Vette's ear. He smiled again when he heard

Jeannie gasp in distress as he lowered his head more and bit the black bitch on her neck. Her

cryin' and begging him to stop turned him on.

"Stop it, Jed! Stop this! She was just tryin' to help me and Sara that day, asshole!"

Jeannie tried to keep her voice down as she did not want Moran and the others to get wind of

what was going on where they were. She also didn't need Jed focusing on them. Jeannie held on

to her resolve, what little she had. If for nothing else she had to stand up to him for everyone

else's sake. Jed had never been stable, but now he was clearly flipping the fuck out. "Drop the

knife! Leave her alone!"

Jed laughed harshly. "You little slut! You don't give the orders. I do. And why should I

not fuck this bitch? Oh..oh, are *you* fuckin' her, Jeannie? That's what ya do now?"

Jeannie took a step towards them. "She ain't got nothin' to do with us, Jed. She don't.

Just let'er go and I'll come back with you. I promise."

Jed sneered back at her. "You still tryin' to tell me what to do. I done told you bout that.

And our little Sara is gone learn, too, while she's still tender. She gone know not to ever order

Daddy!" Smiling maliciously, he then licked his lips obscenely behind Vette's head and rammed

the knife into her back. Vette's eyes grew wide with stunned awareness, her mouth fell open in

shock and then a low moan escaped her lips. Then, he held Jeannie's destroyed and paralyzed

gaze while he buried the knife in Vette as far as it would go. Vette grunted and her teeth

chattered with shocked pain and then her body went rigid. He ripped the knife out while her

body spasmed. Leaning down to her ear again, he whispered, "Best fuck I done ever had."

Vette's eyes rolled back in her head and a trail of blood began to fall from her lips. She reached her hand out beseechingly to Jeannie and Jeannie was already a couple of steps away and caught Vette as she collapsed into her arms.

Jeannie held Sylvette close to her while Vette's body shuddered and without realizing it, Jeannie screamed. As her friend, no, sister, bled all over her lap and arms, shaking from loss of blood, she screamed. She didn't see it, but her scream even startled Jed. He had jumped, obviously jarred by the agonized scream that now echoed hauntingly in the cave. All Jeannie knew was that Vette had been brutally stabbed and Jeannie hadn't been able to stop it. She let her best friend, her only friend besides Miss Moran, be attacked by a man, no a beast, from *her* past. A demon she had brought to these people who had only ever been kind to her. Her throat began to close up and she stopped screaming and looked up at Jed while hot tears coursed down her cheeks.

"Y-You fuckin' bastard! Y-You bastard."

Jed sneered at her and slowly walked towards her and Vette with his knife out in front of him. "You think I give a fuck about your little black bitch? Throw 'er down and get up. Your fuckin' dumb ass let everybody know to come over here now. Screamin' like a fuckin' crazy person. So ya best get your ass over here or I'm gonna shoot the assholes runnin' over this way." With that, he sheathed his bloody knife and pulled his nine from behind his back and pointed it towards the rest of the group.

"Jeannie! Sylvette! I'm coming girls!"

Jeannie started when she heard Moran's voice and realized Moran was rushin towards them. Her first reaction was to feel relief for Vette, but then she equally felt dread. Moran needed to get here because Vette needed help, but Jed would notice her and use her, Jeannie was sure. Panicking on the inside cause she didn't know what to do and Vette needed help like right now, Jeannie stalled.

"Moran!" She looked up and over to her left. Moran was close enough that Jeannie could almost see her eyes clearly. Her heart racing, she yelled out,   "Stop!"

Moran stopped choppily, teetering unsteadily on the rough gravel under her feet. Jeannie's mind raced. Then, suddenly it clicked and she knew what she had to do. She called out, "Moran, come up when I'm leaving. You'll have to hurry. Vette's..Vette's hurt. *Bad.*" Time was short so without looking or saying anything else to Moran, she turned and looked back down at Vette. Her heart aching and terror seizing her heart anew, she carefully eased Vette off her lap and layed Vette down on a mossy patch that was next to her on her right. She leaned over and kissed Vette's brow, silently whispering God's protection over her. Then, quickly, so Moran could get to Vette, Jeannie painfully stood up. She took a quick deep breath, steadying herself. She then looked into Jed's eyes and nowhere else. He lowered his gun, then put it up and pulled out his bloody knife again. He smiled triumphantly into her eyes. He beckoned her forward with the hand that was holding the knife. "Come on now. *Now*, Jeannie."

Jeannie felt a moment of weakness and hesitated as she walked forward. Telling herself she had to do this for Vette, she gulped pass her fear and walked quicker. When she stood directly in front of him, he wasted no time and slapped her across the face with the hilt of the knife.

"Jeannie!" Moran yelled achingly as she watched Jeannie collapse to her knees and then cry out hoarsely as her injured leg bent awkwardly behind her. She cried out again as she attempted to right herself to straighten her battered leg.

"Get up, bitch!" Jed yelled. He reached down and snatched her up. Glancing up, he met eyes with the other older black bitch who openly glared at him. He pointed his knife towards her warningly and when he saw defiant fear creep into her expression, he smiled mockingly at her. He wished he had some time to carve into her, bleed out some of that pride that was shining in her eyes.

Moran watched with dread as the big man who had hit Jeannie dragged her roughly, further back into the shadows of the cave. Moran continued to watch them carefully, her heart heavy with worry for little Jeannie. Then she hurried forward, her heart racing. She had to get to Vette.

Suggs held his .45 out in front of him as he leaned left and looked into the entrance of the cave. An odd sound that was echoing from the cave threw him off for a second cause it reminded him of a scream, but Suggs knew it also could've been many other things as well. So he focused on what was right in front of him and tuned the waning sound out.

"Clear." Suggs called back. Then, he entered the cave briskly, rapidly scanning the area. He looked high and to the side, noticed the walls had collapsed in some places and almost collapsed in others. The ground looked like it had imploded somehow as huge dirt boulders and massive limestone rock appeared to have broken through the ground. There was fallen limestone rock everywhere. Tree debris lay haphazardly all over the ground from what he could see. He wondered if the structure was sound. Maybe there had been a quake because of the blasts and the RPG's that had been deployed. And if that was the case, *were* the girls alright? Was *Jeannie,* alright? Had that been a scream he had heard?

"Clear," he then called out quietly again.

Ranald then rounded the corner, a make-shift bandage wrapped around his head and held his .9 out to his left as he supported his brother with his right side. Kam half dragged himself with the help of his brother and half hobbled precariously alongside Ranald, trying to stay conscious.

"Come on, Kam. We gotta find somewhere to post up man. Keep fighting, bruh." Ranald continued, whispering, "When we get to the girls, Moran can patch you up."

"H-Ho-hope the girrls ok," Kam barely weezed out through his pain..

"Hush, bruh. Don't talk. Don't worry about the girls, ok. Let's just get to'em."

Suggs listened to the brothers behind him with half an ear. He walked forward cautiously and noticed the water level was increasing. It was creeping up to his ankles. And then he began to smell the noxious odor of Sulphur. Why Sulphur, he wondered. The walls around them continued to groan and Suggs was starting to get tired of stepping on fallen rock that the dark water was shielding on the ground. The shit was uncomfortable as hell and if he wasn't careful, messed up his footing.

"Fuck!" Ranald cursed again and muttered grumpily behind him.

Suggs smiled when he heard Ranald cuss and threw over his shoulder, "Yeah, man. They fuckin' me up, too." Suggs thought about Kam and sobered quickly. They needed to get him to Moran and fast.

Suggs had went a little further when the cave finally started to open up a little. Because of that though, he needed to secure the area. He looked back quickly at Ranald and nodded his head. Ranald understood and they both moved over to the right quietly and quickly. Ranald and Kam labored to get behind a jagged, but beautiful and huge, quartz-covered limestone boulder that lay almost against the crumbling wall.

When they were secure behind the boulder, Suggs wasted no time and turned to Ranald. "I need to go and scout the area.   I thought I heard a scream when we first came in."

Ranald replied, "Understood. I'll watch Kam, but if you need me, I'll hide him in here and come in for backup if shit pops off."

"Yeah, well, let's hope there's none of that. We need to move out as soon as Kam and the others are handled. I still couldn't tell who was winning out there. And we've got to get to the trucks. I'll be back." Suggs nodded at a barely coherent Kam and stepped out from behind the rock.

Suggs had walked about 12 feet and the water level was at his knees. He looked out ahead of him with his scope and saw that it thinned out further up. He continued to walk forward and then hit his shin on a boulder under the water and it threw off his footing. His knee buckled and he took the brunt of the weight on his left leg so he wouldn't fall and get his gun wet. Grimacing when a sharp pain went up his calf and thigh, he hobbled forward trying to maintain his balance when the ground suddenly sunk from beneath him. Gasping in shock, Suggs fell back and quickly held his gun high up in the air. He fell on his ass on the jagged rock fragments that covered the ground. The water went over his head and he immediately pushed his upper body forward and stood up on his left leg, gingerly using his right for balance. Still holding the gun in the air he stood there sopping wet and trying to spit out water he had swallowed. What the fuck, was all that kept running through his mind. How the fuck had a whole lagoon formed? Suggs wondered if he should just back up and go around. He didn't know if the ground dropped again further in. Yeah, he decided. He would get out of the water and go around. He could check the left side of the structure first.

Suggs flexed his right leg and grimaced at the pain, but it wasn't unbearable. Hoisting his gun back up on his shoulder he began to move forward to the left. He was about to go into an area of the cave that wasn't lit at all. In fact, the space in front of him looked like a void in the cave. The cave looked different because of whatever had happened and it was dark. Suggs walked into the obsidian space and could see nothing. Standing in the open made him nervous but he needed to let his eyes adjust to the dark. While they adjusted he slowly moved to his left. He needed to brace himself against something if he could. His night vision on his gun had been damaged when the second blast had happened outside. He and the gun had went flying. Gradually, he was able to barely see shadows and vague outlines of things. He had been moving to the left longer than he would have liked and he still hadn't come across anything concrete. Fuck it, he thought to himself. He would just maintain his footing and keep moving forward. He needed to get to the group. So, he kept moving forward and as he moved closer to them he started to get a bad feeling. Suddenly, there was a scraping sound not too far ahead of him to the right. Then, he definitely heard someone grunt or something like that and then more scraping. Suggs knew he wasn't prepared to handle whatever may be coming towards him in the dark because he couldn't fucking see. But he was still sure of one thing, the girls had no reason to be this way so it had to be someone else. He heard a whimper, he thought and scuffling. Was someone being held against their will..dragged maybe?

Suggs quickly turned around and moved forward in the dark, trying to move much faster than whoever was coming towards him. He needed to be able to cross left so that he could move toward the light. Then he would have to post up and wait for the company to arrive.

Suggs couldn't hear whoever was in front of him for a moment and briskly walked towards the lighted area of the cave. Suggs saw a cluster of boulders about 8 feet ahead of him on the edge of the lagoon. Looking back and to the sides quickly, he moved forward. He needed to be unseen when his company came into view. He looked out into the darkness searchingly and then his ears pricked. He had definitely heard a whimper or someone cry out maybe and definitely scuffling and struggling. Who the fuck was walking towards him, Suggs wondered?

Suggs waited about a minute longer and then they were close enough that he could clearly make out one of their voices. His mind exploded with terror and confusion as a big, long-haired white man struggled roughly with his little Jeannie as they walked out of the darkness. His terror and confusion quickly turned into white-hot anger as the man called her a bitch and kneed her viciously in her side and she collapsed onto her knees. Suggs mind exploded with fury and he only knew he had to get to Jeannie. The man was leaning down to grab her as she cowered pitifully on the ground. Suggs ran out from behind the boulders and was coming up behind the man on his right side. Suggs got a little closer and then lunged at the man. Startled, the man started to stand to his full height a moment too late. Suggs smashed the butt of his rifle into the back of the man's head. The man crumbled instantly, dropping his butcher knife and landing right next to the bloody instrument on the ground. His body twitching, Suggs circled him slowly, watching for any signs of trickery. Rage still boiled inside of Suggs and for good measure he kicked the big man hard in the side with his steel-toed boots. The man jerked and spasmed, but stayed out. He really wished he could kill the fuck. Quickly, he cuffed him. Pretty sure that the guy wouldn't be getting up pretty soon, Suggs rushed to Jeannie. He felt rage quicken in him again as he dropped to his knees and saw her curled up in a tight ball, shaking.

"Jeannie," Suggs said quietly. He was almost afraid to touch her because she hadn't even reacted when he called her name. God, what else had he done to her, he wondered? He leaned over her and put his hand on the back of her head gently. Jeannie reacted violently, throwing Suggs completely the fuck off as she jumped up and lunged at him with her eyes closed. Her small body barrelled into him and he had to step back and adjust his stance because she had almost knocked him over. She started screaming wildly and punching him on his chest. Her screams echoed around them jarringly and he cringed. He had to stop this!

"Jeannie! Jeannie!" Suggs shouted over her screams. He grabbed her arms and held them high up in the air while she struggled against him, kicking at him with her better leg.

"Stop!"

For some reason that seemed to halt her tirade and she stopped moving and screaming. She opened her eyes and looked at him without seeing him. Her eyes were wild and owlish with tears pooling in them and then she fainted. That's when Suggs noticed her face. That's when he saw how battered it was. The left side of her face was a brilliant red and her chin was swollen. Her eye was starting to turn a maroon color and blood trailed down and around her eye from a gash that started from top of the middle of her eye down to her cheekbone. All he could think was, oh my God. She needed help and now. He wanted to kill the man who had dared put his hands on her. He wanted to kill the man more than he had ever wanted anything else in his life. But, instead, he pulled her to him and scooped her legs up in his arms. He lifted her easily and then held her close. He took a moment to breathe in her scent and even though he knew they weren't in the green yet, the pain that had been building in his chest from the moment he had realized it was Jeannie whom he had heard being roughed about in the dark (*His* Sprite..his *Jeannie.)*, began to ease. He had her. She was right there with him and she was messed up, yes, but alive. Unbidden, thoughts of the man that still lay knocked out on the floor behind them strayed into his mind again and more rage coursed through his veins. God, he wanted to kill the fucker. Knowing he needed to put distance between them and the guy before he did anything else, he headed back toward the mini lagoon that had formed. As he walked his thoughts plagued him. He prayed she had no internal bleeding. He needed to secure her quickly so he could go and get the others. His thoughts were interrupted by Ranald splashing through shallow water while he ran up to meet them.

"Hey man." He paused to catch his breath. He smiled weakly. "Kam's as good as he can be. He's posted up. What happened over here? I heard some crazy noises." He gestured worriedly at Jeannie. "What happened to 'er Suggs?"

Suggs held Jeannie tight and he knew Ranald could hear his relief as he responded, "Bruh, thank you for coming." Suggs tossed his head to the side as he shifted his weight and gestured with a nod. "You see dude up ahead or, rather, behind me?"

Ranald looked pass Suggs shoulder and did notice a man laid out on the floor, blood pooling around his head and a gun not far off from him. "Yeah, I-I see. Well, shit! What happened, Suggs? I didn't even notice him. And why's he not secure?"

"He's cuffed, but not his damn feet. You'll take care of it and grab his piece?"

"Got it. You're going that way now, too, right?"

"Yeah. I was just heading back to you to explain all the ruckus and get your help, possibly leave Jeannie with Kam, but she'll be better off with us. We gotta get *him* cuffed and get to the others. We don't know what mighta went down over there, feel me?"

They started walking back the way Suggs had come and Ranald's expression grew grim as he immediately thought of *his* baby. Sylvette better be alright, he thought to himself darkly. She just better be alright.

"I don't wanna have to come back and kill this man because he hurt someone up there, Suggs. Uh, uh and he is still alive, right?"

Suggs growled low in his throat with the primal urge to do exactly what Ranald just thought about doing and it showed clearly on his face as they reached the man. "Yeah, the bastard's alive. See, he's fuckin' breathin'."

Ranald pulled his cuffs out his back harness and leaned over the fucker to cuff his feet. He considered the man carefully and knew that he recognized the man, but couldn't place where from. "I know 'im."

<u>Chapter 12</u>

Suggs didn't think he had heard his friend right. "What, bruh? You said, what?"

"Yeah, I know him." He stood up and looked down at the guy. He nodded his head in affirmation and said, "Yep, I know this fucker. But from where?"

"He's probably just someone you busted before-," Suggs stopped abruptly as a thought formed in his head. It was an unwanted, fucked up, crazy ass thought, but…

"Or, maybe he's Jed. Her ex-husband."

Ranald's mind whirled and he then remembered exactly where he had seen the asshole before. Wow, was all he could think.

"This *is* Jed. You're absolutely fuckin' right. I can't believe this shit. He actually got to her, with all a this going on."

Suggs really wanted to kill the guy now, but he knew they didn't have the luxury and they needed to move. "We'll have to figure that shit out later man. And we will figure the shit out, but we gotta get the others so we can get your brother and Jeannie to a hospital. She fainted on me so I'm not sure what all injuries she's sustained."

"Yeah. Let's move. I need to see Sylvette. Even though I'm sure she's fine."

"Of course Vette's fine. She's too scary to fuck with and too fine to approach." Suggs laughed half-heartedly. He knew Ranald had to be concerned.

"Stop ogling my wife in your mind, man. I done told your desperate ass about that. My stain is all over that spicy ass."

"Okay, okay. You got it, Ranald. You got it. Vette is now off limits to my mind."

"You're a real bastard, Suggs. A real bastard." Ranald looked over at Suggs, letting his concern show on his face. He appreciated Suggs trying to help him take his mind off it. "And thank you for it, bruh." Ranald turned back forward and waited till he heard Suggs stop shifting Jeannie around in his arms and then resumed walking.

"Suggs, what about the mini pool that's up there now? I think we may need to take the way you said Jed made Jeannie go."

"Yeah, you're right. That's what we're doin'. The water is everywhere seems like. We'll just stay at the edge of the water as much as possible, but that'll mean goin' further into the dark. But, shouldn't be that farther to go anyway."

A few minutes later, Suggs and Ranald were walking briskly through the murky dark. They both stopped abruptly when they heard what sounded like somebody calling out. Suggs heart sank as he eventually recognized the voice. It was Moran. Before he could even say something to Ranald, Ranald hissed out,'fuck', and was gone. Ranald raced towards the direction Moran was calling from. Suggs didn't allow himself to think, he just took off after him, barely noticing that the murky darkness was melting away the closer they got to Moran and the water was thinning out all around them. Suggs drew his gun while he was running. He had almost reached Ranald when Ranald stopped suddenly again. Suggs finally caught up to him and was going to ask why he had stopped when out of the corner of his eye he saw the madness that was right in front of them.

"Holy Fuck," Ranald said quietly. "My God! Look at this place...*Vette*!" Ranald turned to look at Suggs. "Let's go."

Suggs couldn't believe this was the same alcove they had been hiding in earlier. The area was actually a part of the cave structure, unlike most of the entrance. Limestone rock and jagged boulders lay littered on the ground like they had all fallen from the crumbling walls or maybe from above where a natural, wicked looking cliff had formed. There were tunnels that led from the alcove going in all four directions. Two of them were blocked by huge jagged boulders. To the right of the alcove it looked like a massive eruption had taken place, but all he could make out were sparse pools of water that had formed somehow, just like the mysterious lagoon that had formed close to the entrance. There was a heavy cloud of dust that covered the area and Suggs hoped the shit wouldn't slow them down. He looked down at Jeannie and thought to himself the same thought he had just had. He needed to secure Jeannie somewhere, especially with this mess. He wasn't even sure how he and Ranald would be able to get to the group without shredding their fucking feet. Fuck, he thought to himself furiously. Where in the hell was he going to put Jeannie? He damn sure wasn't going to take her down into the alcove. But they *needed* to check on the others. Quickly, he looked around at his immediate surroundings. He noticed just outside of the wide tunnel that they were exiting, on the right there were a large cluster of boulders that formed a crude kind of circle. Suggs could see a gap between 2 rocks that he might be able to squeeze through. Not wasting another moment, he quickly shifted Jeannie's weight in his arms and stepped into the huge alcove that looked like it had imploded somehow.

A few moments later, Suggs was panting with exertion. He had reached the boulders and squeezed through the opening, careful not to hit Jeannie's legs. There were a group of large stones that filled most of the space and the remaining ground was littered with small, jagged pieces of rock. Thinking quickly, Suggs gently leaned Jeannie as close to the stones as he could. He stood very close to her as he ripped off his jacket and shirt, leaving him with only his beater and vest on. He leaned to his left and laid the clothes on top of the stones. Then, right when he was leaning back down to pick Jeannie up, he heard Ranald.

"Suggs! *Suggs!*"

Ranald's voice echoed through the cave, eerily distorted. Suggs heart grew cold. He had heard the tone of Ranald's voice. Something was very wrong. Suggs quickly finished placing Jeannie carefully on top of the stones.

He leaned down and kissed her forehead. "I'll be right back, baby."

Rushing out of the opening, Suggs yelled back, "Coming. Close, Ranald."

Suggs led the house staff and Moran swiftly towards the entrance. He looked back briefly and saw Ranald and Vette not too far behind. Ranald had to handle Vette carefully. She had already lost too much blood. Suggs just hoped and prayed they could get to the getaway SUV's with no problem. Ranald had radioed in that they would probably be coming in hot and with people with multiple and serious injuries.

When they got close to where they had left Kam, Suggs called to Moran out the side of his mouth so he could keep surveying the area.

"Moran."

When Moran had reached his side, he wasted no time. "How's your injury?"

"It's not bad, sweetie. Why?"

Suggs adjusted Jeannie in his arms. "Can you handle supporting Kam? If not, don't worry about it. I'll get one of the male staff to do it."

"I'll do it for as long as I can. Why did you want me to do it?"

"Cause you're the only one here with medical experience. And Kam is in some deep shit."

"What happened to him, T.J.?"

"Half his arm got blown off."

Moran was so shocked and horrified, if not for T.J. having the forethought to know the news would stop her in her tracks, she would have slowed down or stopped. His strong but gentle grip on her arm kept her moving. She hadn't even felt him grab her.

"My God...Th-thank you, T.J. Yes, I'll do what I can." She tried to prepare herself mentally for what she was going to see. She also thanked God again she didn't have to have a profession. She had never told Sylvette, but she had truly worked one time before as a nurse. She found she couldn't stay unemotionally attached. So, she hadn't done it for long. God, she thought to herself, she hoped she *could* help Kam. She hoped she could.

"I'm okay now. I'm okay."

Suggs let her go and spoke softly to her, "Moran, when I realized what had happened, I almost lost my shit and threw up. But, I didn't. I just kept thinking, keep it together, ya know. That's the only way *you're* gonna be able to help him. And you need to know, Moran, he *is* bad off."

Moran's heart shuddered with sadness. What more could happen?

"I understand, T.J."

"Good. We're almost on 'im."

Ten minutes later they were moving as swiftly as possible through the sodden cave, getting closer to the entrance. Lopez was waiting for them, along with his unit, to the severe left of the entrance. They had SUV's hidden in the woods near a walk-path and a parking lot and were on standby. Suggs prayed everything went fucking right. And he hated his weakness, but his arms were starting to get tired. Ranald walked next to him holding Sylvette in his arms. What a sad fucking pair they made.

Ranald broke the silence, his voice strained. "Hey, I haven't heard any shots or yelling for a minute, I think."

Suggs tuned in and didn't hear any noises coming from out there either. He didn't know what that meant though.

"Suggs, we probably shouldna left that asshole over there."

"What?"

"I'm serious, Suggs. We shoulda killed'im...shoulda killed 'im. He *stabbed* my Vette, Suggs. She's bleeding all over me man. She-she's bleeding all over me. He fucked up little

Jeannie...God, Kam is different, but he's bleeding out, too. Yeah, that bastard doesn't deserve to live."

Suggs knew how Ranald felt. To say that he felt like a bitch was putting it lightly. But as much as Suggs wanted to end the asshole's life, he also wanted him to suffer. He wanted that fucker to rot to death in prison...he didn't like letting him live though. He really didn't.

"I feel you, Ranald. I know you really fucking mean that, too. But *you'd* tell me to do it *this* way, *right*?"

Ranald sighed with obvious reluctance. "Yeah, it's what I'd say to ya, Suggs. But, *damn* man. *Vette..* He *stabbed* 'er, man. He stuck her like she wasn't nothin, bruh. How am I a man if I let that nigga keep breathin' though?"

"I *feel* you, Ranald. But what are we gonna do, put Jeannie and Vette down while we go kill'im? We gonna let Kam keep waiting for medical care so we can go kill the mother fucka?" He paused to take a breath. "Come on, Ranald. I mean, at least he's so strung up he should barely be able to move and that's *if* he wakes up anytime soon. Shit, we can even call in a unit to grab 'im and detain 'im. Shit, our fuckin' dumb asses...don't know why we hadn't thought to do that shit already anyways."

Ranald nodded his head in agreement with Suggs. "Alright. You're gonna have to get your radio. I can't jostle Vette more than I already am."

"Yeah, hold on." After Suggs adjusted Jeannie higher up in his arms and shifted her weight onto his left side, he quickly reached and grabbed his radio off the back of his belt. He quickly readjusted Jeannie and leaned up and over Jeannie and spoke into the walkie.

"...Remember, extreme caution needed. Possible escaped felon. Situation not completely secure. Could be more than one perp and there's definitely more unfriendlys' in the area. Watch your asses. Over and Out."

Suggs held up his hand for everyone to stop and he saw Ranald immediately stop and then start backing up, gesturing to the rest of the group to do the same. Suggs stepped back and turned around to give Jeannie to one of the staff. He walked back to the entrance and waited until he heard no sound from anyone in the group and leaned out of the entrance of the cave. He let his eyes adjust to the full brightness of outside. The ash seemed to finally be dissipating. It took a couple of moments then he was good. He lifted his gun up and looked right, up, left and down. He could hear nothing or see anything besides trees, outlines of buildings and lingering ash and smoke. He eased back in and swiftly turned around to pick up Jeannie. He looked up at Ranald as he was standing back up straight and said quietly, "Follow me."

Suggs leaned forward again and still satisfied that the coast was clear, Suggs eased out of the cave and headed to the left. There was some cover they could take in a little patch of woods on the side of the cave. Suggs headed out, constantly surveying the area and reached the cover. He waited anxiously as everybody quietly hurried over. Once they were all huddled under the cluster of trees, Suggs whispered for everyone to be quiet and as still as possible as he and Ranald continued to scan the area. Frustration began to build in him as he saw nothing and heard nothing. He didn't trust it.

"Ok guys," Ranald began, whispering loudly. "We've only got one shot with this. My contact is going to drive the-," Ranald was cut off.

Multiple shots were fired in rapid succession not but a couple of yards away from them. Everyone in the group dropped low to the ground instinctively. A couple of people yelled out in fear.

"Quiet! Everyone, *quiet*. They're close. We can't let'em hear or see us."

"Fuck! Ranald, I don't like this. I didn't even see those fools over there."

"Don't think they were there at first and at least the trees are hiding us. And, Suggs, Lopez is coming *here* to get us."

"What! That'll blow our cover, compromise everything!"

Ranald narrowed his eyes, "So risk someone getting shot in the crossfire? Those fools up there are *Russian,* bruh. They're not gonna stop until none of them are left to be stopped. They're still attacking us now, man."

"Fuck!"

"I know, Suggs. It sucks, but we can't let them get shot. And we'll be able to get them to the hospital quicker." Ranald looked back at Kam and Billy. He couldn't help but heave out a pensive sigh. Yeah, they had to get Vette and Jeannie, Kam and Torres to the hospital. All of them needed help, pronto. It had already taken too long to get Vette to the hospital. He held her tighter to him, his arms constricting in protest. He put his lips on her neck and felt a slight pulse. Panic had been trying to take him over since he had first seen how messed up Jeannie was, but now in the current situation that they were now fucking faced with he couldn't help but let a little panic leak in. Because, Christ, how much longer *could* Vette hold on?

Suggs squeezed Jeannie tighter to him as more shots rang out. Yeah, they did need to get everybody out of there.

"Are they meeting us around this spot, Ranald?"

"Negative. A little further up, on the other side of the main parking lot. The trucks can only roll over or through so much."

"Ok, Ranald. So we wait for the gunplay to stop and make a go for it?"

"Can't see no other way." He looked down pointedly at Vette. "We can't go back."

Two minutes later, Suggs arms were screaming with protest *and* he was dripping with sweat. Ruthlessly ignoring his discomfort and the blazing heat, he whispered to Ranald irritably, "If those fuckers don't fucking move, find some other fuckin' place for fuckin' cover, they're gonna shoot us before we'll be able to get anyone in the vehicles. And the fuckin' sun is coming back out or the ash and dust're going away..so it's gonna get fuckin' hotter, too."

Eric thought about what Suggs was saying. And then it hit him. "Hey. You're right."

"I am? Well, yeah, ofcourse I fuckin' am."

"Yeah, so that's why we're gonna create a diversion and if we're lucky we'll get to take some of the bastards out as well."

"Wait, wait, what about the girls?"

"Lopez is en route. We need to provide cover anyway." Ranald looked out over some of the group's heads and caught Moran's eye. "Come 'ere," he mouthed to her. "Stay low."

He looked back through the trees and saw the 4 men still about 12 yards away from them crouched low to the ground in a semi state of readiness. Bullets still whizzed by and yet they stayed in their positions. What were they waiting for? Them…?

Ranald looked back towards the group and registered all the fearful and pained faces looking his way. His heart constricted. He had never felt the weight of responsibility so much as he did in that moment. He looked down at Vette, who lay on the ground, her skin looking slightly grey. The maid was tending to her as Moran had been adjusting Kam's makeshift wrap that was on his arm. Knowing he needed to focus on getting them out and to safety rather than the pain and worry that he was feeling, he *tore* his eyes from his baby's face and focused on Moran's grim one as she reached his side. She looked down and squatted low to look at Vette. She carefully pulled back a part of the bandage that was wrapped tightly around her waist. Ranald didn't want to know, couldn't know. His heart was thumping so heavily in his chest. He turned to the side quickly and looked up at Suggs, who happened to be watching him watch Sylvette. Suggs eyes openly showed his frustration, concern and sadness.

"Don't look at me like that, Suggs."

"I-I'm sorry, man. I just-, well..I know how you're feeling..mm..mm. Yeah, so you said something about a, uh, distraction,er, providing cover so Lopez and his team can have time to get them in the trucks."

Ranald's voice was strained with tension as he responded, "Yeah man. Cain't see no other way."

Suggs mind ran with all the possibilities of what could happen and then he ruthlessly shut all of it out. He prayed for calm as he accepted what was going to happen next. All that ultimately mattered was that the Sprite, Vette, Kam and Torres got to the hospital. And everyone knew Vette didn't have long. She needed medical help a long time ago. Yeah, it was time for them to move.

"How far now?"

"We should see them coming any moment."

"Got it." Suggs opened up the duffel one of the valets had been carrying and quickly grabbed 2 nines. He grabbed his rifle and his Colt .45 with the grey pearl hilt. After kissing his Colt, he also stuffed her in his belt. He grabbed a couple of Bowie knives and stuck them in the pockets of his boots and in the inner pockets of the sleeves of his shirt.

Suggs and Ranald were both loaded and ready to move out as soon as Lopez came into view. They waited tense and at the ready when Moran called out suddenly and frantically.

"She's really not good, Eric. She-. She's not good." Then, as if she had been physically holding them back, tears burst from her eyes and she tottered precariously. Ranald reached out and grabbed her as she collapsed into his arms, trying to be quiet as wrenching sobs escaped her body.

Suggs turned his head from the emotional scene and looked back out at the parking lot that lay only a couple of yards from them. Gratefully focusing on that, Suggs saw a partial brick wall separated their little bit of woods from the actual entity. That's why Lopez couldn't just drive through. And as Suggs was looking at as much as he could notice about the wall and parking lot they were going to be running through, he saw a huge black Hummer burst through the woods that lay on the other side of the parking lot. Tree branches and other debris followed after the truck, caught up in it's wind. Shortly after, 3 other monster trucks broke through the woods. Yes, he thought! Yes! Finally, the waiting was over. Adrenaline surging through him, he swiftly turned around and called out, "They're here and they're comin' fast."

As Suggs moved out, Ranald looked deeply into Moran's eyes. "We won't be comin' with you, Moran. We're making sure you get the time you need. Take care of Vette, tell'er I love her, Moran. Do all you can for her and Kam."

Before Moran could say another word, Ranald moved away from her and then he and Suggs were gone, as if they had disappeared into thin air.

Jed woke up with a gasp and immediately started choking on water that he had been laying in and unknowingly sucked into his mouth. Sharp pains racked the back of his head as he choked and tried to clear his mind. He didn't know where the fuck he was or what the fuck was going on. He blinked rapidly in response to the dim light in the cave. He knew that if his eyes had to adjust to such meager light it meant he had been out for a while or he had been hit real hard in the head. Belatedly, he began to realize that he *was* laying in water. It wasn't deep water, but it was enough to choke him. Slowly, painfully, he lifted his head and felt the urge to heave. Automatically thinking to bring his hands up to brace himself on the ground for the spasms, he instead ended up yelping in pain as he pulled violently against the bonds of what felt like *handcuffs*. Immediately panicking, he then tried to move his legs and groaned in misery as the cuffs on them nearly cut into the skin at his ankles. What the *fuck* was going on, he wondered wildly? Why was he in this place? His thoughts stuttered as he heaved again and water rushed up his esophagus, choking him temporarily until it spewed violently out of his mouth and nose. Finally, able to catch his breath, he gasped again and again. His chest hurt terribly and his nose burned so badly he started tearing up. He laid his head back down on the wet ground, holding his mouth at an angle as he tried to breathe through his discomfort. And finally the burning in his nose eased and his chest didn't hurt as much. He lifted his head again and he looked around at the crumbling rock walls and then looked down, noticing most of the ground was pressed earth, except he lay on a ceramic-tiled platform it looked like. He could see a podium turned on it's side pushed all the way up against the wall across from him. What happened here, he wondered?

Dust was thick in the air and there were also iron poles that were all knocked over to his right,

some partially covered with water. He really started to feel panicked as he tried to remember why

he was in the situation that he was currently in. *Where* the fuck was he? What had he *done*?

Jed lay in the water for what seemed like hours, but was only about 20 minutes. His head

hurt badly...worse than before and he couldn't remember anything but his name. Then his

thoughts stopped as he thought he heard something. Yes. Yes! It was coming from in front of

him and it was an echo of something..some sound that he couldn't make out. With renewed

energy, he started trying again to scoot his body forward, his limbs strained against his bonds,

aching and burning in protest. But he had to get some help, someone to get him out of the

damned cuffs. So, rocking himself back and forth on his stomach and chest, he hoped he was

building enough momentum. His chest pain was gradually starting to get worse, but he brutally

ignored it. He wondered if it would be wise to yell and then he quickly decided, no. It might not

be safe to alert whoever might be around that he was there. Hopefully he would just see someone

going by. So, grunting with effort, straining through the pain, he pushed his body forward as hard

as he could and he slid up about 2 feet, rocked a little too hard to his right and then lost his

balance and fell over on his side, his shackled limbs hitting the ground hard.

Pain exploded from his limbs and travelled up his body. He cried out and then groaned

with misery as an ache started to form along with the sharp pains. Fuuuuck, was all he could

think to himself over and over. Fuck, fuck, fuck! His yell of shocked pain echoed around the

cave and it wasn't until the violence of the pain wore down to just the ache that Jed noticed there

had been an echo. He could hear the dredges of the echo now that his mind wasn't polluted with

pain. At least, he thought to himself, now he didn't have to worry about whether he should call out or not because if anyone was around they had surely heard the echo. And, thank God, his face and most of his chest were mostly out of the water. His back hurt from the forced arc in his back, but not as badly as his ankles and wrists. And what worried him the most was the consistent pain he had in his head. He needed help…

Suggs crouched low and held his modified T91 assault rifle at the ready. He quickly assessed the distance to all 12 of his targets and what obstacles might lay in the line of fire. Ranald moved around to his right side and then signalled he was going forward and for Suggs to provide cover amidst the confusion Ranald was going to create amongst the group of Russian men who lay in wait. Suggs heart raced with adrenaline. It was about to go down.

Seconds later, Suggs saw a big blonde man fall to his right, his arms thrown up over his head as he fell back, dead, to the ground. It was like a ripple effect. The men around him jumped up in shocked confusion and then immediately started frantically grabbing for their weapons. Suggs waited eagerly and then saw a man running to his right fall abruptly, landing face down in the mud, half his head blown off. To his left, a small red-headed man fell as he was snatching up his gun, blood spurting obscenely from his neck. Ranald is a bad man, he thought to himself. And now it was his turn. Suggs let go as soon as he saw most of the other men ready to fire. He shot two men in the chest that were to his right with their guns raised, trying to locate Ranald's position. Suggs moved to his left and stopped about 2 feet from the camp. He was almost directly behind 3 men who were whispering to each other in Russian. Suggs waited until the one in the middle looked behind himself and immediately made surprised eye contact with him. He shot the man in the face and then as the other two whipped around, confused, Suggs shot them both in their faces. Suggs ducked low as he saw a man mark him. The man shot wildly in Suggs direction, yelling at him in Russian. Suggs stayed low and waited patiently. The man suddenly stopped yelling mid-tirade as a spray of bullets hit him, tearing him up. Suggs heard him hit the ground hard. Thanks Ranald, Suggs thought to himself. It was time to move. Ranald's hit sounded like it had come from the left of him. So, Suggs moved back to the right, carefully creeping through the little patch of woods. Finding a good resting spot, Suggs hunkered down and brought his gun up. He looked through his scope and saw the 3 remaining men disappear into the woods around them. Great, Suggs thought with irritation. Now it was going to be a hunt. They didn't have time for a hunt. His thoughts were interrupted as Lopez radioed through Suggs ear mike.

"Suggs.. Ranald! We're on'em now!.. We've got them all in now! Fuck! Get outta there! We..we can't wait for you!" Lopez was trying to yell over gunfire. Then the transmission died and Suggs fought the urge to double back and check on them. After all, he *was* doing what needed to be done here, now. He was eliminating a threat to them so they could get away. But he had hoped the rescue team wouldn't have to battle their way out. *Damn.* He just prayed they all got through it ok.

Ranald then radioed him, whispering loudly, "They're tryin' to sneak up on us, Suggs. We gotta get moving."

"Yeah," Suggs responded simply. He pushed his worries out of his mind and moved back towards where they had been posted up with the group, while he knew Ranald would move around the front of the woods. He stayed low and kept his gun ready. He found a tree that was in a good place and shadowed as well. He stopped and leaned against it, staying in its shadow. Patiently, he waited for the Russian that had disappeared to the furthest left. Suggs bet he would be coming his way shortly. You only go that far left to go around. He would have to remember to keep a watchful eye out for the man who had been in the middle. He would eventually come up on his right, if Ranald didn't get him first. Ranald liked to climb trees and shit and shoot. Suggs heard a shot towards the front of the woods and then a second crack through the air. Suggs just prayed it was Ranald doing the shooting. Suddenly, there was a snapping sound on Suggs left. He stilled and listened closely and then his ears pricked when he heard what he was sure were footsteps and then a crunching sound. He was sure they were footsteps, not an animal. That meant his prey was close. Suggs eased carefully around to the right to rest on the opposite side of the large tree. He heard more steps. The man was getting closer. Suggs heart raced as he stood at the ready. The man was getting closer and closer to him and when the man's footsteps were right upon him, Suggs swung out and fired rapidly into the man's neck 2 times. Suggs watched dispassionately as the man was thrown back into another tree a couple of feet behind him, his blood splattered all over the tree, everywhere. Suggs used his hand and wiped the blood of the man off of his face. Gross, he thought. Then, not wasting anymore time, he turned to the left and headed towards where he had heard the shots from earlier come from.

Suggs had walked left for a couple of minutes and then turned to move towards the front. Then, Suggs heard someone running not far from him, in front of him actually. They were coming up quickly so he ducked behind a bunch of gnarled bushes and waited to see who would come into view.

Ranald raced through the woods, hoping the rapid shots he had heard had not been aimed at Suggs cause after that he hadn't heard anything else. He hoped his boy was alright.

Chapter 13

Suggs crouched lower as the person came even closer. The man came into view and Suggs waited a moment to be sure and then felt relieved when he confirmed it was Ranald bounding towards him. Quickly, he stepped out from behind the bush.

Ranald skid to a stop and exclaimed, "There you are! Bruh, I didn't know if they had got ya."

"Yeah man. I was wondering the same thing bout you. So the two shots were you?"

"Yeah, I got both of'em. I was up high in a tree."

Suggs just shook his head. He had known that fool would be up in a tree somewhere. Then, *other* thoughts intruded upon his mind and he turned towards Ranald.

"So..what about Jed?"

Ranald stopped in his tracks, tension creeping into his stance. He faced Suggs and the cold glint of hatred glinted in his eyes. "What about'im?"

"He's there, in the cave. The girls and the rest of them are out. What are we gonna do with him?"

"Man, I wanna kill 'im. I really want to, Suggs. But I need to get to Vette and Kam. I gotta see my Vette. I mean, I-I don't even, hmm mm, don't even know what, I-I mean if she's still-." He cut off and just kept walking.

"I know what you're saying, man. I know. I-I'm sorry, bruh. I just wanna kill that mother fucker so bad, ya know. And no one would know… But, uh, yeah, you're right. We need to get to the girls and Kam." Suggs sighed resolutely and ruthlessly made himself change the subject.   "Just forget what I said. The uniforms'll pick him up. Let's keep heading north and then we'll cut through the gap in the wall. You're gonna radio for a pick up, right?"

"Yeah," Ranald replied quietly, obviously subdued after their conversation.

Suggs looked at his friend and saw tears rolling out of the corner of his eye. Not wanting to draw attention to it, Suggs looked back in front of him and closed his eyes briefly. Immediately, Jeannie was there, filling up his mind. All he could see were her vivid green eyes and her long,curly red hair. She smiled impishly at him, her fullish lips then forming a playful pout. His heart lurched as the reality of Jeannie's present condition intruded upon his images of her. He opened his eyes quickly and looked furtively in Ranald's direction. Ranald was looking determinedly ahead and Suggs was relieved that it appeared Ranald hadn't noticed him spacing out.

They both moved to the right side of the path they were walking on as gunfire echoed in the near distance. Staying low, they hurried to the break in the wall. They were almost there when Ranald quietly yelped as a bullet whizzed by, too close to his ear and hit the tree on the side of him. "Fuck! Get down. They're on us, Suggs. They're on us."

Suggs could see the break in the wall and that was great, but it was really great because it would provide them some cover. "Got it." Suggs ducked lower as a bullet whizzed by him. "Move double time to the break," Suggs yelled over the cracking of the bullets. "We'll have cover!"

They were side by side rushing low through the trees, when they burst into the clearing in front of the wall.

"Hurry, let's get against it!" Suggs kept thinking, cover, cover cover. Bullet after bullet were whizzing past or over them. Suggs and Ranald reached the wall and Ranald took the right while Suggs immediately whizzed around to the left side of the break in the wall and started shooting. He didn't even waste time looking in his scope. He could see the men rushing into the clearing quite well. Ranald was using his scope to get the bastards in the woods who were providing back up for the ones that came out into the clearing. The gunfire was deafening. Suggs knocked down 4 of the Russians and quickly turned back inside the wall to reload.

"Reloading, Ranald!"

"Got it!" Ranald immediately started providing close up fire.

Suggs was done in half a minute. "Going back in!"

"Yeah!" Ranald yelled back. He looked back in his scope and got back to work. "3 left!"

"I got 5 running towards us!" Suggs clocked one guy, making a head shot. He crumpled to the ground. "Make that 4." He saw one guy break off from the group and run to his left. Suggs smirked and moved further up just out the edge of the wall and he quickly moved to the right and shot the *clever* guy in the chest twice. Dismissing him from his mind, Suggs turned to the left as he caught movement out the side of his eye that was too close. He shot twice at a guy that was running up fast, but he missed. Suggs quickly bent down and pulled one of his knives from his boot. Quickly taking aim, he let the knife go and it swirled through the air, landing in the middle of the man's head. The man stopped in his tracks, his eyes rolled back in his head and then he dropped to the ground. Suggs grabbed his pistol off his side and shot the last man as he skidded around to run back towards the main park. "Fucker," he said aloud in disgust. He had only given him a flesh wound but the man howled like he was dying.

Ranald put his gun down and nodded his head to Suggs. "It's all clear for now. What do you wanna do about him?"

"You bastards! You American pigs! I'm gonna kill you mother fuckers! Ahhh! Fuck you!" The man ranted and raved in his deep, barely discernible accent.

Suggs looked at Ranald with a knowing look. "Well, after all that we can't just let him go."

Ranald winked. "No. No, we can't."

"Ahhh! You mother fucking pigs! Fuck you!"

"Well, let's go. I think he's calling us." Suggs and Ranald walked further away from the wall, closer to the fallen, yelling man with their guns drawn, looking at everything.

When they reached the man, Ranald put his arm out, holding Suggs back. "Don't even lift your gun. It's my turn. *You* got to shoot'im in his leg."

The man looked up at both of them and then sneered at them with disgust. The man spit in the middle of where they stood. "Fucking *niggers*. Black bastards! You can't do anything to me! And you think your people got *away*?" He laughed crudely, spittle falling down his chin. "We have people waiting in the woods..They're gonna cut them d-!"

Suggs didn't even see it coming, but he damn sure heard it when it came though. Ranald pulled out his .357 Magnum with lightning speed and shot the Russian right in the middle of the shaking hand that was laying on the ground, loosely holding on to his gun. The Russian's hand seemed to explode in slow motion. And Ranald coldly turned around to walk away before the mutilated hand could fall to the ground with a loud thump, about 3 feet from the Russian's twitching body. Suggs could smell the man's burnt flesh and felt that was his cue to go as well. He looked down briefly and dispassionately at the man as copious amounts of blood poured from his torn up arm, his mouth gaping open obscenely. Suggs turned to follow Ranald and was astonished that his only thought after that horrific scene was, why hadn't the man started screaming yet, because soon, with all that blood loss, it would be too late... maybe he was in shock.

When he caught up with Ranald the tension in Ranald's shoulders and stance were obvious. Suggs just prayed that Sylvette was gonna pull through. He prayed that his Sprite and Kam and Torres would be alright. He wouldn't let himself focus on Jeannie too much. He couldn't. The worst thing he could do was lose focus. What he needed to focus on was how much he wanted to kill all those soldiers, mercenaries, whatever they were. He really wished that Russini hadn't taken it this far. The whole shit was fuckin' ridiculous.

"*Ranald*, are you good?"

Ranald's pace slowed as he walked across the parking lot, occasionally checking his scope for any surprises. "Am I good? *No*, Suggs, I'm not *fucking* good. I shoulda killed that bastard back there *and* I shoulda killed Jed. And Vette...I..*Vette*, bruh." He stopped close to the edge of the parking lot and just hung his head.

Suggs didn't know what to do or to say. And he really didn't think it would be a good time to tell him that he *had* killed the guy. After all, he had been bleeding out at an alarming rate. Yeah, he would tell him that later. He had never seen Ranald like this. After Pogo he had been drunk and belligerent, self-destructive. Now, well now he looked...defeated.

"Man, *Ranald*, it's gonna be alright. Vette's a fighter and-and you just have to fight with her, dog. Ya know what I mean? If you two are fighting together, then you'll win. You can't give up hope. This *is* Vette we talkin' bout."

Ranald lifted his head and looked at Suggs. He realized at that moment, through all his anger, that Suggs was changing. Ranald wondered when Suggs had started to change, and then he thought about it. Of course he knew when it had begun. Catching Suggs off guard, Ranald threw out, "Jeannie's changing you, dog."

Suggs didn't think he had heard Ranald right. He couldn't really deal with it just then though. They had come up on the edge of the parking lot, so he was gonna have to have Ranald repeat what he had said later.

"Ok, Ranald, call it in. We can post up in these little woods while we wait."

Ranald groaned, "More trees, man? Damn!"

"What, *Ranger Rick*! I thought you liked trees and shit."

"Fuck you, Suggs. Look, *damn*, I have *corns, man.*"

Suggs couldn't help it. He just couldn't. Ranald was holding his left leg up, trying to hold his foot up in the air. Ranald was a fool and Suggs didn't get why the fool was holding his shoe clad foot up in the air anyway. Suggs couldn't see no damn corns through Ranald's shoe anyway. Yeah, Ranald had caught him off guard. Suggs started laughing as quietly as he could, but, shit, Ranald was stupid as hell and he needed a laugh...*they* needed a laugh. Suggs figured that they were in shock themselves, so he wasn't surprised when Ranald looked at his face, dropped his leg and started laughing too. Suggs knew at that moment they had both temporarily lost their minds.

Suggs and Ranald were posted up by a big stout tree. Occasionally they heard shots fired, men yelling, but, thank God, it was definitely dying down. Suggs' thoughts were interrupted by the muted crackling and static that erupted from Ranald's radio.

Ranald quickly pressed the button to talk. "Ranald here. Over."

"Ranald...Lopez here. Closest extraction point 2 miles outside of park at burger joint, Sippies...Be advised there is a perimeter set up around the park...Russini's men shot us up pretty badly on our way out."

"Roger that. Everyone okay? How is Vette? Did you get them to the hospital?"

"Were some flesh wounds...Vette and all injured at County hospital...Eric, Vette's not good. She's critical...Get here safe, but fast...There'll be stuff for you guys to clean up with and clothes..change into when...you get to the van. "

Ranald's now numb hands dropped the phone. His mind *shuttered* and he felt his heart tearing in two. He collapsed onto his knees, his gun dropping to the ground next to him.

Hearing the news about his friend's wife and seeing Ranald's pain, Suggs stomach sunk with feelings of dread. He quickly grabbed the radio off the ground and spoke into it.

"Lopez, it's Suggs. How's Jeannie? Who got hit?"

"Jeannie..yes, the little red head...She's in critical care...concussion and an infection is attacking her body from an injury or something like that. I don't have the names of the ones that were hit yet...Sorry for the news guys...Be there, okay...50 mins. Lopez, out. "

On the inside, Suggs was barely holding on to his control. *What the fuck*, he thought wildly, were they ever gonna get a damn break? Betrayingly, he calmly laid the radio down next to Ranald. He looked at his friend and wondered what the hell he should do. Ranald didn't look good...*of course*. And according to Lopez, they still had a *hit crew* to get through before they could get picked up. *And* they needed to be at the hospital like now. Some of the group had been shot! God, he prayed Jeannie and Vette would be okay. And as he stood there in the woods, sweat pouring off of him and the sounds of a fading mini-war going off in the background, he felt truly helpless. He wasn't with Jeannie at the hospital, he had let Jed live and that fucker had *hurt* Jeannie and had probably intended to do a lot more. His friend's wife was fighting for her life from being stabbed by Jed. Lord knows how Kam was doing. Kam was fucked up beyond belief.

Suggs still couldn't believe his arm had been blown off..*Kam*..damn. What the fuck could he do? How did he get Ranald up and moving and focused? Shit, how was he going to keep *himself* together. Now that he was standing still and all the events from the past 48 hours were running through his mind, he started to feel really tired. He started to wonder if they *could* do this. They'd been lucky that neither one of them had been shot yet. Lord knows they had taken enough fire that Suggs was secretly wondering which one of them it would happen to first and possible ways to handle the situation if it did happen. He didn't want to die, he realized. He wanted to see Jeannie and Sara. He wanted to live and he guessed before that moment it had never really mattered to him. He had never really focused on his mortality. But the shit that had went down not too long ago at those peoples house and what was going on here really clarified and brought shit to light for him. But it was such bad timing. He didn't have time to be reflective and do soul searching. He needed to get himself and Ranald the fuck outta there. As daunting as it was and as weary as he was becoming, they still *had* to fight their way out of there. They *had* to get to the hospital. They had to. Trying to pump himself up, he thought about a plan for the layout he and Ranald should take. He wished he could see what the Russians actual formation was, how they had set up their perimeter, but he didn't even know where the perimeter began. They were already close to the outer parking lots and from there were more woods surrounding the place and a break in the woods for the exits to the highway. On the other side of the park was a break in the woods for the street way in and out. Maybe they would be in those woods that bordered the perimeter of the park, right before the highway and street exits, he thought to himself. But those positions would draw too much attention from people passing by. He also wondered why the police hadn't blocked off the areas coming in and out. Maybe the Russian perimeter crew prevented that from happening, he wasn't sure. Lopez said they had given them trouble. The

Hammer had really went all out on this bullshit and *he* had a *lot* of fucking men. Thinking again

that all the shit was crazy, Suggs quickly started trying to stop thinking before he was doing it too

much and bent down to talk to Ranald. He needed Ranald's help to come up with a gameplan.

And that he and Ranald could focus on..pain-free.

Suggs lightly put his hand on Ranald's shoulder. Ranald jumped at the contact and Suggs

quickly removed his hand. "Sorry, dog. Just checking to see if you're as good as you can be, ya

know."

When Suggs stood back up straight, Ranald used that as his que and stood up. Sighing,

because he knew what they had to do next, Ranald leaned back against the tree. His face was

haggard and shining with sweat when he looked at Suggs.

"I was prayin' for Vette, Suggs. For..all of'em. I was prayin' that if she ain't gonna make

it at least I can see her one more time, that God let me see her."

Suggs hadn't expected that response, but he was glad that Ranald's thoughts had been

about getting to her. That meant he was well aware and ready to do what needed to be done to get

outta there. Suggs felt his adrenaline building back up and energy began to flow through him

from an unknown source, but it was definitely building. Good, he thought to himself. *Good.*

Jeannie, I'm *coming* baby. I'm *coming.*

"Ranald, Vette's going to pull through. She *is,* man. You just have to believe it. She's

there, at the hospital fighting right now. You're prayin' for her so all she needs is you to be there,

just like Jeannie needs *me* there. We just gotta get there."

Ranald listened to Suggs and prayed he was right. He did know Suggs was right about

one thing. They were gonna have to fuckin' fight their way outta the situation. And Ranald felt tension everywhere in his body. He just wanted to teleport himself to the damn hospital. He needed to see Sylvette, needed to be there with her.

"Yeah, I know, Suggs. I'm ready. We just need a plan."

"Yeah, I was thinking about that. My problem is, we don't know their formation, *where* they're posted up. And if they *are* in those woods then that puts us at a huge disadvantage because the parking lot is right before those woods, even more so than this one was."

"Hmm," Ranald responded. "They have a disadvantage as well, ya know. They really risk exposure in that location with the ramp and the highway right there."

"Maybe they don't care about that. I mean, shit, *this* area ain't exactly secluded, a bit removed, but not secluded. I think our disadvantage is greater than theirs."

"Okay, what about going outside of them to go around them," Ranald countered.

"But, the highway...how?" Suggs listened carefully to Ranald's response.

"We skim the edge of the highway, then double back to the street side. It'll add about a half a mile onto our 2 miles, but I think that'd be better. The actual highway does provides a huge risk to us as well, so we really shouldn't fuck wit' it like you said. But we *can* skim it and it'll catch them off guard cause they'll probably figure we'll avoid getting anywhere near the highway.

"Okay.." Suggs responded dubiously. "But we're supposed to be hidden, bruh. We don't need anyone seeing our faces or linking us to the department, possibly jeopardizing the protective custody location. Besides that, if we need to, where we gonna run to if the highway's right there?"

Ranald sighed, obviously weary of the discussion. "Ya know what, never mind. We can just not try to avoid the shit. I think that was what I was thinking, but I guess it does risk us being seen." Ranald sighed again, this time with reluctant acceptance. "Alright, Suggs. Yeah, for shits and giggles we can try and locate where they are and see what their numbers are. If it's not many of them we can just cut through and not have to go around that part of the woods. We'll need to find a break in their perimeter though if we're just gonna sneak around them to the street. I wonder how many men it is."

Suggs was still processing Ranald's plan. He really didn't want to go back through the park either, but Ranald was right. His second idea was better. They would have a better position leaving out on the street side. Fuck, he thought to himself. Nothing about either way would be easy really.

"Alright, Ranald. Let's load up and strap up then. We have a lot of open space to walk through, no cover at all in some places."

"Actually, in reference to that, I think we'll be good," Ranald countered.

"How you figure?"

"Suggs, we took out the guys who had come after us. And, yeah, I know we've lost men, but so has Russini. And shit is calming down over there. I don't think anyone else came after us or is posted up waiting for us."

"Okay. Well, we still need to be watching."

"Oh, yeah. We do. I'm just saying I think that part'll be incident free."

"I hope so, Ranald." Suggs stopped to wipe the sweat off his face and then continued, "Let's go."

Suggs and Ranald had just crossed the attractions and were planning to divert right for a bit. There was shooting going on to their left. So, that pushed them to go through the bit of woods that were right before the street. They stopped for a moment at the edge of a mini parking lot. And there had been no problem with the parking lots on the other side like Ranald had said. Suggs allowed himself to feel some relief. Thus far, they had experienced no bullshit, except having to deviate a little.

"Suggs, let's post up around here. Maybe if I can get high enough, I can spot them. Cause they obviously haven't spotted us."

"I know, it's odd. We're close to the highway."

There was a tall tree next to them and Ranald didn't waste any time. Ranald laid his guns down and then jumped up into the air, catching the lowest branch and pulled himself up. And he barely caused the branch to move. Suggs watched Ranald climb silently up the tree until he couldn't see him any more. *Fucking spider monkey,* Suggs thought to himself. Suggs chuckled to himself and then went into cover mode and scoped the area. All appeared good, but he kept looking. And not that he wanted trouble, but where *were* they? Why hadn't they fired at them yet?

He waited on Ranald for about another three minutes and then he heard Ranald coming down. He moved out the way and waited for Ranald to be able to get close enough to jump out the tree.

Ranald landed on the ground softly and immediately straightened himself.

"Bruh, I only counted *3*. I used my pocket scope. Yeah, only 3."

"Hmm. *That* works in our favor. Maybe our guys took some of'em out. I don't know. What were they packing? Where exactly are they hiding?"

"Two of them had RPG's and the other guy had my gun."

"You think they're the ones that let'em off earlier..the fucking bastards?"

"Possibly. And they're on the outside of the woods, not even spread out. They're not that far from the highway fence though."

"Okay. Cool. Let's just take them out."

"Yeah, but we'll have to be real careful sneaking up on'em. From their vantage point they'll see movement in the woods real easy," Ranald warned.

"Okay. Well, we'll be careful. Let's move."

They both grabbed their gear and walked briskly into the woods.

Jed flexed his numb and tingling wrists. They were tied behind his back. He couldn't believe what was happening to him. Five Russian mercenaries stood in front of him, eyeing him coldly. His mind whirled with the terror of confusion. What the fuck was going on, he wondered wildly. They had broken the chain on his cuffs around his wrists with a hand axe and then slammed him into a chair that he hadn't even seen was there and tied his hands roughly behind his back. He had been hoping that he was going to be rescued, but now he was sure that wasn't what this was going to be. He wished he could fucking remember *something* about himself. I mean, what could *he* have done to these soldiers, mercenaries or whatever they were? His next thoughts were interrupted when the bigger guy in the middle started talking, his English heavily slurred by his rough accent.

"Who are you? Why were you here, cuffed? What you do, hmm?"

Not knowing what he should say, he stalled. "Umm, uh, well-."

"Yes! Answer the question!" The man then raised his rifle and pointed it directly in Jed's face.

Jed felt his balls clench as he stared through the barrel of the massive gun and, surreally, all the background noise of the cave faded away. He blanked out for just a moment, but it felt like it had been minutes, at least. He snapped back to reality and struggled to breathe properly, he was so scared. *Fuck it*, he thought desparately. He would just tell them the truth, had nothing else to tell them anyway.

"*Okay, okay. All* I know is my name. I don't remember anything else. I-I don't even know how I got, well, *here*. And, and I'm injured. I need help. I have a bad head wound."

The big Russian man looked at him blankly and then abruptly started laughing. He lowered his gun and turned around to his comrades. He said something to them in Russian and they all laughed, staring at him openly while they laughed and jeered at him.

Jed had no time to react as out of nowhere one of the men came forward with the smallish hand axe and stood over him for a just a moment. Jed looked up at the man and the man was staring down at him. They met eyes and a paralyzing coldness spread rapidly through Jed's bones. The man's eyes were like an ever ending pit of emptiness. Abruptly, the man smiled wickedly and then slammed the gleaming axe blade into his leg, slicing and ripping through his flesh right above his knee. And, then, unmercifully, he twisted and ripped it out, not flinching or showing any emotion when Jed's blood sprayed all over the man's face and chest, his body shaking violently in shock.

Jed screamed before he even knew he had started screaming. Wave upon wave of white hot heat and unbearable burning pain had him twisting and turning, screaming in agony. The men laughed at him again and then a different man from before came up to him, a machete in his hand. Jed was so out of his mind with pain and blood loss, he barely could focus on the other man. His body began to jerk of its own accord and it felt like electrical jolts were shooting through his leg and hips. And then, his heart stuttered in horror as he saw the arc of another weapon, a straight edged machete, as it was being brought down upon his other leg.

"No!" He called out desperately. And then he felt the machete pierce his skin and it relentlessly kept slicing through his flesh until it exited his skin on the *other* side of his leg. And as before, it, too, was ripped out, slicing more of his inner flesh as it left his leg. Jed was delirious with pain and could not even gather the energy to scream this time. His blood felt like it was pouring out of his other leg and he noticed that same leg was going numb, the pain gradually fading. And, somehow, he knew that wasn't good..not good at all.

The middle guy spoke to him again. "Now you see we do not care about your injuries. We want to know who you are."

Jed could barely keep his eyes open, he barely heard what the man was saying. His other leg was starting to go numb as well and his fingertips tingled irritatingly. He felt cold, cold into his bones and woozy. And then, blissfully, as the man started to talk again, he thankfully started to fade out. And...then he could hear nothing, and the pain faded away.

The Russian stopped talking when he realized the man's eyes had closed. He wondered if he was dead. He turned to his comrades and in English said, "I think he dies. Shoot him to make sure. Then, we go." He turned to the side and backed up a couple of steps. He looked at them, silently giving his command and they lifted their guns to the ready. He nodded and then as one, they fired. They shot the man in the chair over and over before they stopped. The man's body was bloody with chunks of flesh missing in some places and the bullets had torn through most of his flesh, causing smoke to come out of several of the bullet hole wounds. The man's body jerked and spasmed, leaking blood all over the floor. And the men watched him twitch and bleed out dispassionately for a moment. Then, just as quickly as the men had come upon Jed, they left, laughing at the idiot American they had just killed.

<u>Chapter 14</u>

"Okay. Coast is clear. Move up. Their backs are still turned." Suggs heart raced as he moved up to the next tree, staying low and barely making a sound. He waited for Ranald's next command. Ranald was up in a tree that provided a good vantage point. The goal was to get as close as possible to the assholes and then Ranald would tag the one in the middle, causing them to scatter. Then, it would be easy to pick the other two off and Suggs would provide ground cover.

Suggs earpiece rattled with static in his ear. Ranald came on.

"Move up, slowly. They've been moving around a bit. Don't think they heard anything or sensed anything, lame bastards. But, just watch it."

Suggs leaned out from behind the tree and got down on all fours. He could faintly hear them talking now. The fuckers really must not be concerned about enemy fire. Suggs moved closer, their conversation muffling any sound he would have made. When he had gone about 5 feet he ducked behind another massive tree. From where he was now, he could see them through the breaks in the trees. He was about maybe 10 feet from them.

"Good. You're close. Do you wanna get closer or just start it off?"

"Well, I can see the bastards from here. Let's just get at it. I can move closer faster once they're confused."

"Got it. Wait for my signal."

Suggs tried to calm his mind as he waited for Ranald's signal. They just had to get through this and they would be on their way. *Jeannie.*

Ranald breathed deeply and put the scope up to his eye. He found his mark through the leaves of the trees and targeted the marks head. He counted off silently. 1-2-3. Ranald pulled the trigger and a moment later the guy in the middle crumpled to the ground. Like roaches, the two other men scattered. They didn't even seem to have any shock, they just took off. Ranald didn't worry about the guy going to his left. Suggs would get him. So, Ranald zoomed in on the guy that went to the right. The guy had stopped for a moment to look through his own scope, trying to catch whoever was shooting at them. Ranald thought to himself that the guy was a fool. He should have ran into the shelter of the trees and then looked. As soon as the guy put his gun down, Ranald pulled the trigger and blew his brains out. The man crumpled to the ground, twitching. Ranald then realized he hadn't heard any other shots go off. What the fuck, he thought to himself? Growing concerned, he slung his gun over his back and started back down the tree. He needed to find Suggs.

Ranald ran swiftly through the trees. He started to hear the faint sound of a struggle just up ahead of him, off to his right. He slowed down and then crouched low to the ground. He moved swiftly and in no time he was upon them. Ranald peered through the gap in the leaves in front of him. Suggs and one of the Hammer's guys were going at it. Suggs was nursing a bloody nose, he saw. He seemed to be fine though, Ranald thought wryly to himself. Suggs was now behind the other guy. Suggs was snarling and ramming the other guy's face over and over into a tree. Ranald stood up and walked towards them. Suggs was so intent upon his business he didn't even

hear Ranald come up. Ranald bet Suggs didn't realize he was snarling and growling, either.
Ranald paused a moment as it hit him that Suggs was *really* affected too. Suggs rarely lost
control. Except for wanting to kill the fuck out of Jed, Suggs had seemed, well, in control.

"Suggs!"'' When he didn't respond, Ranald reached out and shoved him.

"*Suggs*!"

Suggs felt a push on his shoulder and a second later, Ranald's voice. As if someone had
just pulled him out of a tight, pressurized bottle, all his senses rebooted at the same time. His
heart raced so hard it was uncomfortable *and* he was fucking hot. The sudden rush of the sound of
the day and far-off shouting hurt his ears. He must have really been out of it there for a moment.
He looked at the back of the man's head that his hand was on. He belatedly released his grip and
the man slid down the tree and dropped to the ground. Suggs' heart raced as he wondered if the
man was dead like the man that Ranald had wigged out on. He moved out the way of the falling
man, closer to Ranald. He couldn't even explain to himself how he felt at that moment. Before,
when he and the guy had started fighting, he had felt nothing but cold rage. Now, though, with
mosquitoes buzzing around him and the sounds of the near highway that he could see clearly in
his mind..he just wanted to get the hell out of there and get to Jeannie so his life could move on.

Ranald shoved his shoulder lightly. "You good now, right? Cause, uh, bruh had *been*
done."

"Yeah, I'm good...*shit*! *Fuck* man. Let's just get the fuck outta here."

"Right, man. Let's get to 'em." They headed out quickly, leaving the mercenary laying
face down in the mossy grass, rich red blood pooling around his head.

Ranald and Suggs moved out. Sippie's wasn't too far away. They moved right, running along the edge of the woods that trailed the county road that they followed. In .8 miles they veered right and even though the woods grew very sparse they stayed close to its cover as they continued to move towards Sippie's. Suggs felt like his skin was going to start boiling, he was so hot. He looked to his side furtively and damned if Ranald didn't even look like *he* was sweating. Suggs groaned internally. He knew that meant he was fucking doomed. Cause he couldn't be the pussy ass guy who couldn't take the heat. Since Ranald was cool, he was gonna have to be damn cool. *Fuck*, he thought to himself. At least he was closer to Jeannie. He prayed she was alright. He just had to hurry and get to her, he kept thinking over and over in his head. He just had to keep moving.

Suggs and Ranald burst through the dense trees and didn't hesitate as they recognized immediately which vehicle was meant for them. Heat waves radiated up from the newly paved road that Sippie's rested on as they ran across the street. Kids were running in and out the entrance and exit doors, squealing with laughter. Obviously they didn't know they were supposed to be melting. There were two cars in the drive thru, both with caucasian occupants. He also saw a guy with what looked like dreads stuffing his face inside his parked car. Suggs thought that he and Ranald, with their partial combat gear on and bloodstained clothes, *not to mention the guns tucked behind them that were partially visible,* probably seemed very out of place with the tone of the area. And if anybody paid good attention they would see the guns. But no one seemed to notice them as they came up and wasted no time getting into an unmarked black GMC Acadia that was parked on the side of the street in front of the restaurant.

An hour later they were hastily, but freshly cleaned and dressed. Ranald and Suggs rushed up to the nurses station. Ranald reached the desk first and wasted no time.

"H-howdy. I'm Eric Ranald. My wife, Sylvette Ranald and my brother, Kameron Ranald are both here in critical care."

Suggs couldn't help himself. He knew it wasn't his turn, but he blurted out, "And Jeannie!" That damned Sprite was rubbing off on him, he thought ruefully to himself.

The nurse stopped keying things into her computer and looked up at him quizzically.

"Just give me a moment, *sir*. I'm looking up people for your friend here. *Okay*. Oh and I'll need more than a first name anyway."

Suggs felt slightly embarrassed and was glad Ranald was too distraught to notice. He waited for the slow ass nurse to look back up and as soon as she did, he growled out, "Jeannie Derit."

Cutting her eyes at Suggs, she ignored him and turned to Ranald. "Mrs. Ranald is in room 315 and Mr. Ranald is in 323. They are both on the 4th floor."

She keyed in more info and then her cool eyes moved to Suggs and she told him, "And your Ms. Derit is in 314 on the same floor."

Not bothering with a response for the irritating nurse, Suggs and Ranald hurriedly walked to the elevators. They were on the ground floor. Suggs was nervous and anxious. He was afraid of what they might be walking into. *Jeannie,* Sylvette and Kam were messed up pretty badly. God, all three of them. He damned himself in his mind. He should've been able to get to Jeannie sooner. He had been too confident that they would be safe where they were. His mind was spinning with all sorts of not good thoughts. He had to know, but he was afraid to. But they would see them soon anyway, so whether he was ready for the news or not, they would know shortly. *Please,* he prayed silently to himself.

Ranald and Suggs stopped at 314 and 315. For a moment, both of them stood stock still, as if they, themselves, were the calm before the storm. Suggs looked at Ranald and they shared a meaningful look. Then Ranald nodded briskly to Suggs..Suggs reciprocated and they each walked into their respective rooms.

Jeannie was floating in a strange, but mostly pleasant space. The air was spicy and moist. It almost tasted like her favorite, jalapeno potato chips. She looked over at some of the giggling, fat black and white penguins that floated with her. As long as she focused on them and not the blank space that was far away, but that seemed like it was getting closer, she felt almost happy. Happy happy, she thought to herself and then she giggled with her penguin friends. This must be what heaven was like, she thought dreamily. She could stay here forever, she thought to herself.

"So, basically, what you're telling me is, she's in a *fucking coma.* Is that right, Doc? Is *that* what you're telling me?"

Dr. Cross knew he was obviously beginning to show he was getting very uncomfortable as it was *obvious* Mr. Suggs was not taking the news well. In fact, Mr. Suggs seemed angry, very angry.

"Mr. Suggs, please. Please calm down. Yes, she is in a coma, but we are very hopeful. Her body has started responding to the medication and the infection is leaving her body. And when she wakes up, we'll have to do some surgery on her leg and reset some of her bones. Her ribs are also broken on her right side. So, we will also be tending to that. So, see, we have already started planning for her because we believe this is temporary. Now, I'll send the nurse in shortly to go over some other details with you. Oh and are you aware if her family has been notified of this?"

Suggs was still stuck on temporary. "So, you're sure this is just temporary?"

Dr. Cross rolled his eyes and then answered as patiently as he could, "We are *hoping* this is temporary. And her family?"

"Hmm. Family? Oh! Right, her family. I'll take care of that Doc. And her mom is here now."

The Doctor looked relieved as he responded, "Fine then. If you have any questions let your nurse know and I'll be making my rounds again in another hour. Goodbye, Mr. Suggs." Dr. Cross then hurriedly went about his way, muttering to himself.

Suggs watched the short, slight doctor walk away and thought to himself, what a strange little doctor guy. He dismissed the doctor from his mind and was going to go back in the room, when he heard his name being called from the direction the doctor had scurried off in. Turning his head back to his left he saw a tall, young black doctor, or at least he assumed he was. And Dr. Cross was walking back towards him. What now, he wondered?

"Uh, Mr. Suggs!" Dr. Cross hurried over to him. "I'm sorry to disturb you, uh, during this, uh, t-."

Suggs cut the awkward little Doctor off. He was ready to go in the room with Jeannie.

"What is it, Doc? Who's your friend?"

Dr. Cross extended his hand to the young doctor standing next to him. "Uh, this is Dr. Palmer. Yes. Well, Dr. Palmer needs to talk to you about some, er, things."

"What things? Did you find something else wrong with Jeannie?" Suggs looked at Dr. Palmer. "Well?"

Dr. Cross spoke up before Dr. Palmer could. "Mr. Suggs, if you would just hold on, I'm attempting to explain. See, Dr. Palmer has questions about your, er, fiance'."

Suggs was confused and starting to get a little irritated. "Ok. Look, I don't have a fiance' so you're wasting my time. I gotta go guys."

Dr. Palmer finally spoke up and he had a surprisingly deep voice. "Mr. Suggs, I'm hear about Marcella Torres. I need your permission."

Suggs couldn't believe this shit. His *permission* about Torres and his *fiance'*, he thought to himself. What the fuck was going on?

Dr. Cross spoke up abruptly, "Well gentlemen, I shall leave you to it." He turned around and quickly scuffled off again, disappearing into a crowd of nurses who were going around the corner.

Weirdo, Suggs thought to himself scathingly. The doctor really reminded him of a mole with glasses. This shit was really starting to piss him off.

"So, Dr. Palmer, there's been a mistake. Like I said before, no fiance'. And why would you need *my* permission for *Torres*?"

Dr. Palmer's expression had not changed one bit since Suggs had first seen him and even now it was the same. They were both weirdos.

"Marcella Torres was shot one time in her right knee, shattering her knee cap. She was also shot *near* her liver, but close enough to do substantial damage. And I believe you already know about her other wounds. We need permission to operate and if granted we would start right away. *You* are listed as her emergency contact and when we were able to talk to her for a bit earlier, she said you were her fiance'."

Suggs was beyond livid at this point. Dammit Torres! What the fuck was she on? What the fuck was she *thinking*? Suggs couldn't believe this was happening.

"Are you sure you have the right info, Doc? I mean, I am *not* her *fiance'*. I *damn* sure shouldn't be her *emergency* contact."

Dr. Palmer responded, his face still expressionless, "Yes, well I am not here to deal with those particulars. Do I have your permission or not? These surgeries need to get started."

Suggs' mind raced. What the fuck should he do? God, he couldn't believe he was even in this position. *Fuck!* He supposed above all else Torres needed to live.

"Do whatever needs to be done."

"Fine. I will come find you later so you can sign some paperwork. Well, my nurse will. *I* will come out and update you about the surgeries as they happen. Will you be in the waiting room on this side of the hall?"

Suggs wanted to choke *Dr*. Palmer and then throw his ass out a window. All this dumb shit was keeping him from Jeannie. What if she woke up and he wasn't there.

"Look, do what you can for Torres, but leave me out of the rest. Okay?"

Dr. Palmer simply responded, "Right." Then he crisply turned around and headed back the way he came.

"Bullshit," Suggs muttered out loud. Suggs shook his head in exasperation and turned back to Jeannie's door and walked in the dark room. Jeannie's mom was sitting next to Jeannie on a barely padded bench and when she saw him coming back in she smiled wearily at him and stood up. He walked over to her quickly and she reached out and patted his arm soothingly.

"Go on and sit T.J. I'm going home for the night. I'm beat. And I gotta relieve the babysitter. Thank goodness Sara'll be sleep. You sit and talk to Jeannie and just call me if anything happens, alright?"

"Yes Mam," Suggs dutifully replied. "You get some rest now and kiss Sara for me."

She grabbed her purse off the rolling table, hiked it up on her shoulder and looked over Jeannie. Her eyes grew misty and she looked at Suggs.

"Stay with her, T.J. Stay with her." Then she hurried out the room, wiping her tears as she left.

The blank space was getting closer to her. And the closer it got the more stale the air became. It was changing, she was sure of it. And the penguins were slowly fading away. She was starting to not feel so good as well. This place where she was seemed to really be showing its true face. Her euphoria was rapidly dissipating as she began to panic. Where was she? She just realized that she hadn't seen her mom, or Vette..T.J. Oh my God, she thought to herself as dread flooded her system. Why hadn't she noticed before that she hadn't seen them in this space? Where were they? Where was Moran..Kam? Dear God, maybe she was dead. Maybe she had died and only she. Maybe she was alone in this place that no longer held her favorite things. And what was that terrifying nothing of space? Why was it coming closer to her? She had to have died, she concluded. What else could it be? Then she also realized that since Vette wasn't here she must have pulled through. She must be alive! Thank God for that at least, she thought to herself.

It was getting harder to breathe. It was like the air was being slowly sucked away. She still floated and she began to notice something floating not far up ahead in front of her. As she continued to float quickly through the air, her heart started pounding furiously as she got closer to the object. She squinted, trying hard to make out what it was. Damned if it didn't look like someone floating like her, wearing a pink jumpsuit. Then, she saw two more things floating behind the girl in the jumpsuit. What was this place? When she was finally almost upon it, she realized that it wasn't a little girl. It was just a floating jumpsuit. And as the others got closer it looked like they were also floating clothes. Then more and more clothes began to appear. Her heart raced as she eventually was damn near dodging them. What was this, she wondered wildly? Where were the clothes coming from..was it the blank space? Becoming beside herself, she screamed into the thick air, "Help! Please, someone help me!" Only no sound came from her lips..

Suggs held her hand tightly, trying to will his strength into her. Every bit of strength that he had in him he wished he could pour into her to help her fight whatever was keeping her from waking up. He had always thought of a coma as a kind of *war*. The war was internal and spiritual.

He really was messed up. He had never felt anything like this before in his life. He had never loved a woman or cared to. It really sucked that now that he did, Jeannie lay in a coma, fighting the war for her *life*. She might be in pain or trapped somewhere and he couldn't even help her. He couldn't even help her. Not able to fight his overwhelming terror and grief at the condition that Jeannie was in, a sob erupted from his mouth and before he could stop himself, the dam broke. Suggs started *crying* so hard he could barely breathe. He *could not* believe that *Jeannie* was going to die. He couldn't...he *wouldn't*. He laid his head on her stomach and cried, torturous sobs erupting from him.

"Jeannie, *please*," he choked out. "Please come back to me, Sprite. Fight it, Jeannie. *Fight* it."   And then he remembered what the doctor had said. He tried to hold on to that hope. He closed his eyes and said the Lord's Prayer. He'd never been religious, but he hoped that God would hear him. "Please God," he whispered achingly. "*Please*."

Two hours had passed when Suggs felt himself being shaken. He snapped awake and sat up groggily, but quickly. He was surprised to see Ranald standing next to him.

"How's Sylvette, man?" He could see the weariness on Ranald's face.

"She's gonna be alright. The knife missed her liver, but still did a good amount of damage. She's got a lot of recovery to do cause she also lost a lot of blood. But she's gonna make it, man. She's gonna make it. She opened her eyes once and kinda smiled at me. Man, she's gonna be *alright*, Suggs. Whoo..thank God. I ain't ashamed to say I was real scared. Real scared, man."

Suggs was so relieved *and* he understood. Who would've known. He was so happy for Sylvette. He had been worried too. Vette and Kam had been the most critical. He punched Ranald lightly on the shoulder. "So why aren't you in there with her man?"

"I wanted to see how Jeannie's doing *and* some weird little doctor was looking for you with news about Torres' surgery. Go figure. And, yeah, so how is Jeannie? She's still out pretty good, huh?"

"She's in a coma, Ranald."

Ranald's face fell, dismay clouding his features, "Nooo, man. Aww, Jeannie. A *coma*, bruh?"

"Yeah. A fucking coma."

"Well, what's the doc saying?"

"They say she has a good chance of waking up and they *think* she will wake up. So, I guess *that's* good."

"*Yeah*, it's *good*, Suggs. Jeez! God is good. There's hope."

<u>Chapter 15</u>

They both fell quiet for a moment and then Ranald broke the silence. He was staring at Jeannie with an indescribable look on his face. "And, honestly, this is *Jeannie* we're talkin' bout, Suggs. If she ain't the prime example of a spitfire, I don't know who is. She's a fighter, Suggs."

"Yeah, but she has to realize that she's a fighter and that she *can* fight."

"Whaddya mean?"

"You know, a coma is like a war. But what if, wherever she is right now she doesn't *know* that she *can* fight to come back? Then it doesn't matter that she's a fighter."

"Damn, Suggs, you just went way left field, man. *Are* you alright?"

"Fuck you, man. I'm just sayin'. I've been thinking bout this. And stories I've heard about near death experiences and people in comas usually describe being in a different place or reality. We don't know *what* she's experiencing, ya know. It's like when you tell someone your dream and, yeah, they may try to understand what you're sayin', but they weren't *in* the world you were in while you were having the dream. I mean that *space*, if she's in a space like that, it would be foreign to her and terrifying. I feel like when you experience something unexplainable and mystical it's as if you're in a different place or reality, I guess. I just wish I knew *where* she was, because this is a matter of her *will*. The doctor's have done all they can do medically, so.. If I could be there I would fight her demons if they were holding her there or tell her, man. I would tell her she *has* the strength to come back. I would hold her hand, help her in any way I could so she can come back. I just want her to come back, Ranald. I can't believe this shit is happening."

Ranald listened to Suggs with a heavy heart. Jeannie. How had they let this happen to their loved ones? What could they have done differently? Jesus, he didn't want little Jeannie to die. She was finally taking hold of her life and on the road to becoming what she wanted to be. He knew that because she had been so vocal about it when she had first showed up on Vette's doorstep. And those two had been thick ever since. *Damn.* He couldn't believe it had gotten to this point either. Sure, he knew the odds had been horribly against them, but good always pulled through in the end, right? That's what he had always learned in church. That's what his momma always told him. He just didn't understand how good pulled through if there was even one casualty. Maybe he was too idealistic, but he had believed that the girls and the staff would be okay where he and Suggs had placed them. He had been so wrong. Torres, Vette, Jeannie and even Moran had superficial injuries. A couple of the staff were messed up as well. Fucking Kam's arm was damn near *gone*. He was getting surgery now while their parents waited anxiously for news in the waiting room. Kam had been dealt a rough ass blow but he had been joking on the way in to surgery. Ranald thanked God his knuckle headed brother was going to be alright.

Ranald closed his eyes and prayed for Jeannie. His heart lurched when he heard Suggs start crying. Suggs quiet sobs made his chest clench. Damned if he had ever thought he would hear Suggs cry.

He had been with Suggs at Suggs cousin's funeral. Suggs' cousin, Farlan, had grown up with Suggs like a brother. When Farlan had been shot by a 16 year old boy, right in front of the police station, Suggs was actually there at the police station. He and Suggs had been working on a case together. Ranald remembered that when they had finally made it out to the scene, they were told Farlan had died on the spot. Suggs' posture had wilted, but his face had shown no emotion. He had just stood there, still as a rod, staring at Farlan being fitted into the morgue bag. Then, abruptly, he had turned around, walked down the courtyard steps and disappeared into the crowd. Ranald had seen him later that day and Suggs was definitely weary, but didn't seem to have shed a tear. And then Ranald had just asked him about it and Suggs had replied, *I don't cry, Eric. I don't feel enough emotion to cry.*

Suggs belatedly realized he was breaking down in front of Ranald. Ranald was probably very uncomfortable right now, he thought to himself in reluctant amusement. He needed to stop with the shit anyway. It's not as if crying did any good, but he really hadn't been able to hold it in. He just wished he knew how he could help her.

Ranald waited until Suggs stopped crying and said quietly, "You should pray for her, man."

"I did. I keep praying over and over in my head."

"*For real*? You already prayed?"

"*Ranald.*"

"Okay, man. That just caught me off guard. Anyway, I'm going to let Vette know what's going on."

"Are you sure you should do that? Won't that stress her?"

Ranald considered what Suggs was saying, "Yeah, it probably would, but she's gonna want to know when she wakes up, if she isn't awake now."

"Okay. That's fucking awesome that she pulled through, man. And just tell her that Jeannie's infection ran a number on her, so she's still out most of the time."

"Okay. If she finds out, I'm telling her I just went with what you told me."

Suggs rolled his eyes. "Fine, Ranald. At least I'm not scared of Jeannie."

Ranald scooted to the side to get from in between the bench and the bed. When he was at the foot of the bed he turned to his left and said, "You fool. You *should* be." He walked to the door and called over his shoulder, "I'll be back in a bit." Then he walked out the door.

Jeannie was kinda scared, yes, but really, she was starting to get a little angry. Just where the hell was she? She wanted to go back! She wanted to go back! She wanted to hold Sara, hug her mom. Why was she here? Why hadn't she felt this way from the beginning? It had almost been like she couldn't remember anything or anyone, but then she really hadn't tried *to remember. All she had known was what she wanted and what made her feel good. What a strange place this was. Jeannie knew she was going to have to find a way to get out. She hoped it wasn't too late. She should have* been *trying to get the hell out of wherever she was. She was beginning to panic a little cause she knew she couldn't ask for help because she had no voice. How did she get through this? There was no one else around to ask questions to. How did she know where to go?*

"Jeannie!"

Jeannie thought she was hearing things. Then she heard it *again. It sounded like it was coming from behind her. What had she heard?* Had *she really heard something? She listened hard again as she tried to ignore the clothes that were smacking her limbs and her face as they started to race by. She was steadily getting closer to the creepy blank space. She felt a chill growing in the windy air and it was getting harder and harder to comfortably breathe. Something bad was happening or coming, she knew it. She had to get the fuck outta this place or space, whatever it was. She tried hard to remember what she was doing before she had woken up in this strange and creepy space. Nothing. It was like the blank space in front of her was* in *her mind. There was nothing there. Fuck! She tried again to dredge up a memory of what she had been doing. And, then, her ears pricked as she heard* it *again. She heard it, this time, in a way that startled her. The voice was within her. It resonated through her body, causing her fingertips to tingle and her heart to swell and race even faster than it already was. Then, to her astonishment she felt pressure on her right hand. What the fuck, she thought to herself. There was nothing touching her hand, besides the empty clothes. Then she* felt *the voice again. She just couldn't make out what it was saying, but it felt warm and open. There was also sadness that she felt from it. A deep, unabashed sadness. Then,* he *was there, at the forefront of her mind.* T.J. Suggs. *Love flooded her terrified being, coupled with a longing to touch her lips to his. And she knew. She was feeling Suggs. It was Suggs! And then she also just knew she didn't have to remember what she had been doing before she had woken up here. She could hold onto Suggs. And her being was suddenly flooded with peace, a calm that filled her up. She closed her eyes and focused on Suggs, her love for him.*

She knew now that she had chosen this place, this place that makes what you think you want your reality so that you can blindly get closer and closer to the evil space that waited to overtake you. Thus, you forsake your life, sliding into the malevolent nothingness that controls the space.

She had been wrong, cowardly, welcoming the void to a degree. It had seemed easier to let herself slip away, but she couldn't do that. She had to go on. There was reason to live. And she damn sure didn't want to spend eternity here, in this damned place. So, she focused on him. Suggs..

Suggs leaned over Jeannie and as carefully as he could he wiped her face with the warm rag. He knew about being gentle in the bedroom sometimes, but he had never done something so intimate with or for a woman before...had never wanted to. He hoped he wasn't being too rough, but Jeannie needed a sponge bath and he had told the nurse he would take care of it. Besides, he didn't want anyone else touching her. She was his, damn it. He would take care of her. Feeling himself beginning to lose control again, he leaned back and turned his face away from her for a moment, stilling his hands as well. He breathed in deeply and exhaled, doing his best to push the sadness down. He had to focus. He turned back to face her and his heart dropped out of his chest and he thought he was going to have a fucking heart attack. The breath in his body escaped him as if he had been punched in his gut. He felt light-headed and stumbled back, crashing over the bench behind him. It slammed back against the wall, making a loud thumping sound as he lost his balance and fell, backwards, over the side of the bench. Landing on his back, with his legs thrown up in the air, Suggs was stunned for a moment.

Suggs ears were ringing as he tried to shake the fogginess out of his head. He heard hurried footsteps and gasps from someone as if they were far away.

Nurse Rebecca Steeton and her colleague, Julie Jumper, heard the commotion coming from the room where Jeannie Derit was. They jumped up and hurried to the room.

Becky immediately noticed Officer Suggs trying to get up off the floor and rushed towards him, but stopped short when she heard Julie gasp behind her.

She turned back, "What's wrong, Ju-."

"I-I need some water."

Becky turned to her left and saw Ms. Derit sitting up in bed, wide-eyed, but still sleepy looking. "Get Dr. Palmer, stat."

"On it." Julie rushed from the room.

"You really scared us, Jeannie. Really. And then you raise up all wide eyed like the damn exorcist, scaring the hell out of everybody." Ranald laughed and continued. "But for real though,

I'm so glad you're alright. And I told Suggs you were too stubborn to let go of life. Beware of little Jeannie, right?"

Jeannie giggled and squeezed Suggs hand tighter. "Too stubborn, well, maybe. But, oh yeah, I ain't little Eric Ranald and you better not ever talk about Vette that way either. We might as well be just as big as yawl are! *Shit*. We're the ones that make shit happen."

"Woe, woe, woe, Jeannie, now that might be exaggerating things a bit. Come on, Suggs. Back me up, bruh. Stop laughing, man."

Jeannie whipped around on Suggs and even in a hospital gown, her small form drowning in it and the bed she sat up in, she looked ferocious enough that Suggs thought he might give her cute ass some help. *Maybe…* She glared at him, waiting on his response and he felt an insane urge to laugh. He loved to rile her up. She was here, right here, with him, with everybody. She was *alive* and being Jeannie. Thank God. Thank God.

Suggs smiled rakishly and tipped up his Stetson, "Hell yeah, Ranald. She knows that's exaggerating things a whole lot." Ready for it, Suggs held her hand tighter just as she tried to snatch her hand from his.

Jeannie glared at him, baring her teeth at him, not missing a beat, "Why you yellow-bellied-,"

Suggs swiftly moved forward and grabbed her flushed face. She was still going off on him when he closed his lips over hers.

THE END

Continue Reading

for a Sneak Peek

of Erin Lovelace's

3rd Book in the

Texas Heat Series

A Texas Healing

Join Kam and all the others in a story about love healing the most bruised of hearts. Kam and many of his friends find the healing they need from all the troubles they have had. Kam receives his in the most unlikely of situations.

Journey with Kam during his path to heal his body. And experience the struggle of him understanding he also needs to heal his heart and his mind, for he lost much more than he ever realized. When he develops an unexpected attachment for a woman way out of his league, he is surprised at the connection they begin to form..

Coming Soon!

A Texas Healing